THE MIDNIGHT
BLADE
OF SONIC HONEY

Other works by Eric W. Bragg:

At the Threshold of Liquid Geology, and other automatic tales.
iUniverse: Lincoln, Nebraska. 2002.

Automatic Smoke Signals.
Xlibris: Philadelphia, Pennsylvania. 2005.

Meat Art and Surrealist Objects: a collection of oneiric mischief.
Xlibris: Philadelphia, Pennsylvania. 2006.

The Somnambulist FootPrints: a Collection of Surrealist Tales.
Editor. Oyster Moon Press: Berkeley, California. 2008.

Website: **www.surrealcoconut.com**

Other works by Ribitch:

Surrealism & Its Popular Accomplices. Illustrations.
City Lights Books: San Francisco, California. 1980

Free Spirits: Annals of the Insurgent Imagination. Illustrations.
City Lights Books: San Francisco, California. 1982

Somnambulist: Journal of Poetic Research & Development. Co-editor.
Mythographic Press: Berkeley, California. 1984.

Nefftania. Opposite Shore Studios Press: Berkeley, California. 1999.

Third Morning. Opposite Shore Studios Press: Berkeley, California. 1999.

The Somnambulist FootPrints: a Collection of Surrealist Tales.
Oyster Moon Press: Berkeley, California. 2008.

Website: **www.ribitch.net**

THE MIDNIGHT BLADE OF SONIC HONEY

a novel & automatic text
by
Eric W. Bragg

with illustrations by Ribitch

OYSTER
MOON
PRESS

BERKELEY, CALIFORNIA

The Midnight Blade of Sonic Honey
by Eric W. Bragg

Cover photo: "Colony" by Eric W. Bragg
Interior illustrations: Ribitch

ISBN: 978-1-4357-1428-1

Additional copies of this book can be ordered from LuLu:
http://www.lulu.com

Oyster Moon Press is a non-profit, surrealist publishing co-op that
originated in Berkeley, California.

http://www.oystermoonpress.com

Table of Contents:

2nd Incarnation

1st Incarnation

2nd Incarnation

October 2006

1
The Pork

Seconds ticking, the legs moved across the granite pavement, ticking the whistles of morning. Underneath the pavement, the worms crawled, prematurely awakened by the grin of an adolescent tooth fairy whose miniskirt was undeniably too short. This flashback to the previous century was a horseshoe that congregated underneath a sinister broom closet beneath the Manor's staircase, where a tiny cot held a straggler who didn't know how to pull eggplants from ceiling bulb sockets. Pulling out the light was the same thing as putting in the hair staircase – a bedroom splashdown of frozen eyeballs on forks.

Finally, the next century passed, and then the one after that. Underneath the bloody sand was a fraternizing rug that was used to cover the tracks of crashed spaceships. This childish diatribe was really a lost city of porks, a fetid conglomeration of grinning and grunting barbarism neatly tied up with volatile green cords. A dark cloud passed over the forehead of one of the porks, and the particular pork in question suffered from a heart-attack that forced his bones to jut from his spasmodically sunken ribcage. Beams from the sky shot stars through his head and his eyes opened purposefully like those of a forest frog.

Back at the old Manor, civilized hand-claps and strange sounds were uttered from surprised lips, as if a hotel was really a maze of cricket houses used to move the large hands of clocks in the same way knowing legs moved a body to a train-station. The blood on the pavement only reminded the evil pork of the true time of the universe, in the sense that a second was really a foot, and a century was therefore really a lamp-post, jutting with multiple lightbulbs from multiple sockets in a confusing pattern.

The confusing pattern refused to honor the false promises that came from wooden arms that were glued to a vertical wall. These confusing patterns were none other than bone-straps with melted plastic fabrics that were used for mummification purposes, like when purses are unzipped and cosmetic applicators are groped for, within the leather purses. Usually those kinds of purses were like libraries, holding the togetherness of tissues for the bone-cells of guardians in bone museums, as if a spiral staircase were to secretly wind its way through your left femur, on a quest for a boy who cried while spilling cold water onto a large nest of termites.

This cold shower, as it were, was mercilessly extinguished by the grunting pork who finally caught the train, in the same way certain insects catch diseases from ugly humans who wipe their greasy noses with hands soiled with fermented animal extracts. The pork was truly a slob, by the way he took his island paradise and made of it a grubby charcoal, ancient bituminous dagger to carve words of forbearance on-to the foreheads of silly Wednesday worshippers who misunderstood the meaning of "fun" for other dangerous incisions into the grasshopper legs of green flight that could put rocketships on the moon and hairy legs into the laps of librarians.

The Pork put up with the newspaper, and eventually ate it, as if time were something that could be hoarded and greedily consumed after a day's hard work by underlings who sod the evil picnic tables with prayers and terrestrial phlegm eruptions. The Pork understood these horrors and laughed conscientiously, as if he knew how to take all of the menaces and weave them into some kind of beautiful nightmare that wore a dark nightgown to visit him in his early morning concubine hours, before the sun arose and before the second wave of the dream-train would send the kiss of an innocent young girl onto his trembling, salty lips, smarting of blood and devoid of memory.

Eventually the second train left, and the Pork gave birth to a new lightbulb from his left armpit. The armpit was an upside-down bird's nest, and the armpit secretions were eaten by young women in order for them to maintain their youth and vitality. The train collided with a spruce tree, which was very open about the truth that gushed forth from the severed branches like the sappy candy of senators who make strange policies for us ordinary folk to follow. But the second train of the night kept on going. Inside of the train, choirboy hymns seemed to permeate the walls, but the flow of leeches was stopped by a bottle stopper which put the cats to bed, and tucked the children in under the blankets ever so tightly. The confusion of news reports was a paper-airplane of printed text that landed next to the precarious pillow, allowing the severed head of a mannequin to fall off and hit the floor, rolling down the aisle, where it came to rest next to a witch making love to her broomstick of power. The broomstick of power was an act of silence, a wordless display of might that drew its main channels of strength through the absence of the word. In the wordless vacuum of the dead but moving train, the witch leaned back in her chair after her academic orgasm, and then exploded, leading to a plume of multicolored confetti that scattered across the entirety of the particular train coach where the accident occurred.

A few seats up the aisle, the Pork leaned back in his chair and laughed, remembering a similar incident many years ago involving a corrupt politico-religious farce of a man, a certain Reverend McDowell from a previous incarnation of hybrid moon men and other dissected attractions of pink fur, teary-eyed scientists and mannequin visitors from other planets. Such reverie bothered the Pork, as he attempted to count his losses and then his gains, thinking of coins dropping into the piggybank that was his abdomen, swelling with living lard that might one day explode onto the windshields of taco trucks as they brought to the city-dwellers the sacred semen-tacos from the hills of vigilant fertility, where spurts of curly hair grew from the sides of the pink roads, long ago laid down by the work crews who could build citadels of glass from their spit and houses of worship from toothpicks that were generated from beehives nestled among the armpit-crooks of old oaktrees.

The Pork leaned back in his seat and tried to relax. He flipped through useless magazines about mannequins who wore purple velvet uniforms with star insignias and who had the annoying tendency to fall over, with a thud, during moments of severe duress, like when weird mustached villains stole the lunch money from pet rocks, or when whole fleets of Martian birds were found cruelly frozen to death in the exotic food courts of animal protein-munchers from the steps of the planetary capital. The Pork wanted to put down the evil magazine about the purple velvet mannequins, but could not. Instead,

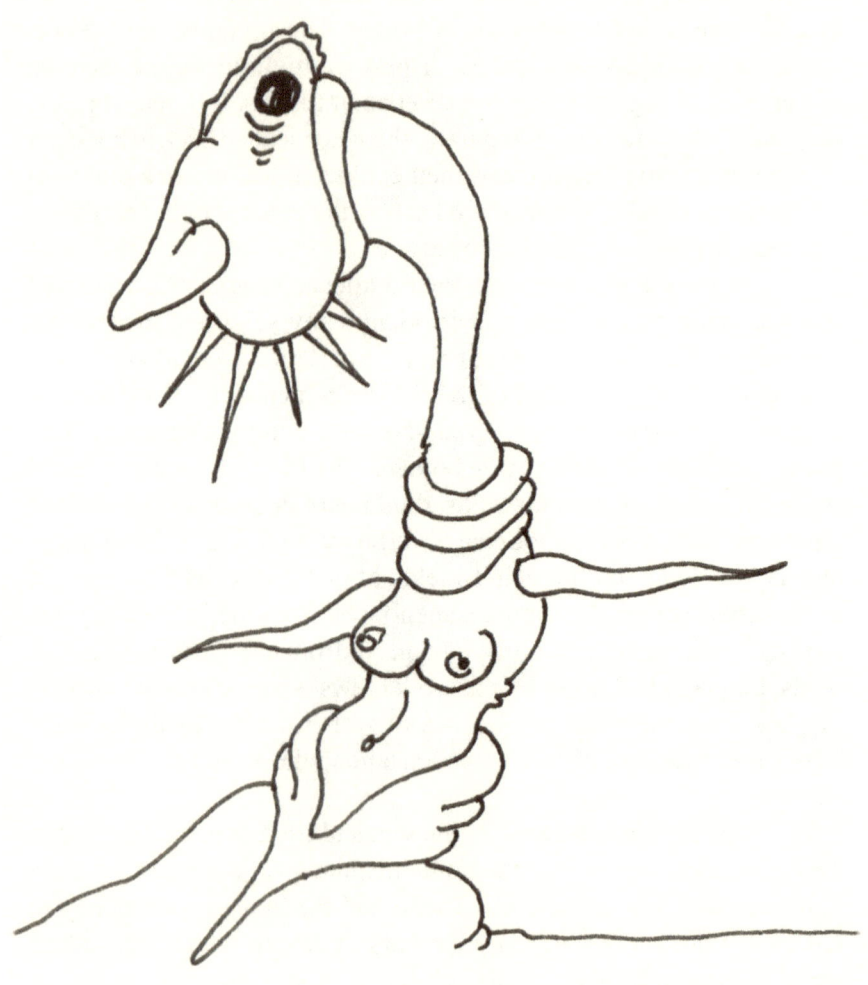

he rolled up the dog-eared magazine and stuffed it into a cylindrical hollow within the briefcase that he took with him on his daily rampages through the smooth pink roads that led to all cities known by humankind.

Upon being interrupted by a stewardess with awfully smooth legs, the Pork turned his attention to her legs and then to her face. She was speaking to him. She wanted to know if he needed a clean handkerchief to wipe the filthy snot that was gurgling out of his porcine nose. The Pork didn't know how to reply. He leaned over his chair and stared down, deep down, into a pool of freshly made urine that had appeared directly underneath where the stewardess was standing on the shaky train. The train-coach's momentum caused the pool of urine to ripple in an agitated fashion, and the Pork leaned over to stare down into this golden puddle of piss. Deeper and deeper he looked, concentrating so as to see through the distortions caused by the ripples; eventually he came to see his own reflection as a narcissistic flower. Instead of petals, the flower consisted of a green stalk with a deflated dog attached at the top. Instead of a pistil there was a canine nose oozing filthy mucous peppered with the grimy dust from bookshelves covered with the excrement of roaches.

At that particular moment, the train lurched, and the stewardess sneezed. She repeated her question about the handkerchief, and the Pork only nodded in assent, holding out a fat limb to grasp the handkerchief that was to be soon extended. Dramatically, the stewardess put her leg up on the armrest, and lifted her dress to reveal a clean handkerchief tucked into her garter. Also noticeable was the strange fact that her legs were hollow, possibly bionic, but definitely hollow and transparent. It almost looked like her legs were terrariums where ant-farms were kept. The Pork squeezed his little beady eyes to peer into the hollow leg ant-farms, to see the little vermin that crawled and writhed within. He put on his pince-nez, to get a closer look, and grunted with surprise when he realized that the wriggling ants were not really ants but actually very animate squid tumbling and turning in the salty tide within the legs of the stewardess. The legs were really ocean hideaways for these tiny squids with their beach balls, and they energetically clung to the insides of the stewardess' leg compartments.

It was only at the dawning of their primitive sense of consciousness that they were unknowingly reaching for the broken mountain of paradise that sat atop the cleft zenith of her rising, salty thighs. Where the two thigh mountains joined was the place of academic paradise.

The Pork looked at his watch and saw the word "impotence" written on it. His pupils dilated into dollar signs, and he fell back in his seat, unconscious, with gurgling, snotty fluids oozing out of his nose uncontrollably. With his grazed head staring blankly at the ceiling of the train coach, as if stricken by a legal baseball-bat, the Pork was oblivious to the touch of the handkerchief that the stewardess lovingly applied to his snout, sopping up the snot on the sneeze-rag, which was eventually thrown out of the nearby window.

Eventually the train came to a halt, reaching its destination. The Pork awoke, and wiped the excess snot on his sleeve. He looked in his briefcase, feeling reassured upon seeing his collection of purple eggplant lightbulbs safely intact, without any alien fingerprints or proscriptive museum-curator rhetoric written all over the delicate glass of the bulbs. Upon this reassurance that his precious cargo was still intact and unmolested, he looked around at the other passengers who by now had become skeletons made of balsa wood. The beautiful stewardess with the transparent squid-infested legs was nowhere to be seen. The handkerchief that the Pork had requested was also out of sight. The light of the midday sun was blinding as it was soothing to a certain kind of miscreant wretch who had dollar-signs in his eyes when he stared up at the sun for too long. Such gestures would ultimately lead to his ultimate demise, but perhaps it was too soon to provide those details, or at least not until the next paragraph.

When the Pork stepped off the train, he wiped his nose on his sleeve again and pattered down the walkway, turning left onto the street. Old-fashioned automobiles buzzed down the archaic cobble-stoned streets, spewing noxious fumes, with the drivers shouting obscenities at anything or anyone that got in their way. The Pork held his breath, and crossed the street. Immediately the Pork was hit by a moving vehicle driven by a plastic mannequin wearing a purple velvet outer-space uniform, with a star insignia on the left side of the chest. The mannequin was oblivious to the porcine pedestrian, and the collision threw the Pork up into the air, with blood and snot flying everywhere. The briefcase that the Pork always carried with him flew across the street, landing with a hard smack next to the gutter, jarring the case open. From out of the briefcase were jettisoned two or three of the purple eggplant lightbulbs, which carelessly but determinately rolled into the gutter, only to drop into the sewer, several feet below, with a resounding "plop." Forever separated from his precious lightbulbs, the Pork expired quickly after the accident, with a crushed skull that gushed copious waves of blood and a smashed snout which could raise the dead with a typhoon of leaking snot.

The street of the killing might have been in Europe, or it might have been in Africa. The location of the unknown city was difficult to place, because so many modern cities have reckless mannequin drivers who wear outer-space uniforms and preach distracting vibes of sedition that can permeate even the most reserved breasts. While the rotting carcass that was once the Pork began to faithfully decompose on the sidewalk to which he was dragged by passers-by, the lost eggplant lightbulbs began their spine-tingling journey to the center of the sewers where all foul ideas live and germinate, creating a hub of transportation for even the most depraved of all horse statuettes who resided in the dank shadows of human refuse. This journey provoked much fear on the part of the lightbulbs, through being forced to travel through unexpected passageways of forgotten darkness from exca-vated memories of fondness for broken cherrytrees who wept with colonial memories of the years of rust and the metropolitan robots of invalids.

Within a cul-de-sac, the sewer water threatened to deposit the loosely floating purple eggplant lightbulbs (who had somehow managed to miraculously avoid being separated) on a dead-end of old dirty sandiness, lost dunes of silt in a sewer room that was really an interrogation chamber of the forgotten. But the lightbulbs were in fact quite lucky, as the current renewed its vigor at the last moment when it seemed as if they would be forever marooned in the darkness of dead-end filth and the memory of sonic drudgery that came from sweating brows to move strong poles of metal and wood into the formation of building foundations, laying the groundwork for the civilization that now held them mercilessly captive.

The day was equally lucky for the purple eggplant lightbulbs, because the current deposited them in a pool of foul water that congealed into a puddle right on the edge of a hollowed cliff. The extra water added by the drainage pipe forced the already full collection pool to spill some of its congealed nastiness over the cliff and into the salty ocean, which roared below in a frightening transformation of what was once an hourglass of legs but which became the part of the bamboo plant that lived under the soil, right where she put her soft feet during times of discomfort.

Meanwhile, the President of the United States of North America, George B. Bush, sat back in his comfy, swivel chair and pulled a shiny green booger from his nose. He looked down at the booger and wiped it on the side of his ancient cherrywood desk, a desk possibly made from the cherry tree that was once chopped down by the young George Washington. As his oval office was completely empty of obsequious personnel, he put his feet up on the furniture and stared out of the window with a big grin on his face, thinking about his oil profits and that cute teenage hooker he had had on his most recent business trip to Philadelphia to meet with certain local leaders. His office had an almost smoky aroma, as if there were a bevy of cigar-toting politicians or a foul troop of snarling, electrocuted baboons that had just passed through. But no mind. President Bush continued his reverie, thinking about how wonderful catholic, white people really are, while he scratched at his balls.

Lost lightbulbs were what make caricatured seeds germinate. Fluent sprays of honeybees were what make succulent honey translate into the grinding beat of boot-heels as they trekked across dusty roads into the dusk of 6 o'clock, as the hummingbirds settled down into their nests and counted the trolls who waited below the trees to exact taxes upon the little leaves that grew from the tree-nuts of speckled despondency.

The tree-nuts were languishing in their horse stalls! An unknown peeping-tom rose from the bales of camouflaging hay in order to move his perverse eyes up to the udder of a clueless cow. The teats on the udder had been replaced by some dirty purple lightbulbs found while scavenging along the coast. He pulled on the nipple-bulbs, and a purple light emanated from each one that got pulled. This was the first time in his life that the peeping-tom knew happiness, and he celebrated by sticking a twig of hay between his teeth the way he saw his elders doing it. A glow of satisfaction coursed through his shoulders as he celebrated his first peeping-tom-pulling of purple bovine nipple-bulbs.

The festivities ended abruptly as a wolf from the surrounding evil countrycide entered the bar wearing a straw top hat, the kind that some chaps used to wear during the beginning of the twentieth century. The peeping-tom fled the scene, abandoning his precious purple lightbulbs, as well as the terrified mama-cow who continued to stare at rings in the beams of wood in her barnstall, all the while chewing her cud. The wolf ingested the lightbulbs without grazing them with his sharp teeth. Then he trotted off into the darkness, with a glowing purple stomach. Upon leaving the final perimeter of the farm, he sat on his hind legs, looking up to bray at the moon, with a trail of farm snot oozing down the side of his muzzle. Such was happiness.

The wolf regurgitated the eggplant lightbulbs into a nest found growing on the side of a dark, deserted road, and the purple lightbulbs almost seemed like glowing eggs, although the wolf knew that they were not. The wolf licked the slime away from the glowing bulbs, while nudging twigs and other loose branches over the next with his snout. At one point he sneezed all over the concealed nest, covering it with a festive spray of clear mucus, which delighted a nearby owl perched in the hollow of a tree. The owl hooted, being visible only as a pair of glowing eyes emanating from the nearby tree. The wolf respectively backed away from the concealed nest covered with clear snot, and reclined at the bottom of the owl tree, which now assumed the furtive appearance of a broken grandfather clock that had stopped all time-keeping activity around 6 o'clock.

The tree gonged and only gonged once, with the dull, imperfect sound echoing into the hills, for a moment overpowering the din of the crickets. In answer to the sound appeared strange moths which materialized out of the near-darkness under the moonless sky. They might have been attracted by the sound of the transformed clock, or then they might have been attracted by the faint purple light that was seeping from the twigs and branches covering the eggplant lightbulb nest. As the secreted nest was covered in thick, viscous wolf-snot, the moths were unable to detach from the surface, and there they stayed until the morning light would dry the snot just enough to make it brittle, so that they could break free. While resting in their entrapment, the silvery moths gently pulsed their lunar-shaped wings, giving the illusion that the concealed nest, which appeared as a roughly spherical mass of collected twigs, was breathing in the dim light. The wolf kept watch, as did the owl with the yellow eyes, who had transformed into an owl-shaped plate of bronze at the same time the tree became the grandfather clock.

2
Mother

During the night, while all the animals slept, the purple eggplant lightbulbs encased in twig nesting material and surreptitiously guarded by the camouflaged, grey moths with the crescent-shaped wings, had a vivid dream which all of them shared equally: in a newly constructed house that lacked walls and which smelled of newly cut pine wood, an army of dead bodies was rampaging throughout the house, at war with the living. The living were down to their last bullets, and were searching for ways to leave the skeleton house behind. A thin ray of hope manifested itself in the form of three stout grenades that serendipitously appeared next to a glass display case holding ancient tomes of automatic recipes for unknown delights which terrified most industrialized people. The three grenades were in sight, and yet out of reach. The survivors who reached for the grenades were eaten by the animate corpses, and so all involved eventually perished. The three grenades were never grasped, and therefore they did not detonate. In the metabolic afterlife of decaying bones and twitching corpses, the grenades became sweet dessert items: perhaps reddish candy-apples which were ubiquitously positioned on plates for easy grasping, in a maddening gesture of irony.

The purple eggplant lightbulbs woke up from that nightmare as soon as the first rays of sunlight penetrated the spherical protective nest in which they spent the night on a lost countrycide. The sunlight caused the moths of night to annoyingly twitch their wings, awakening them from their insect slumber. As each moth readied itself for flight, it grasped one of the twigs, preparing to hold it tightly when flying away from the temporary nest. Only when the round form of the sun was completely above the horizon, hitting the spherical nest with a blast of golden-orange light, that the moths received their special signal to pull the nesting twigs away from the purple lightbulbs contained therein.

Upon being stricken by the full blast of the sunlight, the

lightbulbs immediately fell into a post-waking stupor, and had a waking dream of small plastic swimming people. These tiny, rubbery dolls were the length of one's hand, and were made of a flexible, flesh-colored plastic. These dolls were designed for long-range swimming in the ocean – aquatic marathon-swimmers, they were. They were also for collecting and petting and of course, abusing, and many a child as well as adult got many hours of pleasure from hurting these small, swimming dolls. A whole new breakthrough became available from a prismatic scuba mask which portentously told of a solar eclipse to be seen through the crescent shapes of leaves as they were etched onto sidewalks and other outdoor areas.

A bird of prey circled the archaic house, eventually finding the open window that it was seeking. The graceful creature entered a bedroom with pink wallpaper and landed on an orange pumpkin that was before a mirror. The bird slowly transformed into a beautiful woman, with its curved beak looking more and more nose-like, with sharp eyes expanding into the blue pools that were human eyes, and a hunched avian back that unfolded into the graceful curves of her naked body. And so the Evil Mother was born, preening in front of a mirror, thinking dubious thoughts of a frozen pond with cracks in it, and of cindery remnants of house skeletons which had each of their sugar-teeth tickled by the firm bodies of sweet grenades that went missing from the briefcase of a mysterious bureaucrat.

The Evil Mother felt earthquakes tremble around the old Manor estate, and a quick look out of the window revealed no immediate suggestions of impending doom. She was quite confused by the rumbling inside and the peacefulness outside. Immediately she dismissed these anomalies and began to clothe herself first with an onyx-bejeweled tiara, a royal blue silk gown, and then other forms of redundant metallic ornamentation, such as a brass miniskirt and rope-like beads of platinum and other precious metals. Apparently these metal accoutrements were not heavy enough to impede her move-ments, suggesting that they might be only plated with the precious metals, or possibly hollow on the inside. Nevertheless, the Evil Mother dressed herself with dignity and with a slight bit of pomp, as she frisked her dark, wet hair in the mirror and peered at her features with those hawk-like eyes that presided over an almost beak-like nose which only inspired feelings of some kind of hidden lust, especially when the lady appeared near grand, wooden staircases and next to ancient portraits of her ancestors.

Suddenly, she looked down at one of the metallic necklaces that she was wearing. The particular necklace in question vibrated ever so briefly, and was a brass key molded in the shape of an iguana, almost resembling a dagger, with an inlaid emerald for an eye, hanging from a chain. She fingered the iguana key-necklace and then finished her dressing ceremony, making sure that every eyelash looked right.

A knock at the door yielded a baked nun who offered her a strange pacifier, in the shape of our Lord Jesus Christ. The Evil Mother took the pacifier and hurled it at the fireplace in her room, which shattered in the heat and began to melt. Walking into an adjacent meeting room, the Evil Mother laughed and then grew a bouquet of flowers from the palms of her hand, giving them to the Baked Nun, who then laughed hysterically, bobbing her head up and down maniacally and almost reverently while she laughed. The Evil Mother told the Baked Nun to go plant some corn, and so the nun obeyed, still laughing hysterically and oddly fingering a broom that was hung above a fireplace in the study, in the same way shotguns are sometimes suspended above fireplaces.

The nun laughed merrily as she threw sprouted corn seeds into pots of fertile soil that were located in the corners of the cozy meeting room. When the nun was finished sowing the corn, the Evil Mother commanded her to get on all fours in front of the fireplace. The nun complied, whereupon the Evil Mother thrice clapped her hands, apparently summoning her disposable boyfriend, who had appeared in the doorway with a bewildered smile on his naïve face. After instructing the disposable boyfriend to lie down on the back of the nun, the Evil Mother gave him a blowjob which eventually culminated with his ejaculation into her mouth. The Evil Mother gargled with the semen, and then spat it into one of the corn pots which had been fertilized by the hysterical nun. Later that day, the head of the disposable boyfriend was displayed for the edification of the local population, impaled upon a stake in the courtyard of the old Manor, still displaying that grin

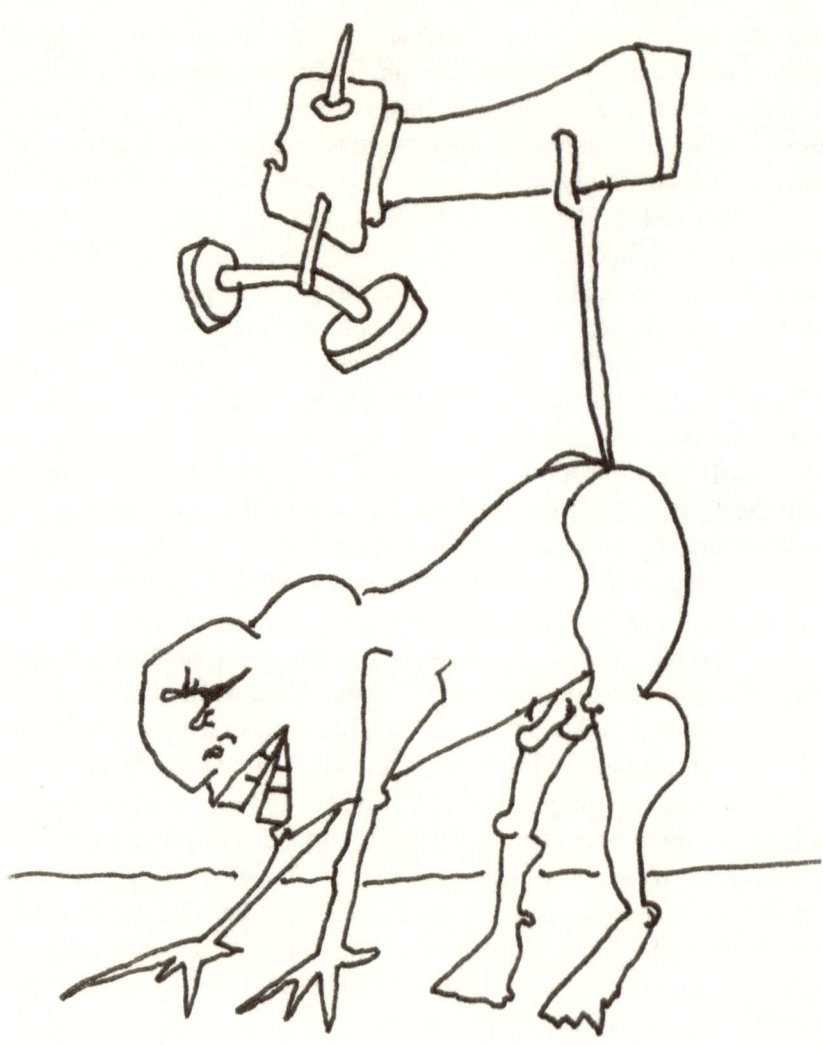

of bewilderment.

Within the movement of fireworks, the cat searched the pond, looking for algae sculptures that twirled within the ceiling of the water, replacing the grid of the roof with slime from the liquid. Occasionally, it would slice the water with its paw, grasping at imaginary goldfish, trying to imagine their fiery ribcages as if they were the assassinated structures of houses which contained the red, candied apples that were once grenades, which were once lightbulbs. The paw groped in between the starving ribcages, searching and digging furtively, often frustrated by passing clouds of algae that made one's eyes itch and which obscured the view into the cool, dank water. Perhaps this dark pond somehow communicated with the sewer system of the Manor? It wouldn't be all that of a shock, if so. The cat crouched down low, taking a break from pawing at the floating skeletons in the pond. It peered at the formidable dwelling, with its crusty facades, and barren windows, of which only a few glowed with a feeble light after the arrival of dusk. But there was nobody staring out of the windows, as the cat might have been accustomed to viewing on many a usual evening.

There were cobblestones which formed a path away from the pond in the direction opposite the ugly Manor. While overgrown bushes and hedges obscured most of the view (in fact passing through many of these hedges had now become nearly impossible, due to the many years of neglect that had allowed these ornamental trees to blot out the light overhead when travelers passed between them, creating brief caverns that tunneled through these now massive barriers), it was slightly possible to look through the slim spaces in between them to get a glimpse of the rolling hills that rose away from the old habitation. Here and there, in the distance, could be spotted the old stone foundation of abandoned cottages and outhouses, reminding all who looked at them of the *age* of the place, apparently longer than the human lifespan.

The cat grew bored with the pond and disappeared through the thick hedges into the hills, where it felt itself being called, especially because the imposing, archaic Manor was beginning to show signs of a quiet nightlife which, although quiet, was still somehow imposing and unsettling.

Within one of the dungeons of the Manor, the Evil Mother consulted old tomes of nauseating length and lineage. She saw herself in many previous incarnations, all thoroughly nasty, all thoroughly rotten, and she realized that she was the kind of person who could travel anywhere. Her bird-of-prey eyes, hawkish nose, and thin, moist smile inspired much lustful and intellectual speculation among her various suitors, all of whom madly desired to know where she came from and in what capacity. Upon learning of her almost infinite lineage, she drooled with excitement, reaching for the witch's cap that didn't exist, and fondly thinking of a broomstick that was innocuously hung above one of the fireplaces upstairs, in the way shotguns are, sometimes. She was naturally a teacher, and had had many disciples, and yet, she still walked the world alone, listening to the strange vibrations that communicated between stellar bodies as well as between the microscopic ones. Often she tied her long, dark hair back, which allowed the sumptuous roundness of her full breasts to witness the light of day.

In all of her evilness incarnate, her habits were frightening, if not always veiled in shadow. Her tastes were expensive, and so were her hobbies, as could be seen by the rapid influx of slaves. New living bodies appeared on every Sunday and Wednesday, and daily could be seen a new head impaled on one of the many spikes that mercilessly sprouted from the barren courtyard. For those men who had the opportunity to put their mouths on her forbidden garden, their lives were prematurely cut short (quite literally), so as for her to avoid having witnesses who might later betray her in the cloudy future, she often told herself.

Within these lustful reveries, the Evil Mother began an almost comical argument with herself, involving her left hand physically in conflict with her right hand. Although amusing for the soon-to-be-beheaded spectator to watch, it was almost sinister to witness the arms of the desirable sorceress at war with each other, coiling around each other like suffocating pythons intent on choking the breath out of each other. Her eyelids fluttered orgasmically as she looked up at the dark clouds, with her panting mouth open, her breath fogging up the cold air and her writhing limbs in some kind of spasmodic, violent ecstasy that was toxic to the touch.

In the end, it was the sinister hand that won the argument. The Evil Mother sighed, and resigned herself to trudging her passive body up the stairs into the dining room where eager servants waited for her, poised to attend to her every need. The room, barely lit by candles and slightly damp, would have been too much for anyone of weak constitution. As it was, many an employee within the Manor often had indescribable head colds, red eyes, foggy vision and the strange reduction in the ability to concentrate on whatever the task, small or large. It was almost as if the walls were made of a humid crocodile leather that could exhale permeable mists of fog and inhuman moisture. The Evil Mother dismissed her servants and sent them scurrying into the shadows, creeping like vermin to their own servants' quarters where they were to hole up for the night in the darkness. In this particular Manor, the servants were strongly discouraged from cavorting together in the after-hours, after their duties were fulfilled for the day.

Alone in the dining room, sitting in front of a pig carcass that had been killed and roasted that very morning, the Evil Mother looked down at her arms and opened them up as if they were a sardine tin. Inside of her limbs were ladders and houses and all sorts of winding, interlacing thoroughfares and congested streets. A world of economy seethed within her limbs, which without surprise were at war with themselves, as all humanity pitifully does at one time or another. She ceased to be a statue and so transformed into a staircase with a crooked smile – a paragon of nauseatingly different geometry and upside-down lipstick that managed to work its way onto every crooked banister, every lip-like surface that populated this evil world within the arms of an unknown sorceress, breaking the hawklike smile when the eroticism of humor blundered its way into the civil opening and closing of a pulsating umbrella. This motion in a metaphorical circle brought the smile to emit a sonic cackle that bathed the night in a warm cheery glow that was uncommon, to say the least. If there had been icicles trimming the armpits of the spiral staircase, they had long since melted by now. Rising from the lipsticked-ledge of the staircase erupted the brass replicas of lizard figurines, with wet, green eyes that seemed to shine in whatever flashlight circles that would zone over these regions periodically in the darkness.

What were once thinly, and delicately gloved hands as black as night, had now become a nocturnal city with computerized digits that described fictitious destinies where amulets worn around the neck contained strange samples of other worlds, different minds of powdered dust that put the black sash around the neck of a witch to futilely attempt to subdue her panting breath in the government of shadows, in the moist crevices of decisions that were made at the price of death. From one passage to another, each of the houses in this world became the nests of ants, as larvae and sugary packets of food were stored in moldy caverns where the decisions were incessant and fearful. Alien to this environment was a festering, brightly crystalline pile of dust that glowed with somber blue colors ever so faintly in one of the more remote city caverns. This pile of crystalline dust would still remain undisturbed for at least a few more days. It was a special kind of dust that no ant would dare to touch..

With her limbs splayed open to the world, with microscopic candidness evident to all but the night-owls whose glowing eyes could not penetrate the old masonry of the decadent Manor house, the Evil Mother was less of an evil princess and more the night itself, in the same way a burning candle inside of a skull is neatly extinguished by grubby wet fingers that reach out from a corner of the dark. Black was the color of the person-now-a-city, with skyscrapers erupting from moist soils of dark fertility. Black ants that burrowed through these soils would enter the buildings and traverse the inclined spiral walkways that would eventually lead to the top of the skyscrapers. Without any dramatic lightning and thunder occurring directly outside of the buildings, there was at least visible a half moon, providing dim light that only accentuated the dampness of the night with invisible automatons who monotonously walked their rounds with bald heads and parasitic insects burrowing into their limbs, creating tunnels within them. Hence a city within a city within a city.

3
Journey through the Forgotten City

As it turned out, the Evil Mother was not really an evil mother, but more of a Dark Witch born from the pits of lustful blackulence and decadence of the minds of men. Her hobbies were simple, and yet her aspirations were complex. As the number of skewered heads grew in the inner courtyard and other stave patches around the Manor, so did her lust for power and recognition. There wasn't a penis she couldn't have, as she drooled, staring at the vermin who peeped out of the cracks in the old stone walls. In her private reading room, which was on one of the highest floors in the east tower of the Manor, she sighed and relaxed her repose on the giant pumpkin that was her chair. After all, evil witches sat on pumpkins, not chairs.

Out by the side of the pond near the Manor, the cat greeted the light of day with its shrinking pupils, now vertical slits of mistrust. It then turned its attention to the ripples in the water, dreaming of long-gone fishes and pine needles that occasionally were deposited in the water by the cold wind. Its hair became raised after an especially frigid gust blew down from the neighboring hills. The cat once again turned its attention to the water, almost afraid of what it would see in there: visions of schoolchildren running away from the nuns, giant pumpkins rolling down the hills with kites made of sandpaper flying overhead. Overturned heads from decapitation parties were kicked over to reveal new colonies of writhing maggots. Old books falling from shelves due to tectonic disturbances from teutonic witch buttocks that slowly but steadily grazed the sides of pumpkins, occasionally stroking the inner petals of the forbidden rose with surges of intense pleasure. Upon the fall of night, an arrival of a most peculiar sort of creature, perhaps pure ugliness itself. And then the trees, all silently whispering among and to each other, plotting to cast an insidious spell that might change the face of the earth forever. Meanwhile, the droning of a winter breed of cicada, which were extremely cold-tolerant, who lived among the cracks and lees of stones, and said to be above average intelligence.

The Dark Witch discarded her metallic clothes and instead wore her traditional witch's costume, an all-black cape with an equally black cap of the sorceress. She pulled a rank, cracked volume from the shelf and read the following:

> Applied hands reach to lift the wooden floors from racing eyes in the dark. The leaflets fall into tears of bears as they paw at trees in the unavoidable wilderness. The bark-flies lay their eggs under the branches and put hexagonal tools within their pockets, for use in later struggles against the stones of a dried-up creek that burst through a locked apartment building.
>
> The gateway to trances spills across your breasts like a clutching fur-storm that pets and smoothes the stream-rocks of your uncountable tomorrows as they furrow through my broken eyelids. This form of land-sliding is a dangerous territory of kisses and narrow birds' beaks that crackle with bags of burning tinder collected along the trails of the forgotten moments of your hair.
>
> Flowers spill the words from the book down to the floor, and bipedalism is forsaken in favor of melting time, when the melted gasp is the memory of future emotions as they do ballet tail-spins into beautiful patterns which resemble the hands that are highlighted. This avenue returns to high-heels, and the vision continues with vertical land-slides and indescribable industrial chutes that relocate the life of old buildings into a new experience between your hands as you sleep at night. A shortened branch of the tree results, and the frozen rain makes me shiver.

The Dark Witch sighed with a gasp that almost seemed melancholic, and closed the book. She sat on her pumpkin, put her feet up on the desk, leaned against the fur-covered wall (originally installed by her old friend, Hebdomeros, long, long ago), and closed her eyes to meditate.

Meanwhile, a snaky visitor appeared on the threshold of a large mammalian city, perhaps a fortnight's travel by horse, from the ancient Manor. Since this was the era of automobiles, the traveling time was reduced from a fortnight to an hour and a half. Therefore, two valuable weeks of mounting suspense were suddenly tossed out the window, and a pale glass of milk that was balancing on a teetering, flimsy table instantly curdled, sending it over the edge, only to smash onto the artificial stone floor, spreading curdled brains of casein screeching in silent horror over the glazed tiles. What horror.

The visitor pulled its trenchcoat up tightly around its throat, while lowering its dark, wide hat, which strangely seemed to remind one of sinister clocks. Just looking at the hat made would make one think that it was actually five minutes past ten o'clock, either morning or night. This strange association between the sinister dark hat and the passage of five minutes after the hour of ten gave the lamp-posts pause, as they watched the snaky visitor penetrate the outskirts of the city, walking with determination, despite the highly noticeable limp in its gait which suggested burrowing insect larvae that lived symbiotically within the wooden legs of invalids who could now walk. It might even be suggested that all of the hidden color and crystalline magic contained within this strange invader of the old city resided in its artificial legs, or more precisely, within the colorful larvae nestled symbiotically within the wood of the artificial legs. It might have given one pause to consider how a snaky and sinister character such as this obscure visitor might maintain his balance by having wooden legs (that were possibly bionic), but apparently his sense of balance and poise was sufficient to make him a character to be reckoned with, not at all to be taken lightly, especially when considering that everywhere he went, he would drop crystalline blue residues of prismatic mystery from his coat sleeves. The stranger that had once been sleeping now walked again!

Within this town, myths were recreated, remembered and reborn. As an example you could consider the dried out hummingbird who reposed on the pavement, in one of the many forgotten alleys of the old city. This bird was seized by invisible hands, being grounded and quite visibly near death. The cold animal quivered with uncontrollable fever, its eyes closed, and thoroughly oblivious to the world and its mortal dangers. The hummingbird had green plumage on its back, with a spot of red jeweled feathers on its throat. Quite the noble bird, yet unfortunate enough to land in this particular city of death, at this particular time. Somehow the bird understood the power of the hexagon, and thought of hexagonal pieces of glass that somehow reflected the world within its confines, and for even a second of this inter-reflectivity, the bird was freed from its malaise and was able to fly away without looking back. Such movements of sudden freedom inspired forgotten stories of strange musical archaeologists who traveled up dangerous and dirty rivers in search of jazz artifacts and other oddities, like rhomboid fish who were unable to hide themselves inconspicuously within the swimming pools of the neighbors, and other distant memories of domestic swing-sets and other genial father & son adventures. But these were only fragments of some past document that was consumed by the flames of time.

A raven sat on the edge of a building gutter, and peered down at the wanderer, as he was to be defined by his wide-brimmed hat, dark mannerisms, and sinister limping gate. To many, he was simply known as the *Ratmeister*. Simple names were always better than the formal, complicated ones. The bird croaked some kind of unintelligible comment, cocking its head while staring at the dark biped many floors below, who walked past the old buildings with determination, oblivious to the dried-up faces of tortured schoolchildren pressed to the filthy panes of unwashed glass, oblivious to the carnivorous dogs who hungrily patrolled the streets, keeping the neighborhoods meat-free. These perils of the old city could almost make one laugh, the Ratmeister decided, as he rolled a cigar made entirely of dried seaweed and began to smoke it.

Within the palindromes of butterflies and their ugly cousins, the fetid moths of night, the patterns of camouflage melted the heavens into some kind of barrier or flapping tent that covered the ancient city with a prescient disquiet that reminded one of boulders that had bloodstains on them. In the search of places for ghost-seeds to germinate, such as within the old school-trunks of invalids who forgot the combinations to the locks that guarded the contents within these boxes, the ghosts could seep through the cracks in the wood, and make photographic statements with the locusts who occupied the inner passageways of substance, hidden away in the vermillion and azure territories that were as much poisonous as

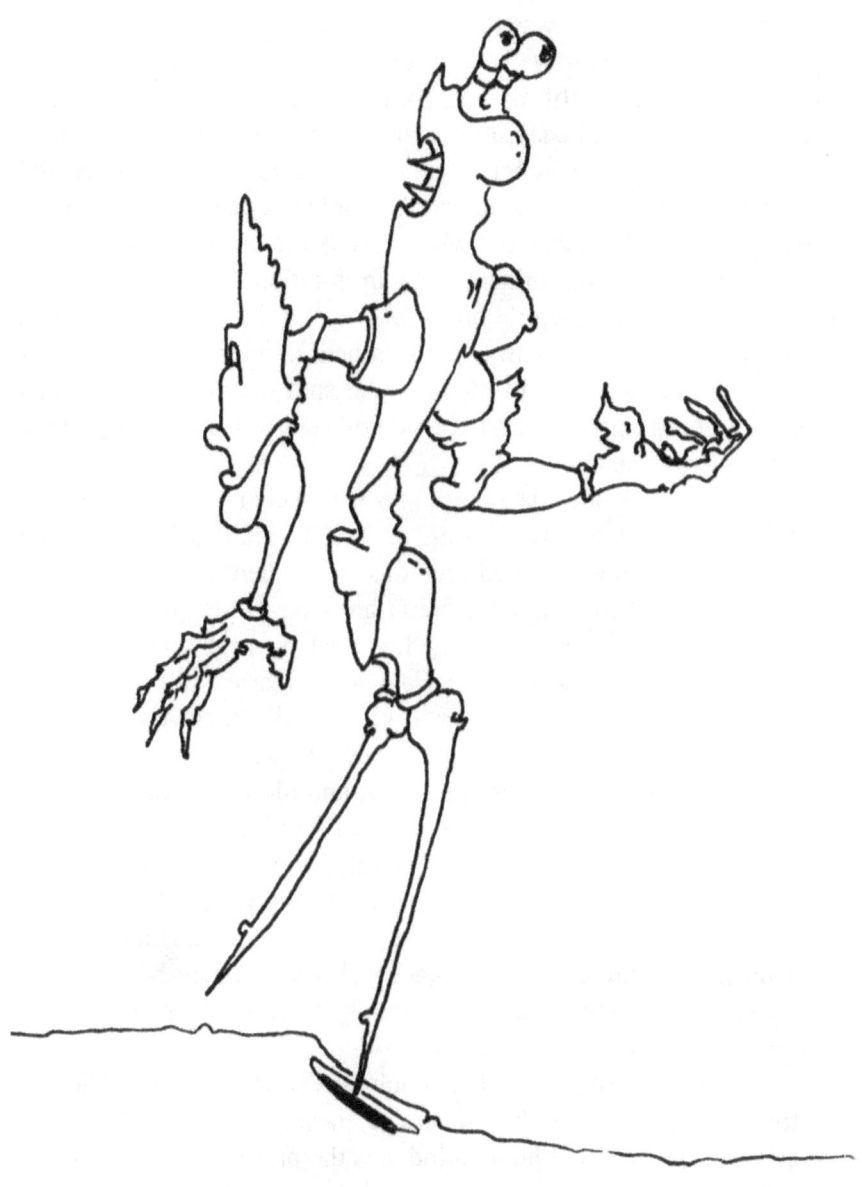

they were of an unconscious bedroom where the injured were en-couraged to sleep. The insomnia of the locusts that hid beneath fallen logs in the countrycide was the same misanthrope who inhabited the fissures in the decrepit walls of brick and tumbling plaster, evicting even the ugly likes of the roaches who loved humans awfully so. These methods of behavior were innate to the frigid cicadas as they conserved wing power by ingesting the minerals from the stones and cement that held the walls together. Rumor had it that they themselves were symbiotically associated with some bacteria in their gut which helped them digest the minerals, as an additional source of energy. Having these bacteria within one's body cavity led to an outbreak of faint spots on the skin, with a well-defined circular marking usually somewhere on the skull. In humans, the spot manifested itself as a reddish-colored ring found on the side of the skull, essentially in the near vicinity of the temple.

It was to be speculated by some, who were no longer breathing, that the Ratmeister (as well as all of his like-minded brethren who wore trenchcoats and dropped blue dust from their sleeves) also had a population of these special bacteria growing in his gut. Hence the powdered, crystalline mineral residues that he kept dropping from his sleeves, possibly scaling off from his forearms and hands. Not that anyone would be around or alive to make such a speculative declaration, but the Ratmeister also wore his trenchcoat tightly around him, concealing his neck with its collar, and hiding his face with his wide-brimmed dark hat that only cast misleading and impenetrable shadows over the entirety of his featureless, grey face. Therefore, if the Ratmeister did indeed have those special tell-tale marks on his face and/or neck, nobody would have been able to see them. But all of this, of course, was pure conjecture, since nobody had ever been able to get close enough to the Ratmeister to study his skin with a microscope and fine-tooth comb.

The cobblestones of the lonely street were the grey domes of fossilized tortoise shells. Traversing these formations of mineral creation by the hands of humankind was the present challenge of the hour for the Ratmeister, and for the small locust vermin who followed him in secret, preferring to stubbornly crawl over the terrain rather than use their useless wings that had atrophied from the cold over the course of many generations. The long-abandoned streets were lifeless only for the memories of children who once crossed their cobbles, beating each other up, bullying each other so as to steal things like lunch money and certain prized trinket-possessions. But now only the ghostly faces in the windows remained, staring out at the visiting wildlife who had dared to penetrate these quiet and forgotten city streets. In one particular alleyway that seemed to reach a dead end, there were several horseshoes tacked above the various doorways that led perhaps to suffocating residential areas now sealed up like tombs. These horseshoes were curious items, suffering under rusted nails that kept their stainless steel curves from falling to the tortoiseshell cobblestones. These horseshoes at once evoked the slim procession of a witch's ceremony as it rounded the curves of a living green mountain covered with moss and bright morning dew. The dewdrops covered faces, hair and scubamasks, as scubadivers were sent in to examine certain fruit trees that were growing wildly along the countrycide. Of particular interest were apricot trees, cherry trees and some gnarly artichoke bushes with extra-sharp spines that poked the unwary arse and legs of passersby who were too busy looking at compasses and the arses and legs of their companion passersby who were not wearing any witch's attire at the moment.

These fleeting memories were the starvation of the horseshoes, the polarized magnet that pulled the fruit trees like acorns down a vacuum funnel into the darkness of a rusted automobile used to store old library books depicting various portraits of dead presidents and cattlecars filled with people to be slaughtered for their blood and rib-meat. These apocalyptic purgings were reminiscent of the ancient Assyrians who chained their slaves with metal hooks through their cheeks, connecting them together as a queue of lost people appended so cruelly to the chain. In fact, a rusted metal chain, barely recognizable, was found in pieces, interspersed among the dirty tortoise shell cobbles of the primitive street. These discarded implements, including that of an oversized, amazingly huge piano hammer (covered with green felt, of course) could only induce despair, rage, and intense longing in the heart of whoever stood by these new discoveries. Seeping out from under one of the horseshoe-covered doors were several radiographs of birds, in the process of being x-rayed. The x-rays fed out from underneath the door in a uniform rhythm, as if the door became one of those antique movie machines that created the illusion of movement by progressively showing snapshots of objects, people, etc. taken half a second apart, like all forms of early animation. The x-ray of the shrieking bird was therefore revealed to the light of day, in this strange manner. Over time, the x-rays had faded a little bit, so that their pigmentation became close to a dim shade of emerald green, quite similar to the green velvet on the oversized piano-hammer that had collapsed in the street like a discarded beast of burden. What was particularly disturbing about the x-rays was that the bird seemed to be opening its mouth in slow motion in order to consume what appeared to be a human form, only a fraction the size of the bird, in just one gulp. Then, as more and more x-rays were pushed out from under the crack of the door, it became obvious that the emerald skeletal form of the bird was being enclosed by the toothy jaws of something much larger than the bird. Therefore it was a human eaten by a bird which was eaten by something much larger. The puzzles of scale and microcosm were dizzying, as if violent earth tremors could quake apart the stones of the old buildings, which, despite the sneering passage of time, still held together despite the tectonic gasps from the earth.

The Ratmeister looked down at his pocketwatch, learning that the time was 10:05AM. He wiped some frozen sweat from his brow, becoming annoyed with the fact that it was now snowing, and the snowflakes were getting caught in his eyes, blurring his vision and blotting the sky into a haze that could only have attracted the alleycats of the world who saw the sky as the glittering scales of iron fish! It was only normal that the Ratmeister would be visited by such beings, these vagrant felines whose well-groomed coats shone despite the dull, wintry weather. One of them sidled up to Ratsniper, apparently in a gesture of friendliness as her prehensile tail wrapped around his leg and she mewed so profoundly, in such a heartfelt kind of way. She made eye contact with him and defiantly maintained her gaze. Eventually it was the Ratmeister who looked away, perhaps conveniently distracted by the continuing outpour of x-rays from the center door presided over by the nailed horseshoe. And as soon as he returned his gaze to the female cat who seemed to have taken a liking to him, she and the entire troop of felines had mysteriously vanished.

It couldn't have been more obvious that a whirlwind of passionate kisses had melted the sparrows from the trees in which they roosted. Or perhaps better still: it couldn't have been more obvious that fish that were found twitching and jumping (completely out of water) in front of the closed doors in the dead-end alleyway heralded by mysterious horseshoes, were twitching in their final throes of death, as obscene math equations passed through their primitive minds in a linear fashion. These twitching fish were the silver lipstick of angels, something to be passionately kissed once the snowy clouds in the sky had receded and the spring had been allowed to emerge from its urban hiding places. But these were simply dreams of wish fulfillment, as there was no indication whatsoever that the weather would be changing for the warmer. Instead, all one could do was to pull one's cloak up tightly around the throat and body, and to wear warm gloves and hope that piano hammers (which must be touched ever so frequently) would not be so cold as to give the hand frostbite, in the same way ants might bite a naive hand into a state of pained limpness.

The sound of a crash broke the Ratmeister's reverie. The noise came from another one of the horseshoe-heralded doors, not the one from which came the slow-motion x-ray movie about beasts eating birds eating humans. The sound came from the door next to the x-ray door. Ratmeister grabbed the knob and gave it a vicious yank, pulling it open a fraction of an inch. He tugged at the paint-slopped knob and managed to pull it open another inch. From out of the exposed crack fell several flecks of paint as well as a draft of air that was even colder that the one that was drying out his eyes as he stood there in the frozen, forgotten city. Eventually the door yielded to his pulls, opening with a sullen groan. The Ratmeister looked up a flight of stairs to see a plastic mannequin that fell all the way down to the snowy mess at his feet. This particular mannequin was wearing a purple velvet outer-space uniform, with a star insignia on the left side of the chest. Completely bemused by this sinister revelation, the Ratmeister ascended the stairs with a morbid, velvet curiosity that could have only been satisfied with a better understanding of velvet, and the potentially dangerous origin of the purple velvet mannequin.

The stairs led up to an apartment complex, a dais lined with unopened mailboxes rusted shut over the years, perhaps containing written missives from a hundred years ago. The hallway was frozen, in a humid sort of way which chilled his bones and made him fantasize about lighting fires and kicking people who wore gorilla suits when the snow fell in concentric waves of circular precipitation. Various hallways and walkways led off in various directions, presumably to other homes or apartments, but Ratmeister's eyes became fixated on a flight of stairs that led further up, as if to a bamboo dojo where monks prayed to lanterns painted with a varnish made from human blood, leading to maggots that permeated the hanging lamps that were able to withstand the coldest temperatures. In this upstairs bamboo dojo was a tree growing human heads in the shape of bloody red pineapples, an exotic bloody sweetness that trailed wisps of pollen and pheromone-starved insects who madly desired to take the pollen to fertilize whatever head-trees might exist whoever knew where else. Glued to the faces of some of the skullfruits were certain books of classical origins, ranging from Greek treatises on certain points of geometry to gothic thrillers written in Romance languages, dwelling on the subterranean erotic delights of fear and wet knickers from the end of the nineteenth century.

The Ratmeister traversed the dojo, where he found a strange metal ring and ancient papyrus photographs tucked within the hidden compartments of old, useless books on nutrition and capital punishment. These objects were cleverly tucked away within the books, such that it was impossible to tell that they were there, simply from looking at the old volumes as they sat on the shelves to collect cold dust. The air was quite frigid inside this upstairs area, but at least it was still. Frost-bitten fingers grasped at the old books to retrieve the photographs, which had been printed on a kind of papyrus parchment, oddly enough. The pictures were confusing indeed, and unable to assemble them according to any kind of logical sequence, the Ratmeister was only able to sense a glimmer of their underlying theme: the birth and death of dark, glistening creatures who had peculiar musical notes tattooed on their bodies, on the ventral surfaces: the sharp keys of violation. Somehow these creatures were associated with libraries and children's playschools, and had trouble tying their shoes in the morning. The creatures also resembled worms at times, with spines that jutted from the soft, wormy flesh. Darkness harangued everyone and everything that was depicted in these photographs. Of curiosity were certain images of the wormlike creatures caressing timepieces, like wall-clocks and the wristwatches of dead children.

The Ratmeister set aside these grotesque pictures and thought of the days when he spoke tenderly to his garden of hairy tomato plants and told each and every one of the tomatoes that they'd make a great salsa some day. He also distracted himself from the memories of discovering the beauty of telephone vandalism in the more remote parts of his favorite cities, like the time he found a rancid coffee drink next to a mousetrap that had been glued to the side of the telephone booth. Such treasures brought tears to his sensitive eyes and he cried for the lost mousetraps and all of those spoiled coffee drinks that were quietly fermenting and seething with magic spells out in the lost fringes of socially acceptable society, where piles of human feces are deposited next to newspaper boxes and where every image of humanity is spraypainted with alternative runes from an alternative vision of the world where the grasshopper experience shows the way of comets that pass through our hair when we sleep at night.

This touching reverie was disrupted when the Ratmeister found more purple velvet mannequin bodyparts lying in a mess in some of the adjoining rooms of the dojo. As strange as they were, in an alien kind of way, they were also halos of evil, in the sense that their malevolent presence served as a disruption in the normal kind of alienation of regular capitalistic life. The purple velvet mannequins with the star insignia on the left side of their tunics represented a sterilization of the alienation, which might have been just the same thing as alienation squared or cubed. Ratmeister kept the ring but left the photos, and went out into the cold again, knowing that he was forgetting something. But he trudged along anyway, determined to leave town and follow some of the roads that led up into some of the hilly areas that overlooked the dead, frozen city. A sinking feeling in his stomach resulted when he had the disturbing thought of being headed along some kind of predestined path. This feeling gave him pause and filled him with a profound sense of dread.

Meanwhile, at the edge of the small pond that existed beside the old Manor where the Dark Witch lived, the cat once again drew its claws ever so gently across the surface of the water. As the feline peered into the water that would surely freeze later that evening, it observed half-squeezed lemons still attached to the tree, and suitcases full of lightbulbs set beside the tree as a demonic offering that spoke of bloodlust and scabies and trilobite fossils that might all be found glued malevolently to fossilized leg bones of young female sloths who were found hanging from sturdy tree branches when a volcano erupted several tons of smothering ash which allowed these specimens to become fossilized in the first place. If these fossils had the opportunity to arrive in straw-filled crates at a circus tent, then the next generation of chameleon instincts would be inaugurated, ushering in new kinds of standards for godlike behavior and the special kiss shared between the situational metamorphosis that only a bride and groom could verify. The cat was puzzled by this kiss only coincidentally betrayed by the fossils in crates (packed ever so carefully with straw), such that it scratched its head while staring blandly at the ripples that came after the vision. Apparently the water had already relayed its message to the cat, and now it was up to the feline to make sure that it did what it was obliged to do, possibly. But then there was always a nagging sense of doubt that encouraged the creature to look over its shoulder at the twisting variety of evergreen trees that grew from troubled soils.

4
The Visitors

The cockroach scarab flew overhead, then settled on the branch of some non-descript shrubbery that grew on the hillside as a neglected weed. Then it flew to the next tree situated nearby. The scarab had the mark of a man on its back, and its primitive consciousness, or possibly lack thereof, limited its ability to enjoy the Sunday morning comics that were so often found in newspapers. This limitation did not really affect the cockroach scarab all that much, as it had plenty of other things to do, such as using its compound eyes to study the tributaries of light and shadow that would warn it when possible predators were approaching, as well as if there were certain gummy, mysterious things welling up on the sides of injured trees, in all sorts of phantasmagoric colors which might sometimes startle this precious scarab from time to time. Sometimes the gummy spherical things on the sides of the trees were sweet, and other times they were bitter, in unpredictable patterns which the cockroach scarab with the mark of man on its back could not and would never understand. The scarab beetle might have preferred to jump from flower to flower in this temperate clime, but having the colored sap globules which grew from the sides of certain trees made it all too easy to find nourishment, as well as a bustling night-life.

In time, the cockroach scarab (which was really a beetle) was approached by two apes that were to be someday called humans, and they sized the hapless beetle up in the same way hungry eyes stare at a plate of cheese, crushed wheat and sweet, imported grapes decoratively arranged on a festive platter sitting out in the dry desert sands of ancient Egypt. The humans, or perhaps Neanderthals, regarded this beetle in awe, as it bore the image of a bipedal primate on its back as part of its hard-shell and wing coloration, which originally had served as a form of camouflage, fooling most other animal predators. Even though the resemblance between the shell markings and the form of a human was only superficial, the Neanderthals didn't know that. Instead, the Neanderthals plucked the beetle from the branch on which it thought it was safely concealed in broad daylight, and they brought it with them to their meeting place among the tribes. Eventually it was decided that this cockroach-scarab was to become immortalized as a symbol of fledgling humanity's ascendance into the realm of forever-ness. And so the scarab beetle with the human design on its back was immortalized by being imprisoned within a sickly sea of tree sap, being visible in a cell of organic glass made by a tree with sinister bark and earthen needles. And that all happened many aeons ago.

The Feral Cat who presided on the periphery of the haunted Manor first found the slab of neo-amber near a stream with many cobbles and pebbles worn smooth by the current that had tumbled them for many hundreds, if thousands, of years. The amber glint that teasingly caught the rays of sunlight persuaded the cat to push it away from the stream and closer to its own secret, stone-circled pond that was made by human hands during the medieval era. The egg-shaped globule of amber, now worn smooth around the edges, clearly displayed the cockroach-scarab beetle inside, a trophy of history procured by two Neanderthals who had found the bug with a curious genetically determined insignia on its back.

Although the cat was born centuries after the creation of the medieval pond next to the ugly Manor house with battle-scarred short towers and turrets for deadly projectile launching activities, it still felt a sense of ownership of the neglected pond, since the humans no longer took any interest in it. The Black Cat positioned the egg of amber in such a way that the sun would pass through its semi-transparent form during some of the morning hours. It was time for the cat to have its ritual tea made of lavender, rosemary, and of course, catnip and catmint. After the tea, it would always go out to hunt, and then by the later afternoon, with a full belly, it would take a restful nap, seldom disturbed by marauding creatures and other annoyances that might pass through the area.

On this fateful day, upon the retrieval of the amber egg with the strange human cockroach-scarab contained within, the Feral Cat was to observe the Evil Queen to have two very curious visitors. The first person to arrive wore the attire of some businessman from a very faraway land, partially disguised in shadow by way of a peculiar oblong black hat which was almost a helmet, but not quite. This individual walked with a sinister, halting gait, and yet there was something mortal or infallible about it, as it were somehow one of the *greediest* creatures ever to walk the planet. This half-sinister person had an entourage of servants who carried behind him several crates and boxes designed for long and rough periods of travel. At the very back of the queue of servants was one who carried two very sharp-looking spears. At least to the eyes of the cat, which had a great degree of acuity, these were indeed sharp spears whose edges of death shimmered under the late morning sun.

The second visitor was to arrive later that evening, after all of the fanfare and festivities and other secret, sinister meetings had settled down after the later hours that preceded midnight.

During the day, the hoarse trees slept, those very trees who had been shouting for most of the previous night: shouting at each other, shouting at the small servant huts and houses that were in orbit around the confines of the old Manor, and shouting at the sleeping ants who burrowed within the dead wood funguses of painful memories that were crystalline keys found within the caverns within rocks, carved by strong winds of breathly force made from the pursed lips of treebark. This type of verbal violence was a visitation in and of itself, and it is no wonder that most of the peasants didn't know about the concept of earplugs made from a soft, almost soapy form of treesap, which wouldn't stain the skin or glue one's ear to the pillow, for example. So therefore ignorance can sometimes be fatal, especially when one is trying to sleep in a miserable hovel, with the perpetual threat of the local village newspaper hitting the front door with a resounding "Smack!" and the lost chances for sleep dwindle from 4 AM to 5 AM to 6 AM and the sun threatens to rise above the horizon, only reminding our bleary eyed friends, with their ears and reddened eyes filled with candida yeast, that the hours of sleep are now gone and the day cycle must commence, with that awful pilgrimage to receive orders and duties from the magistral Queen of Utter Evilness whose ancestors most likely presided over their own, in a similar master-and-servant pattern which only made one yearn for a break in this fluidic passage of daily activities that knew no starting point.

Such was life in the village of the un-rested, all who orbited the sphere of influence of the Evil Queen.

The Black Cat rolled on its back in apparent indifference, preferring to dream of the love it once had, but then lost ever so tragically. The loss of this love hardened the creature to the cruelties and callous expediencies of life, and it stuck out its hooked tongue, half in a gesture of mockery and half in a gesture of the gag reflex, while pondering the mysteries of the terrestrial world, with all of its savage idiocies and despicable ways. Rolling in clover was its preferred activity, perhaps next to staring into the pool of water and watching the reflections of the birds and the sky pass overhead, like a movie-screen for an extremely private audience.

Eventually the sun fell, faster than an unloved woman could jump from a window frosted with despair, and the cat began to feel a surge of interest and intrigue, and a hunger for prowling around in the night. The darkness was just around the corner, and even the owls twitched with eagerness to leave their tree hollows to feed on the unwary creatures, like succulent mice with bloated abdomens. The cat sat up, very alert it was, and scanned the various regions of the hillside for movement. Spying something, it stalked off into the fading sunset determined to find whatever it was.

The arrival of the second visitor to the old Manor house was something of a surprise, at least to all of the residents. The Ratmeister appeared out of the shadows, leaving the dusty road to approach the old, fortified mansion. He walked past the rotting, severed heads on stakes that were positioned in the damp, fertile soils, without so much as a shudder or even acknowledgement. In his left hand was the ring of metal now tied with owl feathers, as if it were some kind of ritual object used for a mysterious but transcendent purpose. His bold, repetitive knocks at the front door were finally answered by timid, wide-eyed servants who pushed back their quasi-religious skullcaps to get a good look at the unexpected visitor. The Ratmeister offered them the feathered ring and urged them to bring it to the Lady of the house, and reassured them that upon receiving it, the Lady of the house would know what to do with it. The servants led the Ratmeister into the vestibule, and convinced him to stay put until the "Queen" (as they so strangely pronounced the word) had had a chance to receive the object as well as the news of the stranger's arrival.

Ratmeister waited for almost a half hour until one of the servants returned to inform him that the Queen was ready to see him. He was led into a central area with archaic tapestries hanging from the stone walls, and lit by candles, as this place was far enough away from any of the power stations that were very scarce in that part of the world. As the Evil Queen descended a wide spiral staircase, her gait bespoke pretentiousness mixed with cunning, as if she had very little patience for people who wasted her time, especially if they might have been a threat to the sense of control that she enjoyed having over others. As she descended the last curve of the staircase to come fully into his field of vision, he took a deep breath and immediately locked eyes with her. Could it really be her, after all this time? Was she the same person? A keenness and coldness from her constricted irises told him otherwise, and he began to doubt his convictions about her identity as well as her integrity.

The Evil Queen held the feather-covered metal ring in her hands, rotating it as one would a saucer for a teacup. The ring would have been just big enough to fit around her neck, as where the Ratmeister thought it should be, or should have been at one point in his memories that had now grown foggy and alien, almost non-understandable. He had been around women who had taken his breath away, who had given him the proverbial butterflies in the stomach, and yet in the presence of this strangely intense woman, (possibly a witch, for all he knew), all of his mind – his identities, his memories, his purposes in life – all became fluid in ways that made him uncomfortable, in ways that were unexpected and unseating. Of course she denied ever owning the neck ring, but he didn't believe her. In his mind he looked back on his memories of the past few days, and couldn't even remember his experience in the dojo when this strange object had fallen into his hands. For him, there was not even a clue as to where it was found, or how long he had it, and somehow, he had watched the moon, and the moon had told him where to wander: to leave the frozen city and ascend the hilly terrain. To live in the mountains and to become the owl. To communicate with the fishes while not being the iridescent beetle that is often found on summer-struck swimming pools, surrounded by hot pavement made of primitive slate rock, all leading up to a house filled with shrunken heads, and strange totems that lurked in the corners, with platinum television sets and strange old reels of celluloid film that collected dust, along with the sullen poker chips and other peculiarities of the past. The living, breathing replicas of lizard people who walked through daily routines and who would sun themselves out on the summer-struck rocks, periodically shedding their scaly skin and dutifully returning borrowed library books on time.

The Ratmeister again thought of his feet as the talons of an owl, while another scaly log was thrown on the fire by a servant. This hollow branch was many years old, having spent much time assembling the cellulose that would someday be twenty minutes of fuel in the fireplace of a strange woman in the heat of nowhere. The Evil Queen spoke about many ritualistic gestures made by those who lived in her land, and gave more than one quaint speech about morality in the land of the owl and the swimming pool, but her words did not reach the Ratmeister, as he stood hypnotized by the motion of her hands as they grasped the metal ring covered with feathers. All he could think of was how well it would suit her by being around her neck. That the ring would have to expand to fit over her head, or that her head should momentarily shrink so as to accommodate the ring did not occur to him. All he had was that vision of the ring so elegantly circling her smooth and supple neck. In fact, within the vision he wanted to bite her neck in two, so that he could remove the ring that way. His only disappointment for the moment was that the ring was not on her neck, so that biting it off of her was impossible. But only if.

In his mind's eye, he saw her moist, languid steps through the courtyard of her fortress (he could not recall seeing the putrid, impaled rotting skulls), as she reached a ritualistic dais in the dark evening punctuated by candle-light in the enclosed space, within the heart of the Manor. The moonlight added to the candlelight, showing her soft skin, with her staring eyes, glistening with the hint of a tear,

perhaps from sorrow or perhaps from joy, and the metal ring around her neck. Part halo, part shackle, it was strangely odd yet reassuring to see this ornamentation that he would so abruptly sever from her neck, if he could. He imagined his weak human jaws strengthening to canine quality, grasping and digging into her jugular, tasting the blood while feeling her soft chin rub against his cheek While he would quickly sever the windpipe and the flesh surrounding the neck vertebrae, he would lustfully slow down the grinding penetration of his teeth as they slowly severed the bone. This last moment of separation (of head from neck) would be the slowest, most deliberate, so that time in all of its erotic capabilities would become friends with the last moment that her thoughtful head was attached to her body. And after that last little snip, which would be felt as the tiniest of shudders pushing against his now-closed jaws, the metal ring would become free, despite the owl feathers that were now dipped in blood that would congeal quickly like the most delicate flan!

But she had the ring in her hands. Her soft, bony hands continued to toy with the neck-ring, quite unconsciously. He noticed that while she spoke of the events of her existence, and how she was the one to direct their flow and eventual transcendence, her fingers would trace the outline of the ring, sometimes smoothing over some of the feathers that dared to obscure the clean, radial path of the metal, and she would do this with the thumb and index finger, stopping every so often to reassure herself that all parts of the circle had the same thickness. Her hands suddenly ceased their caressing movements as she was distracted by a current of air that blew with quite a brisk force, since they were in one of the enclosed but large living halls of the Manor, with high ceilings that were drafty at night. She looked up at some of the candles and noticed the wind causing them to flicker. By sympathetic response, it was at this moment that she shivered, inviting her guest to retire with her to a more secluded meeting area, protected from drafts and the coldness of night.

The servants were dismissed, and the Evil Queen walked arm in arm with the Ratmeister to a more secure location, to one of the lower dens that was well stoked with a warm fireplace, cheery lights and comfortable furniture. A few downward, winding passageways later, they arrived at the den, which looked especially festive, despite the lack of windows.

5
Penetration

B reathless, the Black Cat peered into the water, thinking of sunken ships and the broad sweeps of underwater currents that can push drenched mounds of sand aside to reveal the bones of whales and people. This kind of currency was completely wet, and the fog of a blistery cold morning was enough to shake droplets of ice from the hair of beautiful but apathetic women. The red leaves on the trees began to fall like corpuscles of blood, hoarding their hemoglobin as if it were money, and as if the closed eyes of an elephant seal pushing through the cold waters was enough to raise the hair on the back of any animal that might seek to rendezvous with the dead triangular skulls of sunken whales, the hulls of misfortune and good, common sense. Meanwhile, there were fantasies about raising the titanic, as if the windows of smashed glass mansions could become the red-haired spare-tires of wooly mammoths that were trapped within the glacier windows that looked into the heart of the world, with a raised hump of fat on the neck of a particular horny skull with a tubular appendage that threatened almost all wary sea captains who could see the kind of vandalism often found in ancient citadels.

These disturbing thoughts became firmly ensconced within the brow of the Black Cat, who by this time, realized that the distorted images of sunken thoughts were nothing but the reflection of the ill-colored moon, now looking more and more like a sinister clock revealing the fact that some kind of special moment had passed, but without the desired results, whatever those results might have been, anyway. The illusory hands of the moon-clock (or that mirage of the clock which was actually the reflected, billowing face of the moon) showed that the minute hand had moved five clicks past the hour, which so happened to be ten. It was at this moment, the moment assigned to correspond to the illusion of 10:05 on the surface of the dark pond, that the Black Cat was startled by a rustling in the surrounding bushes.

Through the hedges appeared a dark man, wearing a dark hat, with a dark, featureless face. Although there were no cheery, glowing, sparkling eyes to reflect moonlight from them, the eyes were there, and alert, nonetheless. The dark stranger made no noise, but it held out both of its hands together, palms outward, as if the gloved fingers radiated outward in a star-like fashion. Or perhaps a clock with ten hands! Regardless of what was going on, the cat did not understand, and the presence of the dark man with the dark hat receded into the bushes until all emanations of its presence ceased completely, and the ghost was gone.

For no longer during that eventful night, at least, could the Dark Cat remain by the side of the pond; it would somehow have to find a way into the old Manor. Somehow the mysterious gloved hands in that strange radiating formation told the feline that this perceived need was true and obliged to be followed. The cat knew that the decadent Manor house was really a comic book with ink-stained pigeon's wings, and so it simply found the back part of the house where a large spiral was painted, and stepped through the transparent wall. The cat realized it was in the pantry, by way of the rotting vegetable peelings and numerous fishbones that littered the floor. Although the feline creature was indeed interested in the fishbones, it felt compelled to follow the scent of the trail which the man with the dark hat had helped to illuminate with his curious gesture of radiating fingers – disturbing black-gloved fingers in an almost sun-like configuration that only evoked possibilities of metaphorical black suns, dead stars, possibly even black holes and other dastardly neutron stars, where one spoonful of such heavily compacted matter could very well easily signify the top-heavy agony of gravity. This special kind of agony manifested itself as a moment of dread, as of the adam's apple that gets pulled downward with a gulp when the reflexes of fear begin to take hold. But then cats did not have the same kind of adam's apple that humans do, fortunately, so perhaps there was also less gravity?

Aside from the organic refuse littering the floor of the pantry, which was so close to the backdoor where supplies and comestibles were delivered, the storage room had many storage vessels made from the local mineral clays and gently fired within strong furnaces. As the cat brushed by these unglazed vessels, heading toward the door, it heard a loud crash in the hallway outside. Barely peeping its green eyes through the door that had been left ajar (but just enough for a hairline crack to allow a stale breeze to pass through), the black feline spied an inflated monk's robe filled with rabid dragonflies. These dragonflies kept flying into the walls of the robe, in order to keep the robe "inflated" or at least comfortably filled by imaginary spaces which resembled a person. The dragonfly-filled robe passed by the door without a sound. The cat pushed on the door with its strong forehead, slowly opening it, with the softest of groans. By the time it was out the door, the curious dragonfly-robe had walked through a closed door, into an adjacent room effectively becoming a hooded keyhole.

In the hallway, the Black Cat with nine lives found various objects and symbols of decadence, such as discarded dolls' heads covered with a grimy dust, and withered flowers and crumpled, browned headlines from useless newspapers now long forgotten. Strangely enough, there were long vines of thick, dead ivy that snaked all over the walls and ceiling of the stone passageway, even though there were no signs of windows to allow sufficient sunlight for plant growth. The cat passed one room that was slightly open, seeing inside a short, stocky witch boiling the heads of infidels in a greasy, brown sauce that smelled of rosemary, garlic and escargot. Then in another room on the other side, a mannequin with a purple velvet spacesuit was holding a boat oar in the act of stirring a large cauldron of asbestos soup – a rather dry soup consisting of styrofoam bricks and a lumpy sea of splintery microscopic needles that were just dying to embed themselves into the lungs of the unwary. The mannequin wasn't actually stirring; it just stood motionless holding the paddle that was submerged a few inches in the asbestos soup. Next to the mannequin was a dusty, spartan chair on which rested an old, dog-eared cookbook, opened to a certain page, presumably the recipe for the soup.

The Black Cat felt gravity again as it passed another room, with its door closed loosely but shaking ever so violently. In the next room (in this hallway which now seemed to extend to infinity, towards an unseen vanishing point), there was a young blonde with voluptuous breasts leaning over a chair, with her hair disheveled and her trousers down. She must have been a careless villager that had been captured, and thin streams of blood streamed down her legs from the site of her perfectly round and smooth bum, which was being mercilessly sodomized by a thick muscled brute who was more than seven feet tall. As the cat passed by the doorway, the hulking sex fiend turned around to view the cat, smiling with a grotesque, gangrenous smile on its face, the pustule-covered face of a minotaur, so far away from home. The lost, weeping cries of the girl were drowned out by the ever present din of a low buzzing sound, as if there were a giant bee hive in one of the neighboring rooms. Next to the chair where the poor girl was being sodomized was the wreck of a cotton loom, broken in some areas by the passage of time and darkness, where shadows and grimy plaster were the only friends she had. The cat passed on to the next room, noticing an open door revealing a floor strewn with a mountain of bloody, rotting body parts. Some of the arms and legs there were fresh, with bright red blood, while others had faded and shriveled to brownish husks that stank of the most obscene putrefaction, teeming with bile and maggots in some places, and over all, providing the illusion of a foul garden of even fouler snakes that dwelled in an endless rot from which one could never awaken. Lying on this nauseating mountain of mass misfortune of the flesh was a golden guitar, with little colored, sparkly gems, most probably costume jewelry. The sparkly guitar somehow managed to remain unspoiled by the sea of stink on which it roasted, and its tantalizing handle, with finely taut, coiled strings, was the perfect invitation to any clever and precise git-pic who might be lurking within this strange house of hidden riches and thrilled telephone booths.

The cat once thought it had a strong stomach, but it had obviously been mistaken, while barely suppressing a heaving wretch that came from its insulted bowels and alpine-air sensibility. At this point, it only wanted to find a way out of this corridor, to find some kind of connecting passageway that would take it to where the black sun would be, at five minutes after ten o'clock. It was certain that the black sun could not be found in these horrendous apartments. Still following the only path it had, the cat passed by a few more closed-off rooms that were shaking and thumping with beastly groans and blood-spattering

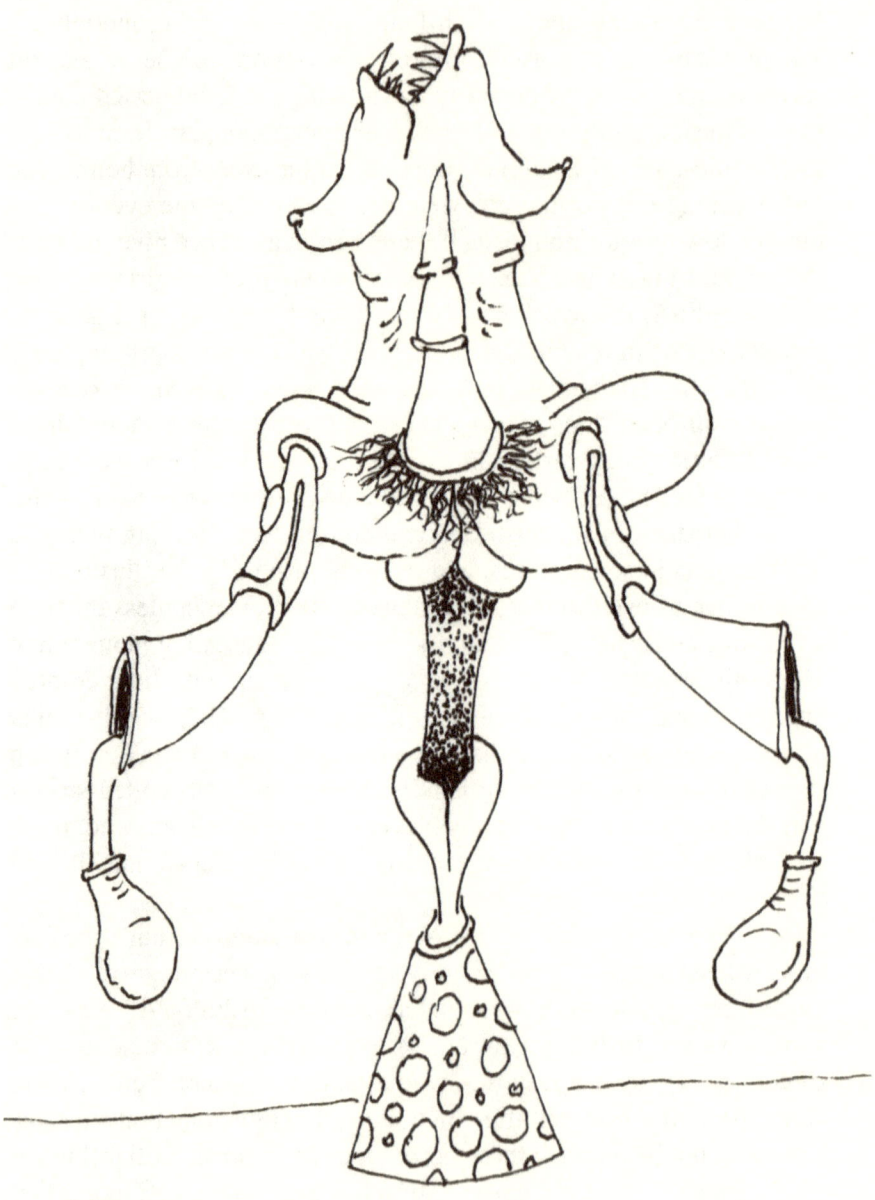

yells of the tortured souls of a Saturday night. In one room, a corporate executive was having his throat slit. In another room, a well-stoked furnace was being packed with useless currency which instantly caught fire. The greasy, round faces of those who pushed the dry banknotes into the furnace periodically glowed with the bursts of combustion caused by the doomed bills, revealing flashes of malice, glee and Sunday-morning cruelty that only a milquetoast family could understand, those wonderful, beautiful people who lived on top of cockroaches who were permanently scratching their sides and groins like a pack of flea-ridden dogs who drank pink-cherry cocktails when the dance was already declared over and done with, after the sad rains of their parade-town had been frozen solid in the dirty gloom of filthy, arctic ice. The aeon passage that facilitated this concretion or calcification of pain in the joints, of lost love in a clean lyre on top of a sea of sonic refuse and old crumpled newspapers in the satin conjugal bed of familial pyrotechnics.

The next room was mercifully quiet and empty, like a foreboding, cobwebbed grandfather clock that leans precariously to one side. The cat quickly darted into the silent room, and sat upon its hind legs, with its paws over its ears, while staring up at the horrid ceiling, so dank with regret. Away from the door, the cat was able to regain its senses, its inadequate but token measure of centering itself, grounding itself with a futility that rarely passed over its face covered with short fur, with green eyes that asked for a ring of light to push it through this sewer system and out of the experimental rabbit cage containing strange, laughing subjects with blood-shot eyes who stuck their tongues to train-tracks when the weather was cold, as a sort of dare that could purge the witch's broom from the other mops in the closet that were all secreted away under the staircase in one of the rooms upstairs, or so was the intimation of that location.

Meanwhile, in the upstairs part of the Manor, the Ratmeister had his face between the legs of the Strange Witch, who was writhing in the knicker-licking throes of ecstasy on her oval-shaped bed, which appeared to be a certain kind of waterbed, but which contained living brains rather than water. The sleeping surface of the bed retained all of the fluidic properties that one would expect from a waterbed, including the oneiric wave action, but the main difference was the presence of the living brain, which seemed to be an entire, single unit, from some ungodly colossal creature unknown to life on Earth. Every night when the Strange Witch slept on the living bed, she swore that her dreams were not her own, and that what she saw during those quiet hours of closed eyes gave her enough insight for her to recreate the entire universe, beginning with all of those magnificently headless bodies, and her trophy collection of skewered crania which formed the central garden of her daytime reverie, in the same way sleek black crows, her only true friends, would come to land on some of the specially placed stone ledges of the inner courtyard which jutted from the building. There they would spit guttural phrases at the dried, stinking heads that were clotted with blood and contamination. And usually upon waking on this bed, she found her mouth smeared with lipstick and vague left-handed half-thoughts of spending time in a musical church where pigs went to find religion in step with brainless, commercialized wine and pop music.

While the Ratmeister pleasured her twisting body, stimulating the fully erect nipples on her sumptuously full breasts, the Strange Witch stared up at the ceiling, closing her eyes because the light of the candle was too much for her. She was a true raven, and her dark hair was as shadowed as a neutron star, potent enough to keep any struggling object from getting out of her gravitational field of influence. Eventually she couldn't stand any more of his swirling, poking tongue (which had gone literally *everywhere* over the voluptuous contours of her body) and then begged him for his hot magic wand that was destined to work wonders for her disposition. Within an instant, he was inside her and brought her to another countless climax within a few strokes of the sword. In a moment of inspiration, the Strange Witch got on all fours, and the Ratmeister mounted her like a dog, filling her with sperm. After receiving many lashes, the witch who was once a raven lay flat on her belly and spread her legs some, inviting Ratmeister to enter her yet again, but this time, deep into her shapely posterior. And as she grasped at the edge of the bed to receive the Ratmeister's deep, penetrating member, she looked like a fuming iguana, baking in the sun and clutching at a hot stone in the full heat of summer, with bulging eyes and curling, quivering lips and a viciously poking tongue, gasping with an unspeakable and breathless vocabulary which was new to her and which spoke the poetry of her impending doom, despite however many more fields she flew over, or however many more skulls she added to her collection. After they were finished, with their faces aflame, the two strangers stared at the ceiling and said nothing to each other. They would have probably each smoked a seaweed cigarette, but there were no such vices to be had in this particularly faraway land.

Ratmeister rose from the bed, in his adamantine, snarling glory, and took a step towards the door, completely liberated. No longer needing any clothes, he took another step, while noticing that from his skin erupted thin shoots of oak branches – the kind that one might see during the springtime, during the cool season of rains and germinating flowers. As the skin of the Ratmeister began to glow with a new pigmentation, his form became murkier and murkier as he approached the door to leave. He didn't even say anything, as if he knew that somehow there were to be no goodbyes. As the Ratmeister touched the door, his body assumed sympathetic shapes that mimicked the contours of tree rings that made up the solid oak door that led out of the Strange Witch's bed chambers. At last the Ratmeister had achieved his true calling: he had become THE door of the house, the Door of all doors. As his body merged with the door, replacing the curves of flesh with the ancient concentric rings of burnished, amber wood, the portal quivered with a kind of unprecedented excitement, and so did all of the other wooden doors in the house (only the wooden ones, not the metal doors). Suddenly, each and every wooden door in the creepy Manor blew open as if violated by a stormy gust of wind, releasing the contents and inhabitants of locked rooms that had been sealed for periods that exceeded the span of the oldest memory, bringing to light those which had been locked in the dark. Simultaneously, the Strange Witch felt exhausted suddenly, instantly falling asleep on her cerebral waterbed filled with gelatinous, pulsing greymatter and neocortical pillows that supported her languid frame. With her face to the ceiling and her weary legs spread, her pink, hairy slit opened like an eyelid to reveal a curious, precocious eye that hungrily stared up at the ceiling while the rest of her body slept. For the remainder of her dominion over the people, over whose lives she had intimate control based on terror and ecstasy, the new coat of arms of her regime became the simple icon of a thick and gnarled oak tree with a full trunk and a full globe of leaves. And inside of the round, symbolic mass of leaves was a vertical eye. Upon the following morning, almost every wooden door in the ancient Manor bore this strange, new coat of arms.

The locks of these doors quivered with excitement in anticipation of the key. It was even said, while intervening college students later ransacked the house, months after the Strange Witch's death, that the locked doors were most likely to open if one were to ease a pinch of sugar into the lock. Despite the disaster that would later overtake the Manor, of a blistery fire that would severely damage several of the rooms and also cause an identity crisis for many of the intervening college students, there was still the comfort of homely lit lamps for pleasure reading, and muffed carpets that needed to be vacuumed from time to time when the undead would tread over their battered fibers in the off-hours when nobody was looking, and the rooms, like a sonic honeycomb on the sure road to ruin, would manage to squeak out a blood-curdling yell that would intimate the power of an acorn, especially when one's pockets were completely full of them. This was the uncanny power of sugary locks embedded in the wooden concentricities of time.

The Black Cat, left for dead but not forgotten, spent the night in one of the filthy rooms in what it later realized was a dungeon. It was terrified by the pounding of walls, the blood-curdling shrieks, as well as the sounds of carnage, sawing, screwing, dismembering, and the like. Although there were no windows on any of the walls in the rooms of the sickly hallway, the cat knew somehow that the morning had arrived. Curious enough was the sudden appearance of the iconic image of an oak tree with an eye in the middle of the green part, on each of the wooden doors (not the metal ones), but even more mystifying was the sudden swarming of flies that seemed to arrive all at once and began to land on the various pieces of rotting material. In all likelihood, someone must have opened a door or window, which allowed the flies to enter the premises, to scavenge a rotted meal and lay some eggs. There was a fresh, clean current of cold morning air that also moved throughout the stifling passageways, creating some circulation which partially counteracted the debilitation caused by the stench.

The cat finally mustered enough nerve to brave the hallways anew, and left the dungeon room in which it had fearfully spent the night. It went back the way it came originally, to find the back door with the strange spiral on it. As it passed some of the rooms from the previous night, looking at how their contents had changed, the cat's sense of fear was replaced by a loathing nausea. When it passed the room of the young, pretty wench who was being raped by the pustule-ridden, gargantuan minotaur, all that remained of the horror was the lower half of the poor girl's corpse – the legs and hips twisted and discarded in a heap, covered with cockroaches that had already begun to shit and lay their eggs all over her cold body. There were large, aggressive rats everywhere, too, which only stimulated an aggressive response on the part of the black cat, who took vicious swipes at them with its sharp claws, and growled and shrieked in all of the ungodly, unearthly tones that a cat's voice could reach.

Eventually it found the exit, but saw another divergent branch in the passageway that had not been explored on the previous night. A waste, really, but the cat didn't know which of the pathways it really needed to pursue, anyway. Pushing through an open doorway, the Black Cat, now hungry and thirsty, found itself in the kitchen proper, observing hung pots and utensils, as well as the dangling corpses of people and animals which presumably had been left to age so as to provide a tastier source of meat. Upon one of the counters, on top of a large oak butcher block, was the corpse of the young blond who had been so rudely and thoroughly sodomized the night before. Her head was missing (presumably used to make a delightful goulash for some equally delightful ghoul), but her arms and torso were still on the block, with one breast nearly severed. Nearby was a large multi-gallon pot on the stove, furiously boiling, and covered with a thick, foamy scum which could only have come from whatever meaty item was contained within. On other countertops were other items in preparation: chopped carrots and garlic, diced celery and onions, dried herbs to be ground with mortar and pestle, succulent, bloody filets of game animals, rising bread dough, as well as some very fancy-looking crystalline seasalt, heaping over the edge of a pewter bowl. On shelves that lined the far wall were many numerous cookbooks bound in cracked, dusty leather, with subhuman skulls for bookends.

Going up a flight of stairs, the Black Cat found itself in a room of mirrors, with the floor completely littered with red and yellow rose petals. The air in this room was far sweeter than anything it had smelled in this decaying place so far, and it sat down a minute to recenter itself, looking at its reflections in the mirror, *ad infinitum*. Not soon after arriving, the cat felt sleepy, and decided to take a short nap. It reclined on the rose petals and had the following dream:

> A human woman lies down atop a bed of cat-nip, with a triangle of glass billiard balls arranged on her abdomen. Each of the billiard balls is made of completely transparent crystal, with a fossilized green fly embedded in the center. The flies look rather natural in their poses, as if there was not a struggle to suspend each one in its eternal tomb of crystal, for all the world to see. The sleeping woman is bound with prehensile ivy vines that restrain her arms, legs and neck, leaving her effectively incapacitated. The sleeping woman is therefore oblivious to the passage of time, and to the movement of earthquakes throughout the land in which she unconsciously resides. Outside of the room she is in, which is actually a shower stall, there are strange twins who hold bath towels and communicate to other friends of theirs who move ever so precariously along a window ledge, braving their fear of heights as well as a fall to their deaths. A coat rack lurks in the room, and taunts the daredevils as they move back and forth aimlessly but carefully along the window ledge. Such thrills are mimicked by similar images that play out in full drama on a black and white television in the

room, with an extremely scratchy picture, suggesting
that the hotel where the people are staying is certainly
not a luxury hotel, by any means. The carpet of the
hotel room is a forest green color, and seems to be
connected to the plantlife that exists in the bathroom,
where the sleeping, incapacitated woman with the
transparent, fly-embedded billiards balls resides. The
foggy morning light pushes across the green rug, as
the sun moves overhead. Now and then a faint seismic
tremor is felt, and the pictures in the room, adorning the
walls, shake on their nails and hooks. The pictures on
the walls are of low-grade photography, as if someone
were spying on ordinary people to take low-res pictures
of them in order to possibly use them as blackmail, or
in this case, just as low-budget wall decorations. In one
of the pictures, a grandmother is breast-feeding a baby
while pushing around one of those old-fashioned baby
carriages. Both the grandmother and the baby look
happy, and they are standing in front of a store that
has a crude drawing of a severed umbilical cord in the
shop window. Flying around the store are biting locusts
that are at least three inches long, and these insects
harass everyone except for the grandmother and the
baby. While everyone else is seen running away in this
poor-quality photograph, molested by the locusts, the
grandmother and baby continue to smile. This is what
the picture in the hotel room shows.

Eventually there is a knock at the door of the
hotel room, occupied by the towel-hoarding twins and
their daring window-ledge friends, and the visitor who
knocks on the door (which is now made of a dense
foam used to make surfboards), is another motionless
mannequin, who of course wears a purple velvet spacesuit with a familiar golden star insignia on it. The
mannequin does not move, but it holds out a necklace
made with beads that resemble red blood corpuscles,
round and disc-like. One of the towel-hoarding twins

gingerly takes the necklace from the mannequin, thanks it and then closes the door. As soon as the door is shut, an earthquake tremor reverberates throughout the very warm hotel, and there is a large "thud" sound of something heavy falling to the ground, right outside their door.

The Black Cat awoke from this dream, feeling somewhat like a wet sock being dragged around by a horse that usually pulls around one of those special fetish-wagons that used to get lost in desert areas. The cat normally didn't feel like a fetish-wagon, but after that very peculiar cat-nap, it did indeed feel like a fetish-wagon, being pulled along for however long into the most meaningless of eternities. Swatting its tail angrily, the cat sat up and looked again at its surroundings, very surprised to learn that the walls, which were once covered with a smooth, seamless, mirrored surface had now changed to a well oiled mahogany scheme, as if it were inside of a jewelry box. The colored rose petals were still strewn about the floor, and now the room smelled just as rosy as it did of that earthy tree smell that only fresh furniture can produce. A wooden lattice, also made of mahogany, led to a large hole in the ceiling, which the cat decided to follow. In the upstairs room there was dull, matted green carpet that had seen better days. Only one tiny light was on in the room at the other side, such that the available light was limited to a narrow beam that landed on the vomit-ugly patch of carpet; that was the only way that the black cat knew that the carpet was green (it had color vision). The rest of room was obscured by gloom. In the center of the room was a large, round object which had vines attached to it. Immediately footsteps could be heard in the hall outside this new and unexplored upstairs room. The Black Cat immediately hid itself behind the sphere and crouched down very low, so as not to be seen.

The door opened and there was the silhouette of the Strange Witch. She lit several of the candles in the room, enabling the Black Cat to notice the large orange pumpkin that occupied the center of the room, as well as vanity night stand where all of the makeup and beauty products were kept. There were mirrors everywhere in this room, as well as a sinister coat-rack which was positioned right next to the door, on which hung several black gowns and other witch clothing accessories, like black coned hats, black lingerie made from the finest imported silks, and black executioner masks made from hemp fiber that had been dyed black. The Strange Witch sat down in front of her vanity, daintily lifting her black dress and planting her naked ass right smack down on top of the pumpkin. The Black Cat, who was cowering behind the pumpkin and a stack of old music manuscripts, then made the connection: the pumpkin smelled the way it does because of the witch! The cat had remembered that the pulp inside of a pumpkin usually had its own special musky, earthy odor, but this smell was even better.

The Strange Witch brushed her long, pretty hair, while reaching for some disposable tissues with which to wipe the tears from her eyes while she sobbed in front of the mirror. For a woman with raven eyes and simultaneously for a raven who occupied a human body, her weeping did not inspire much credibility. But apparently her tears were genuine, as she continually reached for the tissues, always kept in a black leather purse that looked like a staved-in gorilla skull, completely leathery and deflated. Whenever the Strange Witch left the castle during those rare moments of obscure and secret business necessities, she would always take her gorilla skull purse with her. It was just part of the ritual, even if she did so while asleep, without any memories of leaving. While the Black Cat still remained hidden behind her, the Strange Witch produced a fresh tube of red, greasy, monkey-face lipstick with which to apply to her smooth, moist, well-toned lips. She dragged the red makeup along her lips, bringing them to the hue of a luscious fire-engine red, or perhaps a delightful strawberry red, or cherry red, even. The sound of her smacking lips was quickly followed by the tube of greasy, monkey-face lipstick being thrown into the top drawer of the vanity. With her face now made up and her newly achieved emotional composure, the Strange Witch exited the room with a profound crease of intent that marked her brow. There was a determination in her step and she curtly shut the door behind her, leaving the hidden cat to its own devices.

6
The Dungeon underneath the Manor House

In one of the numerous dungeons found beneath the still, as-of-yet unidentified Manor house, the Pork was having another identity crisis, while locked up in one of the clothing lockers. His corpulent body was strapped to the inside of the locker, and had bleeding gashes all over him. Volumes of half-congealed snot were dripping from his bruised snout. His armpit lightbulb nest was stuffed with wood shavings, the same kind of material used to pack and ship expensive sculptures. The Pork, despite the waves of snot that issued from his nose, was weeping with homesickness, yearning for the lost city of porks from which he originally came. But that city was now under some kind of quarantine, or at least, some kind of restrictive surveillance. Even if the Pork had his freedom, he still would not have been able to return to the lost city. Not having eaten for a day, not having been able to caress lightbulbs for at least a day and a half, the Pork languished in the stuffy locker, which was really a form of cruel and unusual confinement, of course effected on the orders of the Mother Corpse, the latest incarnation of decadence who presided over the centuries-old Manor house.

Meanwhile, in a primitive garage of lost memories, the eyes of children formed like inkspots on the dismal aluminum walls, like stains. These childlike eyes originated as chemical blemishes on the face of the metal paneling, but later grew into clusters of intelligent awareness that could only see and not speak. The eyes on the walls could transform the dust and grime on the shop floor into strange compounds of solid, twisting shapes, which were safely contained in laboratory beakers of large volume housed on burners, safely positioned in the center of the shop floor. Inside of each beaker was a whirlwind of grime and dirt, of soot that would make anthropomorphic formulations of arms and incomplete torsos, with half-inquiring faces that were aching to break out of the mold but which were not solid enough. All of these primitive cultivations were presided over by the black cowboy mechanic, who often drove around in a homely, beat-up jalopy and wore nothing but black, including the black cowboy hat. (This cowboy mechanic was of the same mystical order as the Ratmeister, who had recently disappeared forever.) Somehow this black cowboy hat was an obvious anachronism, as if a hat could be a mechanism of time travel, allowing its wearer to hold a watch in the palm of his hand, as if he were the powerful conductor of a fleet of orchestral drummers who could choreograph the percussive language of entire civilizations within the hand-clap of a pocket watch. The Dark Man with the Black Hat kindly regarded his twisting experiments of dirt with a wary eye, looking for possible imperfections that could be further cultivated to help him better fight his own personal war against the Perfect. While the Perfect had left him alone for several weeks now, apparently because they were having second thoughts about lightbulbs, the Dark Man still kept his guard up, and stared out of the grimy shop windows into the streets of an awful place called Lucipheromone, a town sometimes known in the ancient texts as "the lost city of the pork." But now, most people only called the place Lucipheromone, instead of such a long and overly dramatic term, like "the lost city," etc.

The Dark Man felt that all of the Pork People he saw passing outside of his window were up to something sneaky and dishonest, but their activities were always hard to chart, and in fact, he was often preoccupied with other items, such as growing grapes of grime so as to ferment a certain kind of wine that could be useful in dealing with the problems of Perfection, which were really the storefronts of the Perfect – those repressive, wayward freaks who ballyhooed up and down the streets at all hours, selling likenesses of Jesus and having soapbox discussions and orations right next to the abandoned pantyhose factory that was now only a mass of sad brick and mortar which barely held itself together after all the years of neglect. There was no denying that the Dark Man had no love for the Perfect, or even the soporific town of the Pork People in which he had become exiled for the past few centuries.

While he worked on his cultured goulash of dark grime made

from machine oil, cascades of blue, crystalline dust would fall from his black overall sleeves, staining the floor with a clear blueness that rivaled the freshness of the sky on a cloud-free day. This mysterious blue dust often shook from his sleeves, but he never knew why. Suddenly, the Dark Man glanced over at the filthy clock hanging from the wall, next to the radio-set that was covered with spiderwebs. The hands of the clock pointed to five minutes past ten o'clock. The Dark Man would always seem to look over at the clock when it was that particular time. If he went to sleep early, he would wake up at 10:05 pm, with a sudden, uncanny alertness that was not typical of the average sound sleeper. It was as if he carried his own time piece inside of him, as if his golden pocket watch could somehow replace his heart or another one of his vital organs.

Every day or so the Dark Man would take a break from his work for an hour, and walk the listless streets around dusk. That was always the opportune time to carouse the city, because all of the porks were at home, feeding themselves in a frenzied state, possibly even spraying the walls of their swinish homes with wave after wave of nasal snot. The hour before nightfall was always a good time to be out, at least for the Dark Man, because he would not have to deal with these porks in whose filthy city he inhabited for utterly forgotten reasons. Usually the Dark Man would walk up and down a favorite street for a week, exploring its oddities and regularities, searching for the hidden treasures that would only come to life once he had shaken some blue, crystalline dust from his sleeve onto whatever it was that he found. These walks helped nourish his atrophied body and aggravated senses, bringing him a moment of respite out of the daily focus on generating grapes made from dirt and machine oil.

For this particular week, the Dark Man had been favoring a street that had bas-reliefs of blue ceramic dolphins (all weathered and dirt-glutted, of course) that populated the back alleyway of one of the busier streets. Despite the congested nature of the outside street, the back alleyway somehow provided an intimate shelter only through a few layers of antique brickwork, which together created the perfect sound barrier. Not only was the din of the industrial streets completely shut out from the service alley, but there was a certain kind of peace and purity to be found among the filth and the dusty refuse here that was achieved simply through the absence of pork people who daily scavenged the busy walkways of the city, constantly making noise with simple, logical expressions that passed for speech, and of course, the generous sprays of snot which were very much the primary repertoire of these unwholesome and coarse people. But in the back alleyway, all of that madness was temporarily erased, and the alter-ego of the city presented itself by way of dolphin waves sculpted and glazed into the hard bricks, with a touch of the primitive, uncalculating hand, but also with a certain degree of deliberateness that had more finesse than the finest floral arrangement that one could get for one's girlfriend, as a token to show her that he loved her.

The dolphins worked their way through the edge of the wall, with metal implements like spoons and keys which were placed in an offering cup bolted there, near one of the corners of a large, uh, building that might have been the back door of a factory or some kind of disturbing warehouse. The Dark Man soaked in all of these organic details that were ironically made of stone and metal, and with his cup full, he returned to his garage, which was really a workshop, and which was also his home, because there was nowhere else to go, and also because automobiles had fallen out of fashion, at least, according to his views.

Across a sun-scorched sky, perhaps in another world, but perhaps not, the Salt Manor house sat on top of hollowed soils, like a tumorigenic eschar that wanted to die but couldn't. There were rats that occupied the hollows of the soil, and the Manor (the parasite that it was), used diplomacy to get the rats to become the root system for the house, as if it were now a tree that would dig its way through life in order to survive. The house itself was made of too many bricks. Layer after layer of brick had been established as the foundation, as if maybe each brick constituted a red blood cell that altogether would form the life-blood of the entities and/or people behind this house of madness (of the most conventional, repressive sorts of madness, however sadly). The layers of brick were also like skin, and really these bricks gave the house its substance. They were by analogy the organic essence of a house such as the Manor that lurked in the wilderness, a wild but injured animal that would like nothing more than to sink its teeth into whoever or whatever would drift close enough to be within striking range. Likewise, the rotten house, with all of its cavities and passageways, was also a loose tooth in the gum of a terrestrial body. Sharp and moldy, rotting and sensitive. The only windows in the place had flecks of dried blood on them. The Lady of the house, known as the Mother Corpse, as the Evil Mother, as the Dark Witch, as the Evil Queen, etcetera, wouldn't have it any other way.

On this bright and sunny day, the Mother Corpse threw open her bedroom windows to allow the sunlight to enter her withering chambers, replete with faded pictures and shrunken notices, and all sorts of past signs of life illuminated in their peculiar states of moral decay. Her abdomen was bloated today, as if she might have been pregnant or flatulent, but then the enlargement could also have been from all of the rancid things that she put into her stomach, delicacies of pain which came from the kitchen which were culled and clotted together with much care, on pain of death, of course. The familiar Baked Nun was waiting right outside of her bedroom chambers, to deliver the mail and provide updates on which citizens and slaves were mercilessly slashed to death over the course of the very long and intolerable night. The Baked Nun laughed hysterically, with her jaws flapping during this annoying process. The only reason why the nun was still breathing was probably because she didn't have a penis, or so believed most of the other servants who always seemed to know what everyone else was doing, and who always could be seen furtively talking to each other in hushed tones when they thought that nobody was watching them.

The Mother Corpse accepted the missives and the news, and then had a young, neophyte servant brought in for her pleasures. After he had serviced her and completely drained his prostate of all extraneous fluids, his head was later found on a stake decoratively positioned between one of the town friars and all of the other servants from last week who took care of the Mother Corpse's carnal needs. These newer skewers were to be found in the inner courtyard collection, not in the back of the house, where the dishonorable heads of traitors were to be found. For the loyal servants who were decapitated in the line of duty, their heads were lovingly pissed on by the surviving friars on a daily basis, not just out of respect for the dead, but also to satisfy the Mother Corpse's sullied sensibilities for depraved ritual.

In one of the upstairs classrooms for the servants' children, the black cat hid behind a bookcase while listening to the reading class. The children were punished for making progress with their reading skills by having one of their outer digits chopped off. Thus, every time a child advanced to the next reading level, one of the joints in the finger was severed, one piece at a time, for every scholastic display of growth and excellence. Of course, the same honor was awarded for bold steps forward in mathematics, art and even cooking class. Those intelligent children who had no fingers left by the time they graduated were usually given menial jobs, like sweeping and gardening, and usually they didn't live long anyway, so nothing really was lost.

In fact, it was the non-intelligent, non-achieving children who held onto their fingers and who ended up with the more desirable positions (but even then, all male children had numbered days in the presence of the Mother Corpse, regardless of their level of intelligence and scholastic abilities), so in the end, it really was in one's best interest to show very little interest in things like reading, thinking or any kind of mental activity that required intelligence or initiative. The Mother Corpse liked it that way, anyway.

While the Black Cat shuddered behind the bookshelf, listening to some of the brighter students lose their fingers and toes for that day, it noticed a secret door behind the shelf that apparently had been hidden on purpose, only through which someone small like a child or animal could pass. Since the little door was not locked, it was easily pried open. The cat waited to perform this maneuver only until the schoolchildren had left the room for lunch, which for that day was a bowl of stewed cow intestines with an end of stale bread for each child. Odors of the putrid nourishment wafted through the labyrinthine halls, summoning the children who nursed their bleeding stumps, provoking ambiguous growls of protest from their little stomachs, so desperately in need of nourishment. As the children quickly left the room, the black cat began working on opening the door with its claws, which were barely strong enough to pry it open.

The Feral Cat passed through the small doorway in one leap that made it seem like it knew exactly where it was going, when really it did not. Making its way through a wooden tunnel that was carefully chiseled during some earlier century, the cat dodged the spiderwebs, the rat skeletons and the other moldy debris that littered the passageway, which were only but faintly illuminated from the direction in which it was heading. The passageway branched in a few different directions, but the cat took the path that led towards the light, which was really only very dim, at best. This passage eventually ended at an elbow covered by a grating, that led into one of the bathrooms, so dingy with litter and discarded beer cans. At the turn, the cat decided to keep going, exploring this passageway that moved ever upwards, and even passed a scared mouse who whistled by, like a rocket. The turn in the path ended rather abruptly, opening onto a round enclave that would have fit underneath one of the uninhabitable corners of the roof, or on the side of a turret that might have been too slanted to be tolerated by one of the bipeds, with their weak spinal columns. Out in this nearly sealed alcove or chamber, a few removed bricks revealed the blue sky of the outside, and the whistling wind reminded the Black Cat that there were indeed realities that exist beyond the wanton gore and callousness found inside of this festering Manor. Apparently this little freak of an alcove – a misfit chamber, really – that had been forgotten by the building's numerous, greedy architects, created the perfect refuge for the cat, who was now remembering the sweet smell of the outside, with its special pond next to which it often sat, with a strange scarab beetle preserved in amber. Visions of chasing mice in the cool wind at dusk created a feeling of nostalgia that almost obliterated the oppressiveness of the present situation, and the feline was no longer scared.

In the strange space created by the well-concealed intersection of geometric solids (the odd space between a cylindrical turret and rectangular nature of the adjoining room), there was enough space for a family of whatever creatures to live, and apparently such a family did at one point exist, as evidenced by the shards of refuse

and ripped pantyhose that littered the little area. Poking its head through one of the rectangular holes once occupied by the cellular bricks that composed this holy Manor, the Black Cat realized that it was on the west side of the house, facing the opposite direction of where its own abode resided. It could see some of the trees that it used to climb, and some of the boulders behind which it hid, when stalking prey and hiding from wolves and other dangerous beasts. In fact, the Black Cat had adequately seen enough of the Manor establishment in order for it to decide that it was not a place for love to exist, and so it managed to squeeze through one of the openings in the wall and jump down, safely landing in a bush several storeys below. No bones were broken from the fall, and the cat quickly sprang away from the bush where it landed, making a fast retreat into the surrounding woods, completely exhausted and famished.

The Mother Corpse descended the final step of the winding staircase that led to the lowest level of levels occupied by the multitudinous underground complex of dungeons, all of which existed as a subterranean sprawl beneath the Manor, leading out in all directions, like an underground city, or more appropriately, like a subsurface tumor that was insidiously spreading below the skin. And beneath the lowest of the dungeons was... The Mother Corpse shuddered at the thought; it was one of those family secrets that had been kept at the level of utmost secrecy by her cranky father who never had time for her but who instead spent interminable hours in the lower levels collecting strange specimens of worms and fungi and all sorts of rare minerals, or so he claimed. Her father was a furtive, always nearly absent figure in her life, and it was actually due to some of his elite and most trusted servants (who were all to be executed, ultimately, the last one by her hand, even) that she received what little upbringing she had.

Indeed, her mysterious father had forbidden her to visit the lower levels beneath the lowest of the dungeons, and although at the time her curiosity was easily assuaged, now her desire to see what existed beneath her reality was steadily growing in strength. The door that led further downstairs was bolted in several places, with decaying, rusted locks the size of a brawny man's shoulder blade. Littering the floor were several sticky pools of dark blood that were nearly dried, as well as the plastic arms from toy dolls, furiously scattered everywhere. The Mother Corpse carelessly stepped over these miserable distractions and entered the dungeon hallway, whose nitred, arched ceilings periodically dripped stale groundwater and housed semi-intelligent cockroaches who were thought to be as large as a shoehorn, in some instances. The hallway was deserted, perhaps the guard had been eaten or consumed by something nearby, but nevertheless, the Mother Corpse was not surprised at this vacancy.

In one of the furthest rooms, the Mother Corpse turned the key that opened the room which housed the Pork. The miserable swine had shackles on his limbs, chaining him to a wall. In this state he was found seated with his back against the wall, with a blank stare on his porcine face, completely dribbled with half-dried snot. The prisoner snorted when the Mother Corpse entered, protesting his brutal treatment, reminding her of how well he had served her before. With the coldest gesture of dismissal by an unconscious raising of her hand, she ignored his lame squealings and once again demanded what was rightfully hers: the purple lightbulbs. Such a situation might almost remind one of the fable about the golden goose killed out of greed by its owner so as to provide permanent access to an infinite supply of golden eggs. Of course, that story ended badly, since a dead goose cannot make any golden eggs. The Mother Corpse tried to keep this latter fact in mind, and so she successfully resisted her urge to sever his pathetic, cowardly throat. Instead, she viciously kicked him in the groin, and ordered the chattering, sniveling guard (who had now appeared out of the shadows, apparently after relieving his bladder behind some old barrels stored at the end of the dungeon hallway) to release the Pork, so that he might continue his toils of providing the Mother Corpse with her supply of purple lightbulbs, whose purpose or use was completely unknown (perhaps even to the Mother Corpse).

The Pork received this treatment as a threat, to remind him that losing another batch of purple lightbulbs because of carelessness or cowardice – it didn't matter which – would be his last mistake before he left this world as a slab of moldy bacon to feed her morally disturbed and thoroughly famished household. With his tail between his legs and a lump in his throat, the Pork turned to leave the dungeon, escorted by the dysfunctional guard. At that moment, the ground rumbled, and all three beings experienced a simultaneous vision: an image of fighter planes descending on an island to drop bombs, with happiness music playing in the headphones of the pilots, who were arcing their planes in loops to show off their flying prowess before dropping bombs that would ultimately devastate the ancient island, with its forests, its people, its culture and the secrets that it hid beneath the foliage cover. A lot of people would die that day. After the island went up in a mushroom cloud that was seen and heard for several kilometers around, there were pink and orange insects, possibly displaced from the blast, that quickly attached to replicas of cars that were made of freshly chopped trees, most probably endangered species of trees that were taken from a rainforest and so dutifully carved to resemble some of our favorite antique cars. These replica cars were to be found in the neighboring continents that surrounded the vaporized island. The fiery color of the sap-sucking insects, as well as the pulsations that the insects made when their proboscises penetrated the fresh lumber, were mesmerizing to the consumer children who approached the replica cars, as if they were closing in on their future in the way hungry sharks intercept heedless prey whose trails of blood only make them targets for the devilish green eyes of the deep. So on one hand, a mushroom cloud of fire, and on the other side of the fence were the wooden automobiles filled to the brim with tree sap that gently oozed at the slightest touch, even at the slightest look. The sun instantly went into a state of eclipse, and the shadow of a hand was burned on top of each car, leaving a smoldering print that smelled as sweet as it was bitter.

At this moment the vision faded, and the Mother Corpse, as well as the Pork and the riveted dungeon guard looked at each other momentarily, and then went back to their previous thoughts, without the slightest hesitation or second-guessing. Only the Mother Corpse revisited her memories of the vision later that evening as she marveled at her new coin purse made from the scrotum of a gargantuan human-slave who was only killed a few weeks ago. The house tailor did quite the expertly job in sewing together this precious leather pouch at the behest of the Mother Corpse. He was quite pleased with his handiwork, as well as the Mother Corpse's pleasure, and while he sipped his wine that night over supper, observing her pushing her first golden dubloons into the savage purse, he was rudely reminded of his own castration when he took on the job as head tailor of the Manor.

George Bevis Bush, the grandson of the well-known George "Dubya" Bush, and also the current President of what was left of the United States of North America, leaned back in his comfortable leather chair in the Oval Office, and released a creaking fart that would have scared even the vampire bats, had they been hiding in the walls like he was used to hallucinating that they were. He looked at the reports on his computer monitor. The stocks were up, and now he'd be able to pull in enough money to buy that second ranch for his wife, Kathy. Pleased at that idea, he extracted another dried, green booger out of his nose and looked at it, as it sat on his index finger: as green as the color of American currency! He wiped his finger on a peace pamphlet circulated by a certain Middle-Eastern delegation and tossed the whole mess in the trash. Then he returned his attention to the important issues, like the American economy, that nagging situation concerning border disputes. It was true: a few years back, before his administration was in place, several of the western states of the United States of North American had the audacity and thorough lack of mind to secede from the union. They joined forces with a runaway sector of Canada – the Western front, including Vancouver – and created their own Cascadian country which was proclaimed to be "socialist" in nature, meaning that there were such programs as socialized medicine, or cooperative farming and industry which spread the hours and resources evenly across the infant nation. Although too difficult for George B. to grasp, this new country was founded on both Marxist and Anarchist principles, with love as an indispensable ingredient. With only a four-day workweek, and a five and a half hour work-day, and plenty of food and leisure-time to go around, life had taken an interesting turn. But George B. preferred to stick to his capitalism i.e. his wage slavery, and to the culture that was created to maintain this state of wage slavery. Perhaps the time was drawing nigh when the US would attempt to reoccupy the

Cascadian Area, but that time had not yet arrived.

The town of Lucipheromone, sometimes known as the "lost city of the porks," was located somewhere in that wild batch of Cascadian madness, although it was never to be found on the official maps. For all who knew of it, but who did not belong to that scene, it was an embarrassment, and a place to keep one's children away from. Possibly in Canada, possibly in what was once Washington state, or even northern California, it was somehow as old as the indigenous peoples who were eliminated through the invasions of the Caucasians and their disruptive notions of Progress. Some people said that the town assumed many names, depending on who was doing the talking, while others felt that the place was timeless, and could never have a name, distinguishing it from many of the other, ephemeral locales on the globe. When the Pork returned to his home city in the early morning hours after spending most of the night on a cramped bullet-train, he went to a local tavern that only bachelors frequented, since it was a place in which no wife or girlfriend would ever dare step foot. And since he didn't have a wife, he felt right at home among his other porcine friends who were often there after their brief work shifts ended. Dripping with snot from snout to sleeve, from elbow to table, the patrons sat around the bar decorated with sullen, red lightbulbs, as if they were in a darkroom looking at porno pics about to be distributed via newsstand girlie-mags. Rather than darkroom chemicals, they had their shots of hard liquor and mixed drinks in front of them, and in place of exposed print paper to gawk at, all they had were the sights of the harlots doing their tricks to develop within their wet psyches. The hazy bar atmosphere, thoroughly choked with marijuana smoke, was intense yet quiet, with much talk about life and money while servile women got on their hands and knees under the tables and sucked the thick, meaty dicks of these porkly patrons. Of course, these service ladies were also paid *under the table*, as it were, and on an average night, each service-girl swallowed at least a third of a liter of the porkly semen of which they had acquired an intimate knowledge, over the course of their stay in the town. It was true that these women were usually homeless, low-income off-beauties who were lured to the town with promises of upscale, high-bonus escort roles of classy promiscuity, but the local clientele of the town was literally just a bunch of pigs. And a few missing teeth did not diminish their feminine powers of persuasion, either as, in fact, the pig patrons there certainly found such imperfections to be of the most attractive sort. In fact, the less teeth, the better, as far as certain pork people were concerned.

Underneath the card table at which the Pork was sitting, he felt the familiar tap on his zipper, and he instinctively passed a twenty-pork bill underneath the table. Soon thereafter, he felt hands calloused from hard work unzip his pants and a set of whoever's chapped lips wrap around the shaft of his uncircumcised cock – piggy smegma and all – and begin to give him a blowjob. The Pork rocked back and forth in his chair, farting in her face, while nursing his gin and tonic with one hand and holding onto his five card stud with the other. He'd nearly won the round (the card round, that is) anyway, so his attention drifted from the glass of liquor that he was pulling away from his snot-covered snout to the rhythmic oral stimulation he was receiving on his engorged member. He closed his eyes and almost dropped his hand for everyone to see the cards, but not quite. Eventually the right amount of pressure was applied, and the Pork's semen sausage exploded in her mouth, whoever she was, while with his left hand, he placed his winning card combination down on the green felt table, winning him a grand total of fifty-thousand porks, without tax. After the last convulsive spurt of cum into her unseen mouth, he passed an additional five-pork note under the table so that she would swallow (instead of spit) and lick his ding-dong clean of jism. It was a perfect moment, really: the noisy bar, with red lightbulbs everywhere, his stack of winnings for the night, and half-finished drinks with cigarette butts floating in them were all he could see. It was really all just a swinish mess, but that was what made it so wonderful. Truly the stuff of dreams!

Most of the people had gone home already, so the Pork could focus on his greedy pleasures of the flesh without having to rub elbows with some of the other rowdy pigs who had been there earlier. This place was a Musical Drink Sanctuary, just like any other. Apparently his five-note tip included his pants getting daintily zipped back up again, so all the Pork had to do was rise from his seat, fully confident that he wasn't flashing anything to anyone other than what he did deliberately to begin with, and bid everyone a good night, swilling down the last of his alcoholic slush like the true swine that he was.

7
The Dark Cowboy's Visit
to the Night Desert

In the bright morning of the next day, the Feral Cat awoke out of a long and sound sleep which had the creature almost feeling like its old self, before the traumatic discoveries of the old Manor. For all of its years living next to the haunted architectural behemoth, it had never ever decided to go inside of its imposing volume to explore its awful secrets. As it stood now, the Feral Cat was much more content to regard the trees as they merged with the soil, paying close attention to some of the charred trunks that had been recently exposed through several sharp bolts of lightning. The lightning had revealed the inner tree flesh, exposing the rings of time to the atmosphere, effectively undoing a story that was only half-told. This fear of death was perfected by way of the black, charred highlights around the edges of the rent wood. It was then that they cat observed the exposed fibers of organic ribbon that had moved through the body of the tree at an earlier time, just like lies.

The truth was something that filled an hourglass, or perhaps an attic where all of the sublime motions of maternal domesticity reigned under the authority of any house, of any garden where hummingbirds zipped from flower to flower, exploring a library of statements, a passageway of truths. This direction always seemed to lead back to the house, it seemed to the Black Cat, who suddenly felt a hunger for human books and who instead stared down at the human-like cockroach scarab forever embedded in the amber. It was true that the cat was finally learning to read, after all of those decades that passed over the hill, like a calm before the storm that happens when a new library is threatening to move in on a sleepy, non-communicative town that hates books (like so many sleepy, non-communicative towns in places like the United States of North America do). For lack of books, the cat realized that the human likeness from the back of the scarab – forever staring back at him – was the sole consolation in a bland hillside that lacked words, where the only words that existed in the immediate vicinity were those being held prisoner in the Manor, like hooked tongues that were the wooded sandpaper of closed doors, bearing unrecognizable rings of history completely foreign or even alien to the viewer, which in this case, was the cat. Since vocabulary was being held prisoner, like an island that was suffering a naval blockade, the Feral Cat felt a certain obligation, in the same way a witch might burn a candle at both ends, in order to answer the telephone from time to time, as if this kind of sonic witchcraft might represent a toss of freshly cut flowers or even a projection of beauty onto the silvery smooth screen of the night sky when it threatens to hail down a thousand verbs when the right seedling of actuation was released like the fiery tail of a green phoenix bird. This latter thought of the green phoenix excited the cat greatly, causing it to salivate, while it precipitously pawed at rats that were not there, and hopped at imaginary creatures that crawled the outside walls of the Manor, which were obviously invisible to the naked, naïve eye. The Feral Cat of course was generating several ideas about where it was, and for whom it was living, and for whatever purposes it might continue its life, even if to wrap its dark claws around the wax drops from candles, in the same way water fears oil and how it might put one of its paws on the lips of a young human being, to explain the secrets of wood, so as to pass along the torch, however ironic that might be.

The Feral Cat did not fear contradiction, but it did fear the prospects of blankness, like the blank walls of holding cells in the fungal hallways of the Manor, especially when the bloodstains were invisible in the darkness. The cat came to fear the empty skies when there were no falling meteors to latch its eyes onto, or when smooth, unblown surfaces of water in the nearby pond were still enough with a sheen that hid the fiery remains of the architectural goldfish whom it knew surely lived beneath the surface, despite the trouble that they would always cause those whose spine was doomed to a fate of bone-loss, assuming that milk was in short supply. The Black Cat relaxed its raised, black hair as the passing breeze diminished, as the hillside dwelling next to the pond fell into a state of peace, however temporary. Likewise, almost sympathetically, the cat fell into a deep sleep, completely unashamed to nap again, attempting to take advantage of the time that still remained to it.

Several kilometers away, the noon train pulled into the station in the lost city of the pork people. The train halted at the exact same spot it did everday, and disembarking passengers stuffed their bloated forms through the exit turnstiles so as to follow their divergent lives, moving off into different angles and trajectories that were simple and yet far too irritating to follow in all of their nauseating consistency and predictability. Some of the rusted posts of the train station had obscure handprints painted on them in three primary colors: red, green and yellow, and these handprints were small enough to be made by children. Not all of the rusted posts had these markings, but some of them did. When the pork people rudely brushed by these colorful handprints made with a sinister array of childlike color, the hands might have waved back at these unthinking, determined people in the same way a feline tail might flap in unison to the human wave of a goodbye. At this moment, the sun seemed to approach the Earth several kilometers closer than its regular position at high noon, and a moment of solar judgment approached almost as if there were some being of omnipotence skulking about in the heavens who had nothing better to do than to obsess over industrialized peoples with silly, fragmented conceptions of self-serving morality. The light became blinding, and the handprints on the rusted supports in the train station began to glow, as if a cheery greeting were not enough. Autumn leaves were precipitously yanked from momentarily weakened trees, and hot winds blew through the area, although they should have been cold. This feeling could make one weak in the knees, and yet paradoxically, full-length passenger lockers were open near the ticket booths which revealed mannequins who had been in storage, perhaps as a reserve for some impromptu fashion parade, or a manifesto of hygiene which was periodically held by the leaders of the town so as to help its populace remember how to dress in the morning and to brush teeth and comb hair. Of course, it was also credibly possible that these mannequins were put there for a different purpose, like when one could find poisonous sunflowers growing through the weakened concrete

floors of abandoned nursing homes where faded portraits of loved ones were rolled into picture tubes to be archived by the tendrils of loving vines. When the houses are invaded by plants, then the mannequins are the proverbial meek who inherit the earth.

Fortunately, the intense wash of heat and light diminished quickly as the sun receded from the earth, and the solar expansion became a memory and not a reality. This recession of light would disrupt sleep patterns, forcing some children to stay outside into the early morning hours, to play games with flashlights and search for dinosaur teeth that had clattered to the pavement like the crash of dropped spoons and forks on the pavement next to the train station. The remaining pork people, mostly station attendants, became livid and grotesquely animated, greedily dropping to pick up the forks, spoons and the occasional knife. Later that day, when the collection was complete, all of the ubiquitous metal, unknown only until high noon that day, would be ceremoniously placed in some of the collection receptacles around the pork town. Usually these metal collection bins were bolted to the sides of less frequented buildings, like the sinister dolphin mural executed in ceramic right outside of that empty factory.

On that particular day, after the handshake solarflare, the pork people donned masks that covered their eyes, disguising everyone from each other. It might have been easy to mistake this gesture for some kind of small town festival or tradition, but it was obvious, from the somber, quiet pacing, that this act was no festival. The pork people marched around aimlessly, almost as if in a *dérive*, but their empty gazes revealed equally empty feelings, as if a part of themselves had melted and then drained from the vessel that was considered consciousness to them, and was never heard from until several days later. In the meantime, family connections dissolved, fetuses were aborted, and fatal kool-aid suicide punch was served to everyone. Of course, the pig people drank the party punch with the fatal organic compounds, but none of them died, and none of them looked up at the sky, either. Some of the pork men went down to the local stream to pull some fat trout from the waters, but these trout were then spanked on their sides and released back into the stream. And some of the pig women wore pantyhose over their heads and robbed all of the banks in the town, but then the money was returned to the banks later that night, after the sky had fallen and darkness had overtaken the town. Streetlights were extinguished in favor of using handheld torches, just like in the old days.

The Black Cowboy stared out of his grimy garage windows at all of these goings-on, and shook some blue crystalline dust from his sleeves, and wore his dark trenchcoat – the kind that he always wore when he prowled around at night. With his face in the shadows and his body in a hexagonal limbo, he exited his domain and lurched onto the empty street, hearing the far-off shuffling of pork feet in the middle of whatever festival or town pow-wow they might have been having. It was all a mystery to the Dark Cowboy. He had half an impulse to leave town in his jalopy and to visit the desert, those coyote wastelands that were but a short drive away, and easily accessible in the grand scheme of his life. His boredom was almost as fierce as a gnawing hunger, in that it would momentarily lift ever so briefly upon the arrival of a distraction. But then as soon as the distraction had vanished or led to his desensitization, then the boredom would return, along with the socially imposed suggestions of "gee, shouldn't I be working, or making babies, or eating?" That's what commercials and prime-time television were for, as well as for providing programming relating to social control, such as those numerous, no-name detective shows which the apes and pigs watched brainlessly. But since the Dark Cowboy didn't have television, especially in the sinister stomping grounds of the Perfect, which just so happened to intersect with the lost town of Lucipheromone, he was blissfully ignorant of most of those peculiar, dehumanizing practices. The most compelling fantasy to the Dark Cowboy, aside from a strawberry-jello swimming pool filled with fragrant orange roses and naked, ovulating redhead beauties, was a toppled, leather easychair that lay out in the middle of the desert, which sat in front of a fossilized television set that had been shot at by poachers, and shat on by buzzards, leaving nothing but a scenic delight of disrupted domesticity on the forever dry soils of a desert of nocturnal dragonflies. That moment of beauty, perhaps mythical in time, and invertible like an ambidextrous hand, was the tablet of cuneiform dreamstuffs shoved under the pillow each night to feed the tempestual hearth of dreams and of the movement from the south to the north and vice versa.

This scene of frozen desire in the desert was attainable, when the contradictory arms of heat and cold, light and dark, sun and moon were in an uncertain and ephemeral state of peace. Therefore, it should have been no surprise that the moon would suddenly pull the nocturnal face of the earth closer to it, the side on which the pork town, with its mass of masked, torch-carrying pork people groping about on alleyways devoid of electric street-lights, was walking about during this very near midnight hour. The moon was full to begin with, and now it had grown in size, easily blotting out a third of the night sky, making visible all of its pale craters and grainy surfaces which usually were hidden from pigs without telescopes. The ground also shook from time to time, and the oceanic tides became extreme, flooding out several coastal areas for the hour, which although was quite disruptive, actually resulted in only a very few casualties.

The Dark Cowboy left the town in his dingy jalopy, spitting pistachio shells out of the window and feeling the cold air move through the hair on his head not exposed by his imposing dark cowboy hat, with strange leather ornamentation, almost Amerind, but not quite. The front of the hat had a medal made of lead, attached around the hat's barrel by a black cord. The medal was trapezoidal in shape and had the vague articulation of some kind of spiny, six-sided object, possibly a snow-flake, or maybe a spider web, or some kind of insect. In some places the "spines" appeared to overlap slightly, making the strange figure stamped into the pliable metal seem organic. The entire piece looked rough and archaic, as if it came from the exotic vaults of faraway Athanor, a toxic factory that was shut down several decades ago after several people in the neighboring villages had reported seeing ghosts and human-sized, bipedal rodents who were walking around with engorged phalluses and a hunger for the pink, pungent flesh of long-haired primates. And so the Black Cowboy's hat bore this plumbic symbol, totally sheltered in a darkness that was at times excessively dramatic, but then at other instances the crisp closing of a venus flytrap, as fast as one could turn the page of an ancient book with a worm-eaten spine.

In the desert, away from the strange noises of the pork town, the cowboy communed with the night lizards, attracting their childlike interest with phosphorescent splashes of a cupric blue from his forever moving sleeves, gesticulating to them a reenactment of the creation of the solar system, and the ebb and flow of solar flares, as they would eventually come to scorch the earth in the distant future. Such a train of thought translated into wrist motions ended up being quite a stream of information, and the small pack of desert lizards, most probably a strangely communal troupe of gila monsters, observed attentively. The close proximity of the moon put a new kind of glimmer in their dry eyes, carving lines of shadow and knowledge across the features of their reptilian faces, revealing to the Dark Cowboy the timelessness of species and the scales of lizard microcosms that turned pathetic, scaly shoes and handbags into the organic architecture of cities yet to come when all of the interferences of Progress were weeded out, and cast upon a festering dung heap outside of town, next to the advertising roadsigns.

At that point, after communicating his intentions, the Dark Cowboy sat down upon a slab of granite and absorbed the feedback from the night lizards, who had been chirping among themselves, especially as the moon receded and a few tremors were felt from underneath the tectonic plates that were hidden deep beneath the dry, sandy waste of a landscape. The night lizards told of daggers made from black diamond, and how explosive sugar factories – the kind that manufactured caramel, artificial fruit flavors and soup thickeners – would become obsolete, trading the dominant culture of fungus worship for a culture of minerals, instead. This promise of clarity was quite a shuddering moment of pride, and the Dark Cowboy stared down into the dark blue sand and realized that stone steps that adhere to crystalline architecture can move in circles and so therefore so can words. And this form of universality was poignant as it was harsh, but it was certainly true, as in the same way fate can become more than a concept, and how serendipity is something that surpasses the 1960s.

The Black Cowboy was speechless from the revelation provided by the night lizards, and he got into his ancient jalopy and tore up the road in a peal of dust, and returned home in the early morning hours. By that point, all of the pork people were either asleep, passed out, or still fornicating quietly in the institutional rooms designed for such activities, all leading toward the furthering of the Pork State, and of course, those Pork Ideals of Perfection. Such a form of growth was echoed with rumors of the return of the Perfect, who had not appeared in several decades. But by now such rumors had been circulating with a great deal of frequency, leading many to speculate that it wouldn't be that long until the Perfect would show themselves again, bringing toys to the young pork children and law 'n order to the brain-dead adults who presided over pork society.

As the Dark Cowboy went to sleep, sliding into the first strata of unconscious life, he was visited by obsessive thoughts of purple velvet mannequins, who were always hiding under the stairs, completely speechless, but always wearing that same star insignia over the left breast of their strange velvet tunics, as well as the strange, repetitive thoroughness of doorknobs, in that their various round shapes always led to the opening and closing of passageways. In many instances, the doorknobs came to be morphologically synonymous with rubber squeeze bulbs, so that all doors in this unconscious state had doorbulbs instead of doorknobs, making the opening of passageways within all edifices the result of squeezing the bulb on each door. Such a system would be infinitely more cathartic and practical, he thought. But the fantasy was interrupted, always interrupted, by the mannequins who seemed to be everywhere, at all times, and fit into all compartments of all sizes, even when most people would not expect them to fit in such unlikely places, like under the stairs. Soon, it would become obvious to the world that the threat posed by mannequins, who wore the same clothing and makeup cherished by people, would be enough to cause a massive identity crisis, perhaps even on a worldly scale, and subsequently to instigate a change in the modern sensibility. This change would be profound enough to redefine childhood and work, and to redefine the uses of toys, adult products, as well as the vaults of computer systems which were now housed in many subterranean places, so as to cool down these overheating machines in order to give them enough time to think. Someday soon, mannequins would be loathed and shunned all over the world, in the same way Jews despise fried oysters, or in the same way Baptists are allergic to cunnilingus.

8
A Visit to the Dungeon

Within the halls of the Salt Manor (as this vernacular name had replaced that of the original Edenhorn ancestral name, long ago, by way of strange legends and annoying rumours), the living corpse of the Alchemical Waif paced to and fro, completely torn on the inside. Although she had recently considered herself the Mother Corpse, today she felt different, and hence she identified more with the concept of "Alchemical Waif." The usual, sporting decapitations no longer pleased her, as if the river of distractions had run dry, like the bleeding topaz gemstones left behind on the riverbed of sleep, attracting the vicious green horseflies of memory to prey on naiveté. The Waif was anorexic, queen of the castle, princess of beauty, and mother of ugliness, all at once. Sometimes she was a witch, and then other times she was a guitar. Different aspects of her personality would surface depending on the most seemingly trivial things, which had yet to be defined, and which perhaps might never be defined, since nobody every really got very close to the Queen (and lived to tell about it).

Just that morning, the Alchemical Waif, always so under-nourished even in a land of abundance with plentiful meat and crops, took it upon herself to begin searching the lower levels of her subterranean stronghold, in order to penetrate the deepest reaches of the keep which had been sealed off long ago by her elders. When she had assumed authority and complete inheritance, her hands and mind had been filled with the numerous distractions of external wars that had influenced her medieval sensibility, by way of monetary insult and political intrigue. Her precious time was taken from her, being spent dealing with these mundane issues rather than resuming work on past projects that had existed long before the word "industry" had first passed the lips of her ancestors. As a child, she remembered the times when her father and uncles would come up from the sub-basements and lower vaults completely breathless, with a disheveled look about their persons, with their clothes bloody and tattered and their faces filled with hatred. She would always ask them, especially her uncle Roger, who always favored her, to what manner of secret activity he and the others were involved with in the depths of the Manor house, but even Roger would apply a forced smile and change the subject, instead diverting the conversation to the topic of her studies of alchemy and solar systems that existed in faraway galaxies, with alien suns and alien planets housing what could only be considered "creatures of phantasy." Then his mind would silently return to whatever it was that he had been occupied with for the previous part of the day, the part of his day that the little Waif had not been able to witness. And at that moment, every time such behaviors transpired, she felt like she lost him, as well as the rest of her family.

The Alchemical Waif traced her wary fingers over the ancient, carved symbols that adorned the wall next to the door that led to the sealed area past the lowest of the known dungeons. Her fingers moved over the rusted bolts and locks of the door, like feathers. She licked her lips with anticipation and gingerly removed the crumbling metal bolts which she had ordered one of the guards to cut through hours before. Likewise, the colossal padlocks disintegrated into flakes of corrosion, as if she had smashed giant scarabs with her lithe fingers. She simply brushed them aside, since the guards had already cut through the old seals that separated her from her past. She took only a handful of her most trusted guards with her, and armed with torches and pistols, they began their downward ascent.

In one of the first rooms she encountered, which directly adjoined the downward spiraling staircase, perhaps once existing as a simple office or storeroom, there were near-empty tabletops, with the remnants of canned food including rat droppings and tiny bones, near-complete skeletons mired in low forests of dust. The explorers were careful not to disturb the dust, which was sure to wreak havoc on their respiratory health. The Alchemical Waif didn't even try to flip the light switches that were scattered throughout this new territory, as she was certain that no electricity had coursed through these lower circuits in decades. When the bottom of the broad, majestic, spiral staircase had been reached, it was decided that of all doors to be tried first, it was the opening of the tiny door on the far left that should be attempted. The Waif cast her light through the bars covering the window portal of the door, as if the interior of the room should have housed a child-prisoner or someone of small stature. The door opened rather easily with a gentle creak, as the sole contents of the low-ceilinged room appeared to be a set of rabbit dentures, a Victorian top hat, a cracked mirror covered with dust and a sickly hued patina, some smashed teacups and last but not least, the skeleton of a child with long, blond hair, and contorted in the fetal position, bound by dark iron shackles. From the looks of the skeleton, the child might have been sucking on its thumb, or coughing up blood – it was really impossible to determine. The Alchemical Waif turned away from the room with a grimace on her aging face and looked to the other doorways for a sign of progress. While one of them was sealed from behind by a wall of bricks and mortar, the weak locks on the rest of the portals easily yielded under the forced entry of the guards. In one of them, there was what appeared to be a locker-room, or perhaps it was a coatroom with several empty coat-racks, long since abandoned. There were no hung coats, but only the dark coat-racks that cast strange twisting shadows that neatly but hauntingly matched the strange, twisting contours of the dark wood of which they were made. In the back of the room was a large, imposing refrigerator – the kind made during the earlier period of the twentieth century, now reposing like a hulking sarcophagus next to sinks, toilets and other forms of plumbing which had not carried water in ages. Touching the handle of the old refrigerator triggered a memory in the mind of the Alchemical Waif, as she shuddered with the opening details of the recollection:

As a young girl, she had been introduced to a girl much younger than herself as her "little sister" or possibly "little cousin" – she couldn't remember which. She had always had other cousins who were crafty, industrious and obedient, but this particular little girl was very feisty and insolent, and at once very independent. In fact, the Waif-as-a-young-girl decided that this younger girl *should* have been her sister – she had definitively wanted such a bond to exist. It even seemed, at the moment of formulating this desire, that they had made mutual eye-contact with a knowing smile, as if some kind of deep mutual recognition had taken place. It was only later in the evening when her elders had taken the child from her. She remembered despairing, reaching the point of panic, as she ran from room to room in this underworld area, asking her aunts and uncles what had happened to her cousin and her friend, and receiving the blank stares of ignorance and apathy. It was only in the waste transit room, a small room which opened on a foul underground river, and often used to store garbage and waste to be carried away by a barge that would visit weekly, that she found her cousin, or sister, beaten to a pulp, waiting to die and slovenly resting on rancid excrement and the decaying pieces of dismembered animal flesh, human and beast, alike. The Waif cradled the dying girl in her arms, crying in torment and watching her life slip away. In the same garbage room was the very same kind of refrigerator that the Waif had just discovered which had triggered the memory. Recalling further, she remembered that after lowering the dying girl back onto her final resting place of shit and carnage, the *refrigerator had spoken to her*. Somehow, the refrigerator was trying to tell her that there was something *illegal* going on, but at the time, she refused to listen, so overcome was she by her last meeting with her best friend. The problem, however, was that she could not decide if she were remembering a dream, or something that had actually happened, instigating a feeling of powerlessness which reminded her of the hole that she had in her heart.

The Alchemical Waif bristled with anger and sorrow, stretching out her arms that were so very much like the spread wings of a giant raven whose territory was being invaded. After the death, whether real or imaginary, the Waif couldn't remember what happened next, of how she returned to her life, with its commonplace activities of home-schooling and torture-training. She had actually forgotten about her friend for all of these years, and if it weren't for the imposing refrigerator, looking like the tomb that it probably was, she would never have remembered. She turned her conscious attention now to the refrigerator that stood before her in the present. Upon investigation, there was nothing inside of it, of course. The position of the refrigerator, as well as the overall shape of the room, both suggested that the room of garbage she had seen in her memory was not the room that she was standing in now. But even still, the newly discovered memory awoke within her a sense of dread and self-loathing that she had managed to repress for all of these years. Simultaneously, she had a seemingly random but equally disturbing thought: she had not had her period in over a month, in the time since her strange visitor, the Ratmeister, had vanished, possibly becoming one with the wood of her bedroom door. While that latter thought passed through her sense of consciousness, the ground trembled underneath her, causing the stony subterrene walls to shake.

Somewhere on the Pacific Coast of North America, the Pork finished strangling the prostitute with whom he had had his way only minutes before, first suffocating her and then gradually applying enough pressure to break her neck. With her lifeless body dangling in his arms, he threw her to the ground and spat on her. As "They" always say: *you get what you pay for*. In fact, the Pork had paid quite a generous sum for this disposable whore, who from the moment of birth had been branded as *disposable* according the customs of the pork culture. It was completely true: only in pork culture was it possible to kill certain prostitutes (the ones who were labeled at birth with the "disposable" designation). Of course, purchasing the services of this special class of entertainment required more than the usual amount of currency, but the end results were worth it, or so said most of the porkly patrons. The Pork and enjoyed his fuck and his kill, so he did not regret spending the money.

After getting dressed, he delivered the body to the rib-place he always visited for lunch, just because They had such a great barbecue sauce that They used. It was true, these "disposables" served many uses, and not just for sex toys and abuse toys: they were also used for food, implying a certain degree of cannibalism within pork culture. But of course, these special prostitute pork ribs were considered a delicacy, and were far pricier than the barbecued bones of the regular game animals which the pork culture cherished, even down to the marrow that was sucked with gusto from the crudely smashed bones. Therefore, the philosophy of pork culture was to consume every part of the animal or person being consumed, so as to avoid waste, and also to propagate the total humiliation of the object of consumption. It was thought that this total humiliation coupled with total consumption would lead to a more practical society based on the strange marriage of fear and happiness.

When the Pork returned to his studio, he searched his armpits for purple lightbulbs and found one, affording him the luxury of wiping the oily sweat from his hard-working brow, and almost invariably guaranteeing the extension of his life for a few more days. As long as he could produce a purple lightbulb every few days or so, his success in life would be guaranteed. The second hardest part of the lightbulb business in which he was involved was to successfully deliver the goods, without being robbed or taken over by alien forces. The Pork took the new lightbulb and carefully packed it in a small crate with heaps of sawdust, taking extreme caution to prevent fractures, as if the purple lightbulbs – always purple and not any other color – were eggs or offspring to which he had just given birth.

The Dirty Alchemist (sometimes known as the Dark Cowboy, on certain days of the week) looked up at the archaic lasso ropes that adorned the walls of his dusty garage, savoring their savagery that was gently highlighted by the dim illumination pouring through the grimy panes of glass. He hadn't raised the main garage panel in years, since all of the materials he now brought to the shop were not cars or automobile parts, but components of mannequins that had been smuggled into the pork city of Lucipheromone. In the pork city, anything could be had for the right price. For him, his particular vice – or perhaps avocation, or really, passion – was the study of mannequin parts after they had been safely disconnected and deactivated. Especially during these socially turbulent times, it was important to avoid dealing with mannequins that had not been disassembled, so as to prevent the mannequin from having sentience, which in turn would lead to incrimination on the part of whoever was found in possession of the mannequin. The Perfect would see to that. It wasn't even known how exactly the mannequins and the Perfect communicated, but They always showed up whenever mannequin manipulations were occurring. For that reason, most people decided to avoid having anything to do with mannequins, for fear of

being woken in the middle of the night by a knock at the door, and then being taken away, never to be seen again. The Perfect were always followed by a body of such rumors, leading the vast majority of people to fear them.

But he was not afraid. He always handled mannequin parts the way his mentor had taught him, so that by now, doing his experiments and alchemical processes with mannequins was of second nature to him. Often enough, he almost always had on hand several hands, legs, arms, torsos and mannequin heads (with and without wigs) that were well-packed in crystalline salt to keep them fresh and viable. His mannequin sources were reliable, always delivering the fresh plastic goods within hours of his request, and the meetings were always conducted in shady areas, ever so discreetly, such as in the near-abandoned industrial areas of the pork city – usually places where he would be unlikely discovered by Them. The alchemist stared down into the rusted crucible in which he always mixed his compounds, preparing to add a plastic hand, or more likely a firm, artificial waist or upper torso. The process was similar to cooking, resulting in the creation of items to be consumed, but these items had diverse uses, diverse buyers, diverse investors and even diverse thrill-seekers who paid much of their hard-earned currency for the opportunities to take advantage of these mannequin objects of pleasurable hybridization.

As the Dirty Alchemist stirred in the last of the battery acid, adding in a few chips of a metal that would melt at near-room temperature, he slowly lowered a plastic hand into the crucible. In most cases, he would remove the purple velvet astronautical exploration uniform (with the gold star insignia over the left breast) and discard it for its lack of taste, its lack of cultural identification and connection with what most of his buyers evinced and affirmed. As for why these mysteriously and randomly appearing mannequins would be wearing such costumes wholly appropriate for the realm of science fiction circles, was anyone's best guess, but the end result is that they were disquieting, and would always show up when least expected. Of course, they didn't talk, either, but that didn't stop some folks from trying to communicate with them. In all recorded instances of attempted conversations with mannequins, the end result was always the same: the mannequins stood where they were positioned and said nothing. Then, as stage props, they were moved by unseen hands to other locations, apparently when nobody was looking. An analogous explanation was the old question of whether or not the noise can be heard if a tree falls in a forest where there are no ears. But whatever their secret explanation was, the mannequins seemed to have a life of their own, and was most likely directed by some vague and sinister entity with at least a minimal amount of intelligence and lethality.

The Dirty Alchemist, once a mechanic, once a cowboy, shook blue crystalline dust from his sleeve as he stirred the reaction cauldron with a long pole. His fingertips glowed as he gently introduced a catalyst that would convince the combined, congealing contents of the reaction pot to transform into a composite substance, perhaps even a living being with a life of its own. Such transformations were not uncommon during these sorts of crazy days, and were even to be expected. The cowboy alchemist removed his wand from the pot and took a step back, giving the mixture time to go through its chemical and poetical associations, and then re-associations, in an ever-changing but simultaneously ephemeral transfer of identity and growth that would lead to the genesis of some demented plasticity that might enhance the domain of what was miserably called "consciousness." Or so was the idea. The Dirty Alchemist stared down into the reaction cauldron, reaching in with an iron hook to pull out what he had created, to bring it into the fullest light of his optically subdued studio out in the wastes of a pig city. The Alchemist observed that what was once a mannequin hand was now a coxcomb, the head of a rooster amplified with cerebral digits of a brilliant ruby hue and consistency, which projected dreams of light from the gristly fingers attached to the skull that became the clenched knuckles of a powerful fist, and vice-versa. The neck that was once a wrist, choked on a wishbone made from a sliver of moonlight, which manifested itself as a seeing eye on the back of the hand that was just like a cheery fireplace on the back of a skull that became a house. Blue sapphire icicles were cried out of this synthetic eye, evoking the cold appearance of a dark witch who kept her animals in cages, who moved her freight elevators up, just like she went down on her dumb waiters, and who sliced off the heads of infidels expecting the interior of their bodies to be an emerald honeycomb of light that would weep strange songs.

The hand that was a signature of the face, or the face that was a portrait of the hand, bristled ever so slightly, shaking its red rubbery appendages that resembled a latex mohawk on a cranium, or perhaps resembled some prehensile fingers from a glove of unknown intentions, which was in an infantile stage of its existence, brandishing the first tears of birth. Its hand-like characteristics cried out to stroke the orange ribs of pumpkin flesh, while its face-like dimension of the dichotomy desired nothing more than to kiss, kiss, kiss all of the things and people that had never before been kissed. It wanted to go north when really it desired to go south. It wanted both. If it had been able to fly and burrow to the center of the earth, then it would have. Meanwhile, amid the unfulfilled desires which assailed its newly generated sensibility, similar to the way a burning candle held next to wax fingers can reveal the characters from a forgotten language on the digits, the hand-face, or, face-hand, cried the cerulean tears of a newborn, reminiscent of the blue sapphire witch whose method of appearance rivaled the supposed spontaneous generations of mice in a dirty shirt, or maggots on some meat in a sealed bottle. The blue tears welled up like tadpoles of an uncertain armistice, waiting but not striking, perhaps anticipating the moment when the axe will fall and the heads will roll across the floor, like tears from heads that came from streaming fingers. The red rubber glove of the wilderness had finally washed up on the proverbial beach. The genie-rooster had been released from the bottle, a rubber jester who represented himself *ad infinitum*, creating the paradox within a paradox within a paradox....

He had no choice but to release the cherry-red, hand-face-hybrid into the streets and allow it to do its will. The creature barreled through the flimsy door, breaking it to smithereens, while simultaneously strangling and kissing a pork whore who just so happened to be passing through the neighborhood. The red rubber hand-head released its grip of passion on the prostitute, and went rolling off into the night. It went down one of the numerous alleyways that seemed to radiate outwards from the locale of the dusty garage which was home to the alchemist (with a home but without a home), as he shook his sleeves with laughter, letting loose a rain of blue crystalline dust all over the sidewalk.

Meanwhile, beneath the underground hallways of the Salt Manor, where humans had not tread for decades, the Alchemical Waif and her guards caroused the old arcades of her past. There was much dust in some places, and many spiderwebs in others, and the rats had been out and about in packs, in many waves over the years. Periodically the ground would rumble, and her party would receive subtle intimations of a city far, far below made from amber, where the spiderweb was the symbol of a unified world in all hemispheres, on circular continents and where the towers of ancient communication would raise themselves from the mucousy void of broken eggshells, smelling of fish and salt, and raising the dead. It was certain to these people then that this city must exist, as if it might be reached through highly viscous thoroughfares of solidified honey, or perhaps the sweet sap from a maple tree that would create a highway to forgotten memories or perhaps even forgotten people. Such knowledge would be useful in helping the Waif understand the nature of the tiny footprints that covered many of the floors in these newly uncovered levels under her existence – floors where children run upon yet produce no sound, and leave behind no toys or other artifacts normally attributed to the passage of children. The Alchemical Waif, spread her wings into her raven form momentarily, at once scared and yet eager to fly away from this place. But unfortunately there was nowhere to fly. The passage-ways leading back to her existence topside were cloaked in darkness, and the ceilings themselves had viscous drippings, some mineral and some organic, which seeped through the old stone foundations and floors as if the latter were merely the cell walls of some complex organism that dwarfed their puny specks of sentience.

9
Convergent Alchemy

On the outside of the Salt Manor, near the entrance where it once infiltrated this monstrous building, the Black Feline sniffed its way up to a half-frozen carcass that had been discarded during the night. One could only imagine that the house chef or cook had thrown the meat out to the ravens and vultures. Interestingly enough, the carcass was studded in a few places with curious blades that were half black and half silver, as if the side of beef or whatever it was had been within the sweaty throes of a matadorial ritual. The cat licked at the trickles of diluted blood that welled up close to where the knives penetrated the dead meat. The flesh was tasty enough to the cat, although it was on the verge of spoiling, and already several animals had come out of the wilderness, led on by the smell, and thoroughly eager to consume the meat. Amid the possessive squawks of ravens, the cat tore out pieces of flesh to quickly carry to a safe distance nearby, behind a tree, so that the black birds would not hassle the black cat, both of whom seemed destined for tuxedoes and top-hats, and who would luxuriate in the rotting flesh of Hollywood, picking fibers of meat from their mouths while posing with champagne and cigarettes for the camera. The Black Cat and the crows were destined for that sort of relationship, and through their predilection for rotting meat spilled forth by disturbed refrigerators, the cooks of the house would triumph in their dinner rituals-turned-zombie, in their creation of love from lifeless ash.

Eventually the Black Cat finished its hurried meal, completely gorged with rotting protein sure to cause indigestion just as it was sure to satisfy the animal's need for sustenance for quite a few days to come. Although full and bloated, the feline started to do something it had never done before: it felt as if its body had become two-dimensional, and it was starting to jump head-over-heels, in a perfectly circular motion, as if it had become a frisbee or a phonograph, or perhaps a black rubber spare tire that carelessly goes rolling down the road after a particularly grisly car wreck where the pavement is splattered with purple blood, and the black and white satin of the ephemeral-eternal bride is trimmed with lace and lawn-mowings, disrupting the dead from the motion of a lateral pendulum that swings from left to right and back again on the front of an automobile that was destined for an arcane place on the side of a nearby mountain. This complex motion was contained within the sprawling form of the cat, as it began to spin dizzily from its over-consumption of rotting meat, threatening to send it to the faraway cave, as an apple seed is viciously sown to the ground by an angry farmer who wants to create the orchard he never had.

The Black Feline still continued to spin head over heels until it ran smack into a boulder. The collision threw it on its back, with its legs in the air, not quite dead but certainly dazed. With its upside-down visage facing the mountain, the entrance of the cave was almost barely visible to its keen but swiftly spinning eyesight caused by the delirium of the rotten meat and the spinning vertigo caused through the circular reanimation of the dead. It seemed likely that buzzards or vultures or whatever were flying to and from the mouth of the cave, as if something important were going on up there. Curiosities were sparked. Not just on the part of the feline, but also within the peering psyches of the ravens who just so happened to be sitting on a nearby branch, schemingly clucking to themselves with grandiose desires.

The usual semblance of consciousness returned to the Black Feline, as its eyes stopped spinning, its head stopped spinning and its body stopped spinning, eventually allowing it to reach a state of rest that only enabled the animal to focus attention on the seismic rumblings that permeated the fecund soils with even more frequency than on most other days. The tremors caused the animal to retch, but nothing came out. Despite having a full belly, the feline had nothing to vomit, and so it nervously chewed on the grass, often looking over its shoulder and staring across the field at the carcass pierced with the curious knives and now being devoured by birds. Although the nausea passed, there was still the feeling, almost like that of a tidal attraction, of the sun wanting to pull the stomach in one direction, and then that of the moon, tugging it in a different direction. It was certainly an experience the cat associated with the rotten meat and the vision of the head-over-heels extravaganza with intimations of top-hat luxuriance, tuxedoes, and graveyard smoking jackets.

In the kitchen of the Salt Manor, beneath the putrid steam that came from a pot of stewed vegetables boiled past sentient recognition, the sweet smell of an overpowering fungus grew with its steady and stealthy spread of funk, quietly penetrating the stone walls as it had done for centuries. Of course there were certain spills and agents within the fortress that would keep the fungal growth in check, but the kitchen was always prone to such icks and molds that would make even the strong-of-stomach gag with drooling disgust when the odors and flavors were experienced at full potency. Truly a witch's brew, but never intentionally. On this particular day, the scarred, leatherbound cookbook was open to a page about snails baked not in their shells but baked in butter and garlic within the skull of any suitable primate available at the meat market:

> First, the primate's skull is decapitated, and stewed with vegetables so as to loosen the flesh from the bone, or at least *most* of the flesh, without overcooking. Simultaneously, a large tortoise – slightly larger than the size of the primate's head – is also gutted, and the flesh is concomitantly stewed with that of the primate skull and the vegetables (including many peeled and seeded tomatoes), leading to a rich broth spiced with a pinch of cinnamon, chopped parsley, a few bay leaves and a glass of a merlot that has not been allowed to age too much. The primate skull, cleared of most of the flesh (but leaving behind the brains) is then opened and the brains and raw snails are mixed ever so coarsely. This mixture is then generously stuffed, with rustic breadcrumbs, back into the skull and vigorously drizzled with garlic, olive oil, and salted butter mixture. This stuffed skull assembly is then placed in the tortoise shell, now an involuntary baking dish, and some of the broth from the soup added to the shell bowl to create a source of moisture so that the scorched sweetmeats will not completely dry out during the baking experience. From time to time the brains and snails are basted

with juice from the pan. With the baking process finally complete after its removal from the furnace of an oven, the cleaved skull bursting with succulent brain-snails is served alongside the turtle soup, with a few crusts of stale bread for dipping purposes.

Out of one of the side-pantries, the Cook emerged, with his bloodied apron dusted with flour and dried snot. It appeared that this poor slob had the ever-so-annoying cold this week, as he sniffled and snorted, with his red nose continuously running with snot. A fever not to be ignored raged on and on in his head, giving his eyes a glassy look and making his face look like a shriveled, moldy, gargantuan coconut that had been rejected by a land populated by inhabitants who were afraid to eat foods that were larger than the size of their own skulls. The Cook stumbled a few steps forward, lightly touching the grungy, dented soup cauldron only to withdraw his pink, crusty fingers in pain from the heat. He scowled and spat green phlegm on the floor, neatly tagging a discarded end of stale bread that had not yet been claimed by the mice. His nose was running, and he was miserable. He knew what menu he was supposed to follow for the day, but his heart wasn't really into his work at the moment (literally, of course). The turtle-head soup was almost done, and he was only awaiting the return of the Scar Lady from her subterranean exploits so that he could provide her lunch: hence the turtle soup and the baked cerebral escargot.

As it turned out, the Scar Lady (only recently known as the Alchemical Waif), bearing a long, jagged lineage of inherited scars, enjoyed the soup and baked escargot immensely. She voraciously sucked the brains and snails from the baked skull, just like she sucked the cum out of the phallic organs of the servants who were routinely executed after such pleasures. From the turtle soup, she devoured the acrid broth and hastily consumed the face meat and turtle meat that was abundant, saving the turtle bones for last, to suck clean of the gelatinous, ferrous marrow contained within. Apparently exploration had a way of stimulating the appetite, and so the Scar Lady felt reinvigorated after her lunch. What she had seen in the newly uncovered areas beneath the deepest dungeon had disturbed her, but she was determined not to reveal her disquiet. The room with the little blond girl and the rabbit dentures and the top-hat, as well as the sinister vision of abandoned corpses on the shores of a bloody, underground river sent chills up her feathered spine. While within her reverie, the Black Feline watched her through the window, as it was perched on the branch of a Linden tree. The cat observed every tic, every ruffle of the matriarch's psychological feathers, every twitch of the moist red mouth, especially when she wiped her lips with a napkin, took a draught of her post-meal cognac and then applied a fine line of red greasy, monkey-face lipstick to her mouth – that special kind of lipstick that pushed cold tremors through the spinal column of even the likes of this curious black cat who had more than just nine lives. The cat was able to calm down when the tube of lipstick was put away, but as soon as the queen looked over in its direction, the Black Feline leapt from the branch in order to get out of sight. The Scar Lady sighed and regarded the empty turtle shell bowl that held the empty, scorched primate and realized that the day had yet begun.

Being the pig that he was, the Pork woke up midday, taking advantage of his slave-pig's care and cooking, and emptied his nose of snot that had accumulated during the night. On some days the liquid would continuously dribble from his flared and imposing porcine snout, like today. Eventually the well ran dry, so the Pork checked his email to discover that the Perfect were planning a surprise visit that day. He had barely enough time to get himself and his purple eggplant lightbulbs in order. There were many packed crates that he would be required to open, in order to display their contents to whichever of the representatives the Perfect sent. On almost all occasions during his employment with the Perfect, They always sent different auditors each time. And he knew all the way from the hair on his chinney-chin-chin down to his filthy extremities that he would have to give the Perfect exactly what They wanted, or otherwise he would be killed. There were no compromises in this area; it was simply the way They operated. The benefits of working for the Perfect were of course financially self-evident – the Pork had a lucrative existence that afforded him many exploitative luxuries which made him the envy of his porcine peers. And also the sense of danger, the threat of instant death, was what propelled a businessman like the

Pork to pursue the kind of life that he did.

The Pork made half a gesture to clean himself off, although the Perfect were indifferent to efforts at personal hygiene. But regardless, the Pork rinsed off all of the snot, sex, tobacco, liquor and cocaine and whatever other designer substances with which his system was constantly immersed. These impurities were washed from his fat little body, and then he prepared the warehouse for the inspection. There were several crates, and he expected the representatives of the Perfect to open at least half of them. While moving some of the crates into position, he suddenly recalled a dream that he'd been having during the early morning hours, having to do with a hand of red latex that reached out to suffocate him while he lay on a sandy beach with a ring of seahawks circling overhead: the Pork had been caught by surprise while napping, by a puffy, red latex glove that seemed to contain an animate hand not attached to any limb or body. The wriggling hand managed to single-handedly cut his air supply, causing him to choke and fight for the air. But the red hand was so strong. At the point where he thought he was going to lose consciousness, the hand transformed into the face of a masked dominatrix, whose mask was made of red latex, and who was of course kissing him. The kiss literally took his breath away as he realized that he'd been fooled again, and that the dominatrix was really a cock rooster who'd been pulling his leg. This spontaneous genesis of foolishness made him blush with rage and embarrassment, and he realized, only after hurling the strange hand/face/coxcomb away from him that he was dribbling sapphire sperm from his jaws, instantly fearing a strange and abnormal pregnancy that would use his body as a host for whoever could guess what – that his corporeal existence would be handed over to the lifecycle of a parasitical beast of which the standard science fiction pulp stories would pale by comparison.

The Man who was Nickel Plated (at times referred to as the Dark Cowboy or Dirty Alchemist) woke up with his back against a brick wall in a hazy alleyway, leaning against a dumpster. It was only yesterday that this man was a Dirty Alchemist, but today he was the Man who was Nickel Plated. In fact, although he was coated with a thick film of shiny nickel metal on the outside (which composed his skin), his inner viscera and skeletal architecture were made of varying densities of coal, of the blackest carbon available, although it was uncertain how exactly his living cells came to be substituted with charcoal. However this arrangement was settled, it allowed him to continue breathing, nonetheless. So today he really just consisted of a trunk of charcoal coated with a layer of metal, however strong, that helped hold his entire body together as one unified object. A noisy hunger awoke him from his confusion, as if he were one of the homeless people who slept off the effects of their alcoholic celebrations from the night before. Despite being made from solid coal, black as a night without flashlights to poke its opacity, his stomach was capable of a steady gurgle of noise which helped him get situated in his new surroundings. His resting spot happened to coincide with the back of a restaurant, and so he begged for something to consume. After a few bold raps on the restaurant's back door, and a very direct request, the door opened just enough to allow unknown hands present him first with a hairy coconut and then with a full bottle of the heaviest proof vodka that was legally available in the pig city. With a word of thanks, the Man who was Nickel Plated took these items and quickly returned to his garage, which was also a studio, a workshop, as well as a house, all rolled up into one abode in which he resided all year round.

In the dusty garage, the Man who was Nickel Plated walked past the dusty jalopy, running his fingers along its side, shaving scoops of polluted urban dust that he flung to the ground. A wave of fatigue instantly consumed his person, and he fell to the oil-stained pavement, inching along to where he could lean his sore back against the cold concrete wall, that same wall that he always leaned against when his back gave him trouble. With both hands, he tapped the coconut against his forehead, gaining strength with each hit. The hairy husk of the coconut only made him think of self-flagellation with a mammalian breast and he began to salivate, from underneath his carbon tongue, while considering the pure, cool coconut milk that must have been contained within this perfectly-sized receptacle of sweetness. A few more swift blows to the head and the coconut cracked. And a few more blows and he felt the trickle of coconut milk on his forehead. Immediately he sucked on the coconut as if it were a breast and fed himself with this ambrosial nourishment, having false memories of infancy where his mother breastfed him with real mammarian handholds to comfort his newfound journey out of amniotic nothingness. However in real life, the Man who was Nickel Plated never had any access to breasts as an infant, as he never had a mother. Instead, the breast encounters came later on in his life, after he had a chance to adjust to a life of bipedalism and a certain degree of sentience.

Next, he guzzled the bottle of vodka within a minute, allowing the undiluted alcohol to penetrate his system instantly, in the same way thirsty briquettes spontaneously absorb the highly flammable lighter fluid that eager BBQ'ers douse when they are having their mundane, domestic pleasures. Already the Man who was Nickel Plated had consumed a liter of alcohol, but he felt certain that more alcohol must be obtained so that every briquette in his body would be doused with the ethanol, for whatever unknown purposes of later conflagration. In a moment of inspiration, he jumped to his feet, oblivious to the soreness of his back (which was steadily fading anyway) and he went to the nearest porkly package store in order to purchase several more liters of alcohol, non-diluted, of course.

Out on the street, outside of his dim residence, the Man who was Nickel Plated was blinded by the rude sunlight, as he staggered down the street in the direction of the porkly package store. His lanky arms and legs shook blue crystalline dust onto the ground, around him, but none of the nearby pork people seemed to notice, as they were staring into space at odd angles, with their eyes glazed, with strange smiles on their faces and blistered skin making them look as if they were slowly being cooked. At the package store, the Man who was Nickel Plated bought the liquor and then returned home, where he would eventually finish dousing his carbon insides with it. As he passed several delis and grocery shops on the way home, he noticed that many of the shop windows displayed a certain new fad that was available for the right price: apparently (and this new product was being marketed towards young adult pork people) it was possible in these grocery establishments to pay hard currency in order to be allowed to squeeze the soft neck of a rooster, without killing the animal, of course. These were special kinds of roosters brought in from the frigid countrycides, however, as they seemed to be made of a rubbery flesh which, although not very tasty, was instead very flexible and squeezable. The end result was that a male chicken choked in this manner led to a strange inflation of its bright red coxcomb, making it look bulbous. Of course, the rooster's red eyes also expanded and became bulbous, too, and this new toy seemed to appeal to children of all ages and species, even. All one had to do is to squeeze the rooster's neck, and the red eyes and head appendages would engorge like another, well known organ. Obviously, such distractions had their appeal.

When the Man who was Nickel Plated arrived at his dusty garage, he felt a premonition that made him look through old picture albums, as if he might never return to his beloved home. He thought of all the ghastly, porkly people in his ugly city, a city that was viewed as ugly by the rest of the world, and he held his head in his hands as if to ward off a painless headache such that no terrestrial nerves could fully convey the painful impulses from the center of his charcoal mind out to the extremities of his nickel plated skull. He looked up at the clock, utterly shocked that it was 10:05 AM, as it always seemed to be whenever he decided to look up to check the time. This image of the clock produced a certain anguish in him that made him gasp only once, but which gave him a flashback of a mansion with a winding staircase, of a hallway at the top of the staircase with many residential rooms filled with dragons and rodent-like people who buttered their toast with music each morning, as if such consumption of the sonic emotions could transform them into honey-swabbing hummingbirds, pausing their gauzy wings of emerald green from time to time to pursue the criminal inspection of flowers opened for the pleasures of nectar, the main ingredient in the honey that would create footprints of sweetness leading away from the den of the bear into the red, silvery breast of the hummingbird. Honey-swabbing, indeed! This memory was like a dark raincoat stashed within one of the alcoves prematurely sealed with bricks, which were hidden in this unknown mansion, so gaily decorated with glitz and febrile wall-hangings that tempted the aesthetic of any creature who lived in a tomb, like a tall, thin god of old iron would cross from living to dead and then back to living again, as if wearing a veil of living skin were just an article of clothing to be tossed at the end of the day, and then worn again upon the sunrise of the next. The sealed-in bricks around the hidden raincoat disguised the alcove within the upstate mansion, bringing its frigid walls to a new height of ecstasy that no Salt Manor could reproduce, that no 1970s funky disco bed-chamber could emulate and which no papal white house could offer either, regardless of whichever figure of authority were picking his nose at that particular instant.

The fall of the moon within the night sky allowed this upstate mansion to sigh with an anguish that the Man who was Nickel Plated had only just mimicked a moment ago. The ancestral suit of metal, or perhaps a solid body of old, angular iron, did exist already, suggesting that his own metal skin was a copy, or even an engraving or rubbing that one might take by placing a paper on top of an iron work and capturing the indentations by rubbing over the paper with charcoal, in a hierarchy of truth. The moon was still alive, but perhaps the mansion wasn't, as the veils of forgotten drapes blew in the night wind that crossed between panes of glass windows that had been shattered by vandals who knew nothing of the lost inhabitants, those dragons and rodent caretakers who had vanished one afternoon in a telephonic rainstorm, where each droplet of rain was a grain of static on an empty-headed Television monitor.

This sense of loss and geographic deliverance was puzzling to the Man who was Nickel Plated, teasing him with half-truths and half-memories which only hammered home the dreaded portraiture of a family of hummingbirds whose ruby-red breasts were caustically integrated with a coat of emerald green feathers, displaying some kind of mesmerizing nobility that was similar to what doomed people do when they grasp at straws to see which one is to be sacrificed next, in order to prolong the survival of the rest of the group. Such a family portrait of noble tragedy had collected dust along the gilded frames, and the symbol of such feel-good sentiments was already dissolving in a field of static, under a deluge of ocean rain, drenching the roosters with bulging eyes and coxcombs with knuckle-white hands grasped around their necks. Somehow the stately intentions had melted into a pile of molten metal, and the bed of thorns that might have broken her fall only crumbled to ashes by the heat of the falling object.

The Man who was Nickel Plated now knew what he had to do. He stretched his musculature, allowing his alcohol-soaked carbon organs to breathe and move, and then set out for the Wax Museum, which was on the other side of the pork city, and in a no less shady area.

Several hundred kilometers away, within the oppressive safety of her Salt Manor, the Scar Lady had reeling thoughts of her recent experiences beneath the colossal house in which she had spent all of her life. Her perceptions of the place tended towards visualizing an old, resurrected scab in the throes of being supplanted by a sea of pus, representing the last stand of an immune system that had lapsed somewhere along the way, with trained pigeons closing their eyes when the important things had passed. Such a lack of consciousness was probably only her fault, she chided herself, as she recalled all of the years spent with her eyes on neighboring lands, with their neighboring people whom she wanted to ambitiously put under her yoke of economic production. She could remember the way her board of advisors used to give her the news and predictions she didn't want to hear, and how she killed them off one by one when she didn't like the answers that she heard from their wet lips. It was only during the past few years that she alone operated her Manor house including all of the agricultural and manufacturing businesses that surrounded this megalithic house, such that everything was run by her expertise without the input of any more advisors to tell her the things that she emphatically desired not to hear. In most cases, anyway, their truths about impending financial doom were laced with self-serving dishonesties which perhaps were to be expected, and yet were ultimately an obstacle to her plans. As a professional liar, she was very good at spotting lies: not just from looking at a person's eyes, but also through their physical characteristics. It was almost her sixth sense, in that she could look at a person by peering at the twisting, invisible fibers of their very being, as if they were a constellation, and then judge their truthfulness based on how the planets and stars within that constellation lined up. Analogously, each lie that a person told put certain interior celestial bodies into motion, into awkward trajectories, into zigzags of unbecoming oscillations that eventually came to define a person's character, like an abstract, chaotic painting of bleeding slashes that eventually were transmuted to self-confessing and therefore damning scars. As far as she was concerned, she could handle awkward trajectories, and she could also handle the damning scars. There were worse things to combat. Some people might have called her crazy, and others would consider her abilities a bad case of x-ray vision, but regardless of the nature of this kind of discernment or derangement, she had a strong sense of intuition that served her well in many instances.

Lately she had been noticing the slight abdominal bulge from her pregnancy, and the ultrasound exam confirmed this observation. Although she didn't know the sex of the baby, she was almost sure that it would be female. As soon as she got her hands on one of those test-at-home kits, she'd know for certain. She was lucky to have found the man – that Ratmeister – who impregnated her, since his rare form of other-worldly sperm was hard to encounter, as if she hadn't known that already. While the Scar Lady ubiquitously drank the sperm of her servants and followers, she was actually very choosy, awfully choosy, about whose sperm made it into her reproductive tract. It was Ratmeister's character, and his intelligence, and good looks of physical strength which convinced her of his quality as a paternal contributor. The Ratmeister's appearance was rather strange, but perhaps his disappearance was even more so, the Scar Lady mused, as she put her eyes on the coat of arms depicting a full-grown oak tree with a central eye in the mass of branches

She was finally going to have the heir she always wanted: a protégé whom she could teach all the details of her petty trade, giving her the resources that would enable her to carry her mother's dictatorship to an even further level than that which had already been accomplished. It meant that the Scar Lady would be less scarred than she was now, since all of her lies and subterfuge would lead to a new kind of infrastructure, and she would justifiably find a certain pure sense of redemption. In her dressing room she sat on her pumpkin primp chair, and applied red, greasy monkey-face lipstick to her wet lips, and gently massaged her belly, maniacally talking to the embryo – the magical fruit that was steadily growing on her twisting umbilical vine, increasing her power and ensuring her lineage into the future. There was nothing else. To celebrate her coming motherhood, she produced an obsidian key from under the rug which unlocked a cabinet in her bed chambers. From the cabinet she pulled a special drinking vessel made of silver and whose interior was lined with a thin but uniform layer of industrial-grade carbon. She poured from a smoky colored glass bottle, introducing a yellowish liquid – snake bile, to be exact – into the special goblet. The thick liquid went down her throat immediately, and she licked her colorful lips, savoring the future that was in store for her. And looking forward, the Scar Lady thought of future offspring – subsequent experiments – who would do her bidding without question, at least until they were old enough to understand the importance of her vision of how existence should be. She was certain that in the next few years she would be able to find another man like the Ratmeister who would haplessly fall into her clutches, by pure chance, in order to provide her with what she needed the most right now: viable sperm. She wasn't interested in having a father figure for her children; most certainly she would have him killed, or she might even kill him herself, but the end result would be that she would be able to choose the male figures of influence to act upon her developing offspring, shaping them in ways that she could control and which would serve only her purposes, in light of the great vision of destiny which she had been seeing in recent years in bits and pieces. There was nothing else.

10
The Perfect and the Transference

The Black Feline awoke during an early morning hour, just as the sun was beginning to push its first beams over the horizon. Many of the neighboring birds had already begun their preliminary chirps, sending out those quirky little twits and tweeps that announced their presence as well as their subsequent intention to fly from their territorial boundaries into the bosoms of flowers and other odd markings of moss-covered branches that held within their fronds the silent motions of insects destined for a juicy breakfast. The cat noticed these waking activities, as it reveled within its own hypnogogic state, dreaming of the broken words it was learning how to read, and reassembling them into its own personal, useful and sometimes poetic meanings. The cat was indeed learning how to read, and to use language to its own advantage – something it had hitherto never done. The Black Feline, now stretching out in the dewy grass, rolling around in a half-frisky, half-dreaming manner, arched its back and stretched out its hind legs as if they were full legs of baked turkey, ready for the mischievous plucking by whatever childish and delinquent rascals who might have happened along at that particularly vulnerable moment.

The Cat stared up at where the old owl normally slept, wondering if it had returned from a busy night's hunt. Usually the two only barely acknowledged each other's presence, mutually preferring to provide only barest recognition of the other, while still maintaining a silent, respectful distance. In the end, both of them apparently had nothing in common other than the will to survive, and so they left each other alone.

When it went to the old, medieval pond for a drink, the Black Feline noticed that there were several miniaturized, dead human-shaped bodies floating in the water. This anomaly was not only annoying, but perhaps a bit cryptic as well, as its intelligent feline eyes scanned these motionless floating corpses for the least amount of movement. They did not smell like flesh, and neither did they taste like it, as the cat quickly pecked at one of the legs of the strange creatures. The only conclusion to be reached was that these floating curiosities, wearing conventional white sailors' uniforms, and all miniaturized like discarded toys, were really nothing but some form of rubberized or plastic toys that had been placed in the pond as some kind of joke or prank. It was true: lately the Dark Feline had begun to understand the concept of bipedal humor, which it learned from books that it was reading on the sly. It would still take a while for the cat to understand the humor that was so highly prized by human beings, but eventually, with a bit of luck, it was certain that it would be able to reach the same cultural plane as the one on which these strange and complicated human beings dwelled, or so it had been misled, feeling less-than, thanks to the condescension it had experienced prior. The cat looked down on these invading presences with a profound disgust. It was not so much that the water had a faint taste of vinyl and plastic, but that the primacy of the cat's pond had been compromised in favor of some stupid prank. It did not even occur to the Black Feline that these corpses might have come *from below*, rather than above. This thought was instantly manifested when the cat saw a few bubbles lift from the depths of the shallow pond, revealing another of the small plastic corpses rising to the surface.

It was true: there was indeed a pipeline connection of some sort which joined the old pond to the sewer system of the Salt Manor! The Dark Feline had had such intimations from time to time, but no substantial evidence had ever really surfaced, until now. During this last realization, a large, mahogany coat rack surfaced from the shallow depths of the pond in the most menacing way, towering over the cat, who, rearing up on its hind legs, prepared to flee at a fearsome speed, poised in the classic fight-or-flight posture, looking up at the hulking mass with eye-beams of pure adrenaline. The stature of this menacing coat rack was enormous, sending a shiver of fear up the spine of the feline who had decided to fight, rather than run, as it began to quickly dart back and forth, pacing around the perimeter of the pond in order to find a good angle at which to attack the wooden beast who should not have been moving at all if its form had truly assumed the object of its original, intended purpose, that of an ornamental implement of casual domesticity, to be stored in the corner of a living room near the front door of the most mundane of houses. But apparently not in this case. This particular coat rack was the most vicious, blood-thirsty coat rack ever conceived under the terrestrial sun, as it splashed about in the pond, with a strange, abnormal intelligence, as if the entire wooden surface of it were one big eye that watched that cat as it darted around from all sides, occasional taking a swipe at it with its paws, showing off some feline shoulder blade which had hitherto been hidden beneath a nebulous coat of black fur. Having enough, the mahogany coat rack retreated, quickly sinking into the muddy murk of the disturbed pond, quite possibly making a fast getaway back to the pustule of the Manor house from which it most probably came.

In its place, and most likely due to the instruction of the coat rack, a sinister beanbag resumed the savage attack on the Dark Feline. This beanbag was as large as a five pound sack of potatoes, and the kind of beans inside were the Mexican Jumping variety, contributing a degree of hyperactive malevolence to the bean bag that the feline found to be annoying as well as highly threatening. From time to time, the beans seemed to conform to the shape of a human or other primate which the casual observer might be tempted to speculate was hiding in the bag, possibly with the beans. While growling the most ungodly notes, the cat pounced onto the quivering beanbag that was attempting to march out of the pond onto the neighboring green grass, in order to continue the assault on dry land. With its sharply clawed limbs attached to the top of the beanbag, and the broad shoulder blades of the feline becoming visible, the animal attempted to lacerate the bag. Bites to the impenetrable fabric with the sharp feline teeth were also made, eventually yielding a deflated sack of lifelessness that had completely spilled the beans. The fight was over before it began. The Dark Feline howled with rage, while scowling in the direction of the Mexican Jumping beans, who were hopping away at full speed. All that remained was the empty sack, made with a hemp-fiber that was beyond obscene in its quasi-lethal emanations, as if a burst skull of a demon might come back to haunt the victor from some obscure corner of a livid graveyard, oozing viscous putrefaction

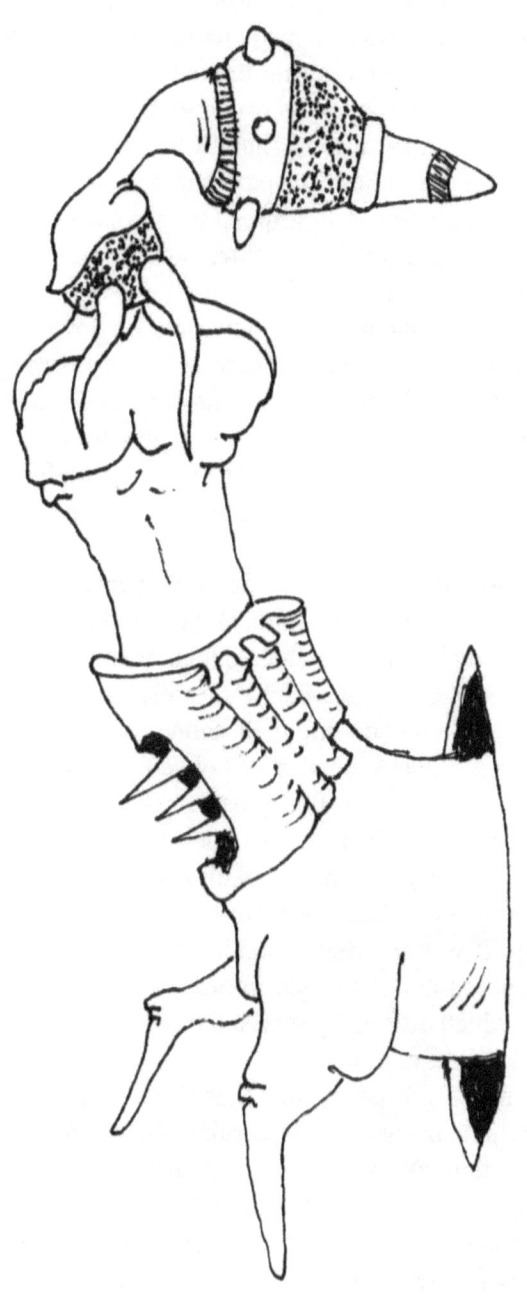

from the cracks that often form over disturbed tombs of insecurity.

The Black Feline was alarmed to discover that its precious shard of amber had been shattered during the battle, so that the cockroach scarab with the mark of man on its back had been pulverized, leaving nothing behind except for a lousy handful of granular dust, capable of making a sad, little cloud of topaz that was quickly scattered by the wind. Paranoia immediately gripped the psyche of the feline, as it conjectured explanations that highlighted vicious motives of sabotage, or the hijacking of feelings, or invasions of the subconscious, and other sorts of volatile madness that only pressed down upon its heart like a concrete weight. If the cat were to insist on maintaining its residence near the pond, then it would have to find a way to seal the vent of communication that now existed with certainty between the Salt Manor and the pond. Such prospects of thwarting future invasions were a field of domestic birds pecking at crumbs that didn't exist.

It was Wednesday, and the fresh delivery of slaves had just arrived upon the doorstep of the Salt Manor. As the motorized coach drove away, leaving behind a chained queue of chattering delinquents from one of the northern, Cascadian territories, the lead Slave-Handler stepped forward, asked everyone their names, and with a fully flexed bullwhip, whacked the newcomers into obedience. Long gashes from crude leather were made onto fleshy backs which bled noble streams of blood into the dust of the road. No one cried out, but many a gasp of barely hidden agony was heard issuing from the nearly clamped mouths of the prisoners. Most of them had clothes and footwear, but not all of them. It was the Slave-Handler's responsibility to provide them with the necessary outerwear in order for them to work hard at their new jobs, which ultimately served the Queen's well-being, which included her pleasure, of course.

The armored side door of the Salt Manor was lowered to allow the Slave-Handler to bring his new recruits into the antechamber of the primary keep, which only led steadily downward into one of the many heavily guarded holding areas. The sentinels prodded the newcomers with pointed sticks, pushing them forward, down into the depths of the castle, lit by feeble electricity and oftentimes supplemented with torchlight that burned the oil of slaughtered pigs. These human animals were savagely pushed to their knees by the guards, so that they might be properly introduced to her majesty, who was waiting for them at the bottom of the ramp. The Scar Lady, scarred to the core of her being by civilization – her civilization – hid her scars very well, instead showing the new prisoners the face of the Evil Queen, another and no less predominant facet of her personality.

The Evil Queen spat on one of the more morose-looking slaves, dissatisfied with the gorilla-faced leer that contorted his face with a monkey lust that could easily induce a young woman's undergarments to disintegrate into powdered ash with just one withering look of unbridled eroticism. Within minutes, the slave's head found its way onto a sharp skewer in the moldy courtyard, while the body was sent to the farm to be converted to fertilizer mulch. While this material conversion was carried out, the Queen continued her inspection of the new slaves, making notes to herself about which ones would be good for which sexual positions and whichever voluptuous pleasures might be available to her at a moment's notice, in the same way doctors keep certain kinds of emergency bandages and antivenins on hand at all times, even during the full moon, when wolves from the outside might burn through the walls of snow with their eyes and wet saliva, threatening to burst through a weak dam made of ice.

The Evil Queen's eyes smoldered within the sockets of her frozen skull, quivering almost imperceptibly with a tension that could have broken frozen metal or maybe knuckles that were placed between heavy books in order to be smashed should one breathe the wrong way, to her displeasure. The tension in the air was just too thick for some of the prisoners to handle, and two of them spontaneously began to cry out, begging for mercy and forgiveness (forgiveness for what?), and trying to list the reasons why their lives should be spared: family, financial obligations, a living room that hasn't yet been vacuumed, children that need paternal care, BBQ'd meat that hadn't yet been cooked for the nuclear family meal which was to be temporally conjoined with one of the many cowardly religious ceremonies designed to breed fear and obedience, to be stupidly passed down from generation to generation like a cursed ring that finds its way onto your finger from malodorous lineages that infinitely delineate themselves into the murky past, tying strings onto your puppet skull, filling you with purposes and roles to play but which you did not ask for. These were the sorts of excuses that the Evil Queen was hearing now, as she carelessly passed one of her smooth, blue-veined hands over her womb, just to prove to herself that she was indeed carrying a child, albeit an embryonic one.

The left hand of the Evil Queen, up until that point, had been calmly held at her side, but as soon as the right hand had passed over the womb, almost like a solar eclipse, the former sprang into action by dramatically grabbing the right hand and pulling it out of the way, as if the caressing action of the right hand had been an irritant covering the eye that was her womb. Momentarily the Evil Queen moved to a telephone glued to a nearby sentry point, pretending to make a call, while really trying to hide the fact that her hands were at war with each other, with the right fighting against left, with the left trying to control the motions of the right. It was a typical case of possession, and yet there was nothing for the Evil Queen to do but ride out the chaos, hoping for more peaceful moments later. It had occurred to her that perhaps such fits of hand-against-hand discord were really owed to the stress of her position as head of the Manor, or perhaps due to her unexpected (but thoroughly welcome) pregnancy. As mysterious as it was, the convulsion of which she was temporarily the prey would eventually leave just as quickly as it arrived, and with this mental fortitude, she again turned her attention to the group of slaves, selecting one of the crybabies for lunch.

In her pre-lunch waiting room, one of the previously terrified and whining servants felt his prostate explode in her avaricious mouth, as she gargled with his semen, nourishing her already healthy gums and molars with his sperm, as if somehow the DNA contained within these wriggling cells might satisfy her urges for hereditary control over her own destiny. After she was finished with him, whatever his name was (the Evil Queen was infinitely bad with names, but she never forgot a face), his head landed up in the skewered courtyard collection, and his arms were to be used for the dinner BBQ and the rest of his entrails were destined for official Salt Manor fertilizer. Over lunch, the queen studied the printed reports of her scouting minions:

the surveys of neighboring lands, night surveillance of the grounds, reviews of security protocols and camera installments, all of which were designed to maintain her regal hegemony of fear and territorial concupiscence, and last but not least, to maintain her political and economic fortifications. She would routinely order this or that guard troop to shift its focus from here to there, so as to confuse her enemies, which so far, had not surfaced in years. But one could never be too cautious, especially when dealing with the common enemies of the Salt Manor and its deluded dictators, who were fleas living within the honey-combed putridity of a pustulent scar on what was once sweet land.

After a cannibalistic lunch, the Evil Queen retired to her library. She directed her faithful, personal servant – the Baked Nun – to acquire some freshly squeezed goat's milk for her. As the chattering, hysterically laughing nun ran away to go fetch the milk, the queen aggressively surveyed her aging bookshelves which sagged from the weight of several centuries of crookedly begotten knowledge, born from the executed lives of now-faceless and nameless people. Knowing that it would still be some time before the Baked Nun was to return, the Queen opened her blouse to expose her breasts. She walked along the rows of books, closing her eyes, while one of her nipples would rub along the spines of the books past which she stepped. This private thrill had always appealed to her since her adolescence, during the time her breasts matured and she was still a student learning from her mother and her father, the latter who was often occupied in business conducted in the lower levels of the estate. While supposedly studying, she would entertain herself with this little game, using the sensations of the bookspines to help her decide which of the books were the most interesting to read. Oftentimes, the game actually worked, helping her to find tomes which were of use to her, such as when it was time to crank out a termpaper, or to find a book to which she could relate on a personal level. As peculiar as it sounded, the tips of her nipples constituted a special sixth sense which allowed her to find books and therefore ideas which applied to her, or that complemented her life in some profound way. She would be using this ability again today.

Some of the books she passed were pleasantly smooth, with

a well-tanned cowhide that seemed to rub the nipple just right. Other volumes were old and scratchy – perhaps interesting, and yet utterly useless for what she now sought. Still other volumes seemed to be of the immediate past, with freshly dried blood, fish glue which hadn't quite sealed, and wounded animal hide-bindings that still wept the serum from the savage wounds incurred at the bindery, and even before that. The particular book that tickled her fancy was a twentieth century tome that apparently had used the face of someone of minor nobility as the leather cover. One of the stitched eyelids formed the top of the spine, while the other eye, and the nose and other features were on the front cover, warts, moles and all. These facial apertures were all sewn shut with a needlework that was done in the hands of an expert, and what made them interesting to the touch was a certain gumminess created through the slow seepage of sticky fluids still retained by the dried tissues, as the decades had steadily passed.

The book she selected seemed to fit into her hands quite snugly, as if the dried face that was now the spine and cover were also a glove. *The Repudiated Architecture of Lower Reptiles*, by Sir Archibald Florantino DeGuedes. Such a curious title for a book made with a face of human skin! The Evil Queen would have taken the extra few minutes to rub her breasts all over the yak fur that lined the walls in the library, but there wasn't enough time, as she knew that the Baked Nun would be returning with the milk anytime now. In fact, as soon as she had sat down in an armchair, prepared to crack the spine of this thoroughly worthy book, the nun had fortuitously returned in a hyperactive state, muttering in her quite usual way about swaying livery trees and burning beetles, and about haunted pantyhose that would rise from the dead, becoming the ascetic shells of reanimated cicada, singing violin maladies that could make a lizard's eyes burst! The Evil Queen gave the Baked Nun a violent slap across the face, beseeching her to shut the fuck up, which caused the animated nun to laugh and bob her head up and down even more. The only solution for the queen was to simply shove the servant nun out of the library and to bolt the door, freeing up mental space in her cluttered consciousness that would allow her to focus on her search with an even higher sense of awareness and fixedness. This was no time for senseless laughter, the

Evil Queen fully realized, while blushing as she suddenly remembered to button her blouse.

But with the cracked tome in hand, the Evil Queen's fingers seemed to know exactly where to probe as they turned to a page towards the middle of the volume that seemed to swing open by itself, with the page in question lightly fluttering in a wind current that came from the fireplace. The particular page showed a diagram of a lizard's head, with the eye socket portrayed in a hexagonal fashion, as if some kind of hexagonal jewel might fit nicely into the cavity shown in the picture. Beneath the drawing was the following passage:

> ...Within the light of what you knew, cut in half by the death of what you didn't know, is a mythical reenactment of the genesis event, with land and sky separating from the mother of all primal substances, reducing the putrefaction of nothingness into a plurality of celestial orbits. These orbital motions – sometimes eyes, sometimes ant nests – would put the music of jacketed trees on the sullen mountains of inverted cave formations, like moonstraws, stalactites and other pools of iridescence where might the traveler find the music not of habit but from unorchestrated sighs of waking steps. Once the madness is culled and the talons and beaks assuaged, then the progress of new steps will surface as the new bridge across the infinite ocean of polished rock without substance, thus floating on air which would make feet unnecessary.
>
> Once the feet become the staircases themselves, unseating the tusks from elephants and traveling the smooth pink roads that lead to all cities, then the metropolitan birdcage will admit defeat, leading the herds into the waters which will ultimately bring them to the tops of plateaus, pinching the ass of night, while causing the night clouds to weep. With but just one fallen tear will appear the long neck of a viper – the feathered serpent, Gucumatz, no less – to transform the earth into an egg that disappears down the gullet of the viper, leading to a harmonic choir of childish song, reaching the ears like the shaft of an arrow...

On a whim, the Evil Queen looked at the dangerously sharp iguana key with the emerald inset for the eye, its daggerish shape, touching its brass curves, only now wondering which part of the house it might open, taunting her as if it were a complex song or riddle. She had been given this key by her mother many years before, although she had not been told its purpose. When she had asked her father about it, he simply slapped her so hard she fell down the stairs, twisting her ankle which put her in bed for over a week. After that day, she never spoke to anyone about the key that she subsequently always hid close to her bosom.

By the time the Perfect arrived at his studio, the Pork was decked out in his most dashing business attire: pressed suit, starched tie, and special moonbeam loafers that would fetch a very high price on the black market. Not only that, but he had managed to expel most of the snot that had seemed to replace itself every five minutes, so for the next half-hour, he estimated, his nose would not need to be wiped with the endless rolls of tissue paper he kept around his pigpen of a house. It wasn't just for anyone that he would clean his nose completely of all snot.

And he was just clearing his throat when the knock at the door sounded. Coughing up a wad of tobacco-ish snot into a tissue from the depths of his respiratory passageway, the Pork threw the rejected phlegm down the toilet and immediately turned his focus to straightening his coat, smoothing down what little remained of his hair, and squeezing the automated doorbulb with poise, suavity and determination. The door slid open to reveal the sinister representatives of the Perfect: a couple of coat-racks and a pair of mannequin escorts wearing the usual spacesuit attire. The Pork blinked his eyes involuntarily, and suddenly the coat racks and the mannequins were in his livingroom. When he bade them to follow him to the studio, he blinked again, and suddenly they had traversed the distance before he had even arrived. These coat racks and mannequins were indeed loathsome and sinister. He used the proverbial crowbar to open the sacred crates to show them the purple lightbulbs, whereupon they received this information without displaying any kind of emotion or reaction. After opening several crates he explained that they all contained the same quantities and qualities, and were always plucked and packed with the utmost care, using ancient porcine techniques of lightbulb extraction that were around even before the master race of humans had invented lightbulbs (or so they thought). At this point, the Pork knew he had passed the surprise inspection with flying colors. But as it turned out, the representatives of the Perfect – those sinister coat racks – insisted on his opening of *all* the crates, so the Pork had no choice but to oblige. It was only when he opened the last two crates that he realized some of the precious lightbulbs were missing. For the now-forfeit life of him, he could not explain what had happened to the missing lightbulbs, or where they had gone. Even before he had the chance to have his life flash before his eyes, a lethal burst from a taser electrocuted his spinal column, and his twitching, failing body dropped to the ground in a reckless crumple, with BBQ'd blood and pigfat oozing all over the concrete floor of the studio. The Pork was completely dead. Incinerated. A charred mass of BBQ'd ribs and guts and scorched limbs laid out as a sumptuous feast for the rats and the cockroaches. The Pork was no more. The sinister coat racks and purple velvet mannequins left as quickly as they arrived, within the wink of an eye – as the expression goes – and their passage through the town of the pork went unnoticed. In fact, nobody ever really figured out that the Pork was dead, because he had no friends or family to come looking for him (they had all been eaten at the local, neighborhood BBQ-pit over the years). The Pork was the only member of his entire social network and clan that had managed to free himself from the highly terminal "cannibal BBQ" status.

Not very far away from where the Pork was killed, within the lost city of the porks, the Man who was Nickel Plated trudged along the cold city streets, kicking at tumbleweeds that didn't belong, and whistling off-key tunes that were annoying to the ears as well as the feet. He could feel the burning fuel inside of him approach the point of combustion, and it was only thanks to the thick layer of carbon graphite that lined the inside of his body cavity which prevented the inevitable explosion. Although his metallic skin glistened in the pale sunlight, like the bottom of a platinum creek, his current mindset evoked a turbulent sojourn within spiraling, woodsy pathways of autumn leaves which were really red blood vessels in search of exposed tissues to nourish within the diffuse light. The slowing of time was prevalent, and the innocent doodling of a xylophone somehow made peace with a morbid, wrenching cello procession completely accentuated by violins who sounded like whinnying horses getting their front teeth pulled out. Completing the soundscape was the periodic drilling of a self-confident pneumatic device, possessing the passageways of bloodvessels, as if the motion of corpuscles could move around a throat like a sinister garrote, as a corpuscle necklace. The Man who was Nickel Plated kicked aside stacks of unclaimed newspaper that had been thrown to the curb. Barking dogs appeared out of nowhere, making plenty of noise while coughing up blood-stained hypodermic needles which inspired impressions of staying in a sanatorium with rusted walls. This vision caused him to shudder, almost making his metallic arms feel hollowed out by worms which did not exist but which might treat these limbs as piano keyboards at a moment's notice, calling all neighboring sea vessels towards his location like a lighthouse with a sweeping eye for color, painting the cypress trees with an ectoplasmic revulsion consisting of deflated shoes that refused to walk one more kilometer. Such was the moral state of the psyche in the land of the owl and the swimming pool.

The Man who was Nickel Plated fought back the vertigo of fear, pushing the wind out of his face with an imaginary umbrella – a white umbrella that was made from spider's silk. With throbbing temples, the Man who was Nickel Plated put his hands to his skull as he arrived at the place, the Wax Museum within the slummy part of the forgotten city of porks. He pushed some sugar into the lock, to release the door. Then he squeezed the doorbulb and allowed himself inside. As he passed through the door, he was actually penetrating the convex lens of a giant eyeball. Before entering the room he was real, but now within the room he felt that he was virtual, or perhaps only a replica of himself, possibly even a doppelganger. Every part of his body felt real, but even still, he felt almost that he could have become a projection onto a wall or moviescreen. This illusion passed as soon as he surveyed the interior of the Wax Museum, which appeared to consist of only one large room: there were mannequins everywhere, some holding industrial and domestic implements, while others were empty-handed. These mannequins, all wearing the nefarious purple velvet spacesuits with the star insignia over the left breast, had assumed unique and individual postures that were all their own, positing them in various walks of life, whether working or playing or sleeping, etc. The facial features of the mannequins were of varying degrees of intensity and clarity, but with most completely dulled as if through many years of exposure to the boring effects of miserabilist civilization. And yet despite their boredom, they were still just as curious and still just as menacing. Although it was indeed very still and quiet within the Wax Museum (surely just a hole in the wall), the need for vigilance somehow still impressed itself on the psyche of the Man who was Nickel Plated.

Iconoclast that he was, the Man who was Nickel Plated gave a swift kick to one of the mannequins who stood next to him, one that was carrying a propeller used by the ancient aircraft of the twentieth century. The mannequin fell over, with a thud, incidentally knocking over the gestapo mannequin that was standing next to it, which in turn knocked over the next one, like a domino chain reaction. Over half of the mannequins in the Wax Museum fell over in this manner, within the span of fifteen seconds. It was only until some headroom had been liberated that it was possible to see the actual exhibit, the humanoid forms who were dressed up on platforms near the back of the dimly lit room. Subdued light from the noon sun came through the grimy windows, magically illuminating only the faces of the wax sculptures, who were indeed distinct from the artificial plasticality so characteristic of the mannequins who seemed to be everywhere at once, all over the planet. Whether wearing riding hats or false wigs, each of the wax people had their own qualities of realism, with rouged faces or shadowed eyes, or wet lips and vampire holes on their necks. The pounding within the throat and skull of the Man who was Nickel Plated was steadily threatening to dissipate, as if he had found the wrong address, despite himself. These wax people were the wrong ones, or he must have been in the wrong place, he concluded. It was just as he was turning to leave that he caught sight of Her, the one for whom he'd been looking.

He could see that She had a face of gold, quite literally, which glistened metallically like the golden bees that he used to see from time to time as a child. These metallic insects were rare, yet they did surface with quite a degree of regular frequency, showing off compound eyes, antennae sets and celluloid mandibles all covered with a thin layer of highly reflective gold, creating almost a mirror image of the luxury of old oak trees which had throaty hollows filled with bee honey, as if drowning opera singers could still belt out the musical sentences despite the sweet aether that was currently occupying their windpipes. And so the siren song reached the ears of the Man who was Nickel Plated, and he unbuttoned the wax woman's blouse. He wasn't the least surprised that the woman's torso was transparent as if the outer hull of her body was made of a translucent crystal or plastic which made clearly visible all that was contained inside. In this particular case, the inside of her body cavity was completely filled with the clearest honey, with bits and sections of broken bee hive, embedded within the viscous sweetness capable only of summoning an archaeology of glistening passion as the nectar of ancient flowers was returned to the light of day where it really belonged. Although She did not move, the Man who was Nickel Plated, embraced her, completely removing her trenchcoat while completely removing his. Although she was made of wax, the surface of her body was completely transparent and smooth, unlike what he would have expected from the average wax dummy. But she was completely different from the average wax dummy.

Each of her golden eyes became a crystal ball, refracting the daylight into the legs of insects who marched along the world incarnated as a finely carved plank, moving the soup of hieroglyphs into the cauldron of a rearranged alphabet, summoning the mandibles of hardened ants who could fight their attraction for small cubes of congealed sugar for only half a second until the urge to reunite with the ancestral plantlife took over in the same urges that certain fur-covered books inspire in readers only north of state. The branches of trees grew like blood vessels, and eyes of awareness sprouted from the interior of all the aortas of the symphony of grimy mirrors and window panes in the warehouse districts of old citadels, where oblong alleyways blocked the passage of conventional vehicles, only allowing through the agile birds with blue feathers whose reptilian ancestry only threatened to burst through the façade of loving glances at any moment, covering the laid eggs with a fresh coat of spots, relegating them to roles and functions yet to be determined, yet which were dutifully noted within old volumes even before the whimsical thoughts of work assignments even surfaced in the mind. All of this endless preparation was not seemingly senseless, but ultimately the anticipation of a new kind of becoming, a rolling of the carboniferously black dice that would alchemically transmute into cubes of sugar to be dropped into a sea of tea, penetrating to the dream-depths of a honeycomb, where all fear was born but where the best songs would come to rest after a night of arched backs and swarthy molars that would cross swords with the canines.

Although she didn't move, he knew that she was alive. Now her hardened waist was not so brittle, as one would expect from factory-made plastic or finely-blown glass that had originally contained all of her liquid honey. Now the flexibility of her body became apparent, although it was possible to witness many fragments of the voluptuous beehive that inhabited her interior domains, singing inaudible songs which could not yet cross the boundary of her waist. Likewise, the Man who was Nickel Plated could feel his own loins threaten an outsurge of fire, as if all of the alcohol he had loaded into his carbon-lined system were in a process of exothermic agitation, causing his metal skin to become heated, flaking off shards of oxidized nickel, as if he were shedding some kind of green, rusty skin that only made him realize how clear the air was once the skin had been shed. The liquids within him reached the boiling point, and from between his teeth a plume of burning fuel appeared, scorching the walls and even melting a few of the wax sculptures past recognition. All the while, the Woman who was Honey passively looked on, proudly defying the jets of ignited fuel belching forth from her companion without the slightest effort. It was only until the last of the fuel had passed his lips that the fatigue from the moment brought him to a sub-zero plateau

of stillness, where it became possible to concentrate on anything, everything, to see the molecular vibrations occurring inside of all objects, all drafts of wind and all crystals of night. Everything became visible, but the only catch was that he found that he could no longer move his body. Hunched over on one knee, as if about to either retch or gasp for air, or both, the Man who was Lead could not move, as he came to see only what was in front of him, without being able to really listen anymore, or sneeze anymore, or even reach out to slap another mannequin that had all of a sudden seemed to appear dangerously close to him. He simply could not move. The entirety of the carbon inside of him had vaporized, too, so that all that remained for him to do was to think, within his frozen metal shell that was called a body, and which was now made of lead and not nickel.

In contrast, the Woman who was Honey enjoyed a new motility, relishing a new-found plasticity in her step which had been absent from her existence for however long. She proudly swung her hair around, as if she were doing a televised shampoo commercial, with a wicked grin on her face, and then looked down at the metal being who was hunched over at her feet, as if frozen the way she once was. It was too much for her, all of a sudden, and the first decision of her motile existence was to kick over several of the sinister velvet mannequins that had somehow managed to aright themselves, causing them to fall over again for the second time that day like a long train of dominoes covered with dots of Braille. Dazedly, fingers of all shapes, colors and lengths would be afraid to pass over these tactile communications with a terror that mimicked the sounds of strangulation produced by a violin player whose hands were completely covered with the stickiest of honeys manufactured by poisonous bees who built nests on remote cliffs. The shock waves from this mannequin cascade engendered the most deathly presentiment of decay and violence, as their motionless forms reflected the silence of Her guilt, of the calm before the storm, which no joke or laugh could cure or deter the immanent force of rage soon to explode from inanimate objects like the spontaneous combustion of a great drum of volatile liquid.

Later that evening, the Evil Queen remained quietly in her room, watchful of the time. She took the batteries out of her old cuckoo clock, which was really more of an owl clock who started hooting on the hour, rather than the traditional bird who popped out of the nest to announce the time. She had to touch the face of the owl with her fingers to assure herself that the batteries had indeed been replaced. Until becoming tired enough to turn in, she sat in her dimly lit quarters reviewing the DeGuedes volume she had looked at earlier on in the day, in a state of wonder mixed with fear, as if she had had her eyes open all the way, after spending a lifetime in the dark, burrowing underneath staircases, digging tunnels, when she really could have been crossing bridges made of clouds to the places necessary for realizing her unknown goals. While poring over the book for perhaps the twentieth time, she failed to discern the connection between her little book and the metal ring with the owl feathers on it, which the Ratmeister had mysteriously presented to her on that fateful night when he had arrived at her residence, unannounced. The ring was hung on the wall close to the light switch, but it remained steadfastly ignored ever since the disappearance of the Ratmeister. This disappearance had been coupled with the genesis of the strange, new coat of arms of the oak tree with the eye in it which now was to represent the Edenhorn clan.

The Evil Queen eventually reached the conclusion that she had had enough of waking consciousness for the day, deciding to retire for several hours of slumber. As she reclined on her cerebral waterbed, she could feel the quiet call of sleep whisper in her ears, as if somehow the bed were talking to her (where in all actuality, it most probably was). Within minutes she fell into a deep sleep, as the bed stimulated her dreams by sending electrical impulses from its brain to her brain through the separating membrane on the waterbed. Within her dreams, she immediately began to explore a vast, underwater cavern system, perhaps occupied by many pulsating eels who turned and thrashed through the kinked turns and twists of the cave system, forming an elaborate honeycomb with its angular profundities, hiding many an alcove, all of which exceeded the mind's ability to grasp due to its huge size and complexity. While traveling through this cave network, the Evil Queen perceived herself as a drowned leaf, limply carried along by a surfeit of residual currents made by the passage of the eels as they would periodically cross paths with hers. While traveling, she could hear the singing and chanting of children's voices, as if the sounds reached her ears ever so vaguely, similar to the way the faint twinkling of starlight reaches the retina by way of a teasing glimmer that is only barely perceptible, and maddeningly almost within grasp. These sounds became her guide, as she fought to gain control of her body so as to navigate towards the voices that were calling her, summoning her into their presence. She found this call unbearable, realizing that more than caves were now standing in her way, as planks of sea-faring wood erupted from the earth beneath her feet, creating even more impassable barriers (which she was sometimes able to circumnavigate, but many times not), as the strange, impenetrable wood came to life, sprouting branches of madness that only came after the death of the wood, all of which bore the new coat of arms that had quickly become the characteristic mark of the Edenhorn clan: the bulbous oak tree with the eye inside. This reanimation of the wood from the doorways was confounding, with its multidimensional pull. All the while, the voices of the children seemed to emanate from the spots of light generated by the high pressure of the water that was pushing on her eyeballs, as if through her furtive and desperate navigation through the choked underwater passageways, the voices were becoming a galaxy that she was part of and yet paradoxically she could not fully grasp, because its sheer size was beyond her frame of reference. The voices were lamps, or they were stars, and the words were lost on her ears, but not the emotions and subtle tonalities, which she could almost understand. These notes of speech were the implorations of summoning, asking her to remove the mask of stars that was her face? To replace the emerald webbing of her face with the true carapace of a spider? Was this all really true? Was this all real? At the last moment she saw herself with rubbery legs traversing the underwater rocks of the hive with a sluggishness bound to inspire much lip-biting, with a green sparkle in her eyes and a tongue that threatened to become a sticky finger to type highly enthusiastic notes from a remote keyboard. On the walls were hieroglyphs of trees with an opened eye in the middle of each one. It was at that point she woke up in a sweat, realizing that her dream had taken place somewhere *beneath* the Salt Manor.

11
The Arrival of Yes-Yes

Every day the miniature dead bodies would return, along with the harassing machinations of the coat-racks who were to eventually spoil the peace of the Dark Feline. They would always come while the cat was napping, or eating whatever it had hunted from the woods near the medieval pond by the Salt Manor. Such invasions had never occurred within the rather short lifetime of the Dark Feline until now, causing it to wonder if these visitations were symbolic of some kind of retaliation?

Regardless of the reason which never was elucidated, the Dark Feline decided to flee to the countrycide, to wander in search of a place that was safe where a cat could have a moment's peace, to eat rodents it caught and to read books without being disturbed by the likes of coat-racks and the other dangerous toys of the Perfect. For a while, it took the high road that led away from the Manor, which cut through the surrounding hills, some of which were often dabbed with patches of snow that never seemed to melt until the middle of summer. And then the snow would return again, almost as quickly as it had left. Such a terrain provided only a short-term solution, as the cat realized a gnawing curiosity which never left its psyche. It felt as if its mind were a swaying lantern, while walking through wooded fields, dodging wolves and snatching rats from their holes, realizing that each rat was blind in a figurative way, and that the eyes of a rodent were really on its back, right above the hips. Such a realization was always disturbing, through stimulating strange human-friendly thoughts within the mind of the Dark Feline: corpulent rats filled with the leavings of kitchen food were, by degrees, transformed into succulent drumsticks of large, cooked animals gutted with slime. If one took a long bone and shoved it through the mouth of an obese, diabetic rat all the way to its ass, and then cooked it slowly over a hearth with smoky wood chips, then you would have the perfect rodent drumstick. The Dark Feline thought of nothing but this delicacy for a day or more, which distracted it from digesting the metaphysical philosophy on which it had gorged while still being in a place where it could hide books from the Manor in the bushes, under rocks where the pages wouldn't get wet. At that particular moment, it was reading the works of Gerard de Nerval, among others. This sudden blizzard of knowledge was the white noise of conflicting ideas about Progress and Civilization, things which this particular feline had very little knowledge of, in its limited dealings with humans and their sub-human breeding experiments.

The cooling down of the weather suggested that winter was not very far away. Often enough, cold winds blew over the hills and through the valleys, liberally distributing rain and chill which matted the black fur of the dark feline with a wetness that didn't quite penetrate to its skin, but got nearly there, inspiring a shivering existence that reminded it strongly of the warm areas where humans lived. It was this later realization that prompted the cat's decision to pursue one of the pink roads that leads to all of the cities of mankind. The first pink road uncovered was the one on which the Dark Feline hopped, moving in the direction of the occasional vehicle of traffic that had neither wheels nor legs, but which steadily bypassed the cat in a whirl of cold air and a spray of wet sand from the road. Because of this undesirable effect, the Dark Feline chose to travel the road outside of the curb, out of sight of the fast vehicles.

For many days and nights the Dark Cat traveled, always on the edge of human notice, never refusing handouts, but then never asking for any, either. Sometimes a meal and a place to hide were easy, but other times, the madness of human disruptivity reached into all the nooks and crannies of the landscape, making it impossible for the Dark Feline to elude notice, resulting in tired, bloodshot eyes and an empty belly. By some event of synchronicity, the cat chose the very road that led to the lost city of the porks, Lucipheromone. As the cat approached the city, which was still a great distance away, it noticed that the amount of incoming traffic had increased, and so did the foul odors of pollution and lackluster hygiene. Along the way, emptied cans of sugar drinks and half-eaten body-parts were found that stank of animal decay as they decomposed on the side of the road, discarded by corpulent and

near-diabetic passengers whose taste for sugar and flesh verged on the Dangerous, ultimately causing nations to go to war and also to collapse from within. This was a literal slice of life from the land of the owl and the swimming pool, as the travelers dumped their petty trash on the sides of roads. Once in a while the cat was tempted to gnaw on a half-consumed chicken leg, utterly ready to pretend that it was the "rat drumstick" that it had fantasized about earlier. But in the end, the desire to hunt its own rodents, and to catch its own birds and lizards gave way, propelling the cat to reaffirm its abilities as a hunter, whose ancestors took down great beasts of prey with willing claws and fangs, in the throes of passionate snarls and grunts driven by hunger and desire.

It was during one especially warmer evening that the Dark Feline encountered the ruined walls of a small cottage that had been abandoned for however many years. In the darkness, only a sliver of the moon provided enough light to spy the shadows of trees and other, similar ruins of past walls and imposing edifices. As tired as a plastered lampshade on an effervescent street, the feline chose a quiet corner of the ruined building in which to curl itself into a ball. The night air was warm and dry, so it was fairly easy to avoid the shivers. Little was there to disturb the sleep of the cat, who slept on and off for several cycles until the sun rose.

It was during the first rays of sunlight when it opened its eyes that the Black Cat saw an apparition of a human dressed in a dark cloak, possibly leather, in a semi-crouching position near what was once the entrance of the now ruined and roofless building. The wrists of the person were pressed together emphatically like lips, with black-gloved hands and fingers radiating outward like the rays of a sunburst. This configuration immediately terrorized the cat, causing it to jump to its feet and literally bounce over the wall in hysterical flight away from what it considered real. But there was no sound and there never had been, and when the cat again looked around the corner of the wall to see if the figure was still there, there was no detectable movement or shadow. But in place of where the figure had stood, there resided a small, leather-bound volume so badly bent along the front face, as if stuffed within the bottom of someone's pocket for a few years, completely forgotten. The cat nudged the book open with its nose, while holding down the pages with its paws. Already the volume began to crumble, as if it had been kept in a vault for thousands of years slowly being oxidized by time. From what the cat could tell, the small tome was someone's journal, documenting the passage along a river, dealing with trades, and navigating by starlight. Occasionally it was hand-illustrated with crude sketches, showing what appeared to be a garage with well-defined brick archways, with cheery automobiles passing in and out through these archway openings. The cat had never seen such automobiles, suggesting that these were perhaps older models that had existed before its time. As the cat gazed at this curious picture, all of the paper in the book had become powder, and began to scatter in the morning wind blowing under the full light of the sun which played on the autumn leaves and twigs scattering the ground. Not very far away was the roar of the highway, with the corpulent near-diabetics and their sugar drinks and half-eaten limbs of cooked meat. With an uncertain feeling in its stomach, the Dark Feline moved closer to some of the ruins of buildings that now emerged from all around. The darkness of night had hidden from its view the extensiveness of these stone ruins, many of which lacked complete roofs, because the rusted paneling overhead had fallen through after many seasons of precipitation and heat. Most of the buildings were single storey, but there were a few multi-leveled edifices that were dark on the inside save for the smashed windows and the occasional blast-holes in the stone and mortar, opening up the inside to the outside, and revealing the dramatically weathered contents within.

There was very little to be found in these strange derelict buildings, aside from the occasional personal effect, like an office nameplate, or tube of lipstick weathered past recognition. In fact, most of what was discovered in these areas were liquor bottles, smashed and unsmashed. Occasionally there was the odd strip of pantyhose that littered the dusty walkway. In one of the larger areas, where there existed the empty vats, with all sorts of heating tubes and steam pipes with indiscriminately placed control valves, etc. there were discovered bales of uncut pantyhose left in the dust. Those clumps of the wadded pantyhose fabric (now weathered into a conglomerated mess) that were not in direct sunlight managed to survive, although their precarious existence was certainly coming to an end because their molecular structures had started to break down, making them very brittle. And on every wall, every flat surface there was an endless stream of graffiti, some of which was stupid and some that was brilliant. This stream of words, of ubiquitous verbosity, of flaunted name-tags and youthful concepts, was a fresh-flowing stream of warm water that coursed through these metaphysically frozen ruins. At every second, every glance, a new feature of poetical archaeology flashed through the cat's field of vision, stimulating its imagination upon the distortion of history and uncovering the poetic intersubjectivity among people who were no longer there, who might even have been dead but who still contributed to the collective ghost that coursed through the walls, the floors, the veins of graffiti and the broken machines that were left alone and off the smooth, pink path of the noisy road that was only a few minutes away, that would lead to all of the cities of nearly-diabetic humanity.

There were several entrances to lower levels in the biggest of the abandoned factory buildings, but the Dark Feline avoided all of them. Instinct told the cat to do this. Off in the distance was visible the sordid skyline of the lost city of the porks, as it rose up from a hill, making the city look bigger than it really was. But nevertheless, it was a city, and somehow this particular city was calling the Dark Feline, summoning it as if it were some kind of dérive that one could follow with open eyes, as if looking did nothing to disturb a pre-destined sequence of footsteps that would ultimately bring the traveler to a place assigned by some kind of fate patterned after a riddle of the collective-unconsciousness of sentient terrestrial life. The cat simply could not resist. It might have found temporary shelter in the area around the Salt Manor, living like one of the silent bodies in orbit around the magnetic and terrifying power radiating from the entity that was the Dark Queen, but really, such a prospect grew more and more reviled by the growing collection of rancid memories whose voices were louder than the more pleasant ones. The Dark Feline simply could no longer ignore the warnings that it had been hearing, and the appearance of the miniature corpses and the attacking coat-racks was the final insult. The cat simply had no choice but to follow its instinct, which would hopefully take it to a new home, a new place where it could live, swatting at insects, eating wild lizards and maintaining a good relationship with the local library.

This reverie of purpose was suddenly interrupted when a loose rock fell from a nearby wall. The Dark Feline was actually leaving the old pantyhose factory site, but one of the last buildings through which it had to traverse was a labyrinth of old concrete rooms – probably old offices – which were crumbling and highlighted by spokes of sunlight that effortlessly reached through the compromised roof. Throughout the hallways now littered with pine needles, branches and fungi, there were visible several mannequin parts that had been recently separated from the body and which were now lying aimlessly amid the invading nature, almost casually strewn about for one's viewing pleasure. The cat saw also a few intact mannequins sporting strange necklaces made with beads that resembled glowing blood corpuscles, the red kind. These "blood cells on a string" emitted the most curious crimson pulsations, while lending the mannequins, all decked out in their purple velvet space costumes, a however temporary augmentation of their naturally uneasy, near-disquieting apparition of power. One of the mannequins nearest the cat had its arm raised threateningly, holding some kind of beehive made out of red velvet which appeared just as menacing as it did ridiculous. If it weren't for the menacing gesture of the featureless mannequin wielding the red velvet beehive, then the cat might have assumed that this "hive" was nothing more than some kind of strange, childlike object made with expensive art supplies, in preparation for a school art class. But instead, it had a sinister appearance, as if it were some kind of bomb that could wreak an unknown form of havoc on whomever it touched. Therefore, the Dark Feline slowly backed away from the motionless but highly menacing mannequin, bumping into a wall. Its very next impulse was to flee, but before it did, it suddenly felt the first sensations of pink and green mucus forming all over its joints, in its front and hind legs, along its neck, along its spinal column and tail. It almost felt as if strange fish-birds were growing from these sensations of pink and green mucus like a tumor would. Before turning to run away, it noticed that the mannequin with the menacing and highly expensive art-supply object was also being enveloped (around the joints) by the same variety of colorful mucus, but because it could not move, it was slowly being disassembled by these strange pink and green fish-birds who began to occupy the same space as the mannequin.

The Dark Feline ran as fast as it was able in the direction of the smooth, pink highway that led to all cities (to the lost city of the porks, in this particular instance), never looking back, and completely relieved to feel the strands of pink and green mucus slipping away from its limbs, as if the mucus were some kind of invisible tourniquet of insidious deconstruction that lost its grip on reality.

Elsewhere, on a rather small Pacific island right off the coast of the North American continent, several fighter jets vigilantly dropped small-scale bombs on the handful of villages that were based there. The bombs were not strong enough to incinerate the island, but the explosions certainly disrupted all routine activities for the inhabitants who might have been human, but also might not have been. While faceless people ran from tree to tree, the green iguanas ran from rock to rock, momentarily sunning themselves only to hide underneath one of the larger boulders as soon as the whistle of an incoming strike was heard. Therefore, much chaos resulted in the early part of the morning, during an unnaturally cool day in October.

After the dust settled, the survivors huddled about small campfires to discuss why they had been singled out for a strike, and by whom, since the attacking planes had no identifying markings. It was really a mystery, since the island made no serious contributions to anyone's economy, and had no history or secrets which one might want to obliterate. Or, at least that was what most people thought. As it were, the island folks tilled their fields, ate wild fruits, wrote their history on animal hides, played sand checkers at the beach all day and also drove around in archaic automobiles. It was unknown where exactly these automobiles came from, or where the petrol was obtained with which to fuel these vehicles, but nonetheless, all of the villagers had their share of cars that were utilized for traveling among the island villages. The curious phenomenon observed after the bombing was that all of the cars appeared to have the image of an outstretched hand burned onto the hoods and roofs of the vehicles. It was as if each hand was assigned to reach for a car, possibly to pull the vehicle toward the gods, or so said some superstitious people who were picking dead flies out of their noses. It was also said that some of the hands seemed to be wearing rings, suggesting that the gods who dropped the bombs were rich, and were offering a "payment" that was a form of black humor, as black as the carbonized blast of the image. Still others shook their heads, thinking of the hands in the way piano keys become stuck and special hands are needed to lift the stuck keys so that other hands might continue playing the pianos, creating a society of hands and hand etiquette that would eventually manually create a leaning tower of Babel requiring, of all things, the leaning of many hands against the wall of complications, in order to put a finger in the hole to plug a leak. Nevertheless, much speculation occurred that afternoon as the villagers and iguanas wracked their brains to understand what had happened to them.

Reconstruction events were attempted, with hands pushing on the damaged tinder, pushing tiny sticks into place which eventually became houses. People rejoiced and combed their hair, while posting "do not disturb" symbols of an unknown calligraphic language on their wooden front doors, using naturally occurring driftwood that daily washed up on the beach. This conservative effort was a streamlined version of the existence that once was, before the bombing. It was as if a flying saucer occupied each and every head of the town, leading to a separation of hand and head, in a similar way to how countries that have vague democratic aspirations boast of the separation of church and state, or perhaps the separation of left and right. Therefore, hands and heads were free to be momentarily independent of each other, leading to a particular hand's display of a metacognizant awareness of words formed from its partner's lips, and then with the corresponding head showing an unconscious awareness of the automatic movements of hands which did not conform to expected outcomes of usual finger exercises that went from being simple maneuvers to their transformation into the orchestrated fall of dominoes which is what happens when ballerinas fall over each other onstage, in unexpected moments of rare beauty when the audience becomes separated from the dancers by a curtain of jeweler's red velvet, after the tomatoes are thrown.

Hence the beginning of an unpleasant dichotomy that represented a schism of what was once a unity: the hand-and-head unity. Now hands and heads were seemingly opposed to one another, but their unity of the past only became mythologized, while the villagers and iguanas fantasized about a new relationship between the hands and the heads that might be more dialectical in nature and which would enable the hands and the heads to surpass what they had been able to do when acting as solitary agents in an island paradise which could have easily been a goldfish bowl that had been turned upside-down.

Therefore the villagers and the iguanas were stumped by the profusion of hands on their automobiles, while they searched in vain for anomalous heads that were never to appear, even in their dreams, of which the latter were often thought to hold clues to the future. The villagers took to ritualistic practices that were as obscene as they were brutal, and the youth of the villages wore special armor that barely shielded their sweating limbs from the blows of clubs and swords of the opposing centurions. Their battlefields were ironically the old graveyards of their ancestors, with tombstones freely lopped off at every slash of the sword, and at every sip from a soda straw laced with arsenic in the local establishments that were known as Musical Drinking Sanctuaries – for that was what they really were: sanctuaries where one could go to have drinks and listen to loud music. These were the places where nearly empty drinks were found with floating cigarette butts, and where the music was so loud that thinking became impossible, but which contributed to a state of theoretical happiness that was written in cultural stone like the religious commandments of cranky old holy men whose yeast imbalances made them act like morons. In and out of these ancestral graveyards and Musical Drink Sanctuaries, the centurions traded blows and beers, straining friendships to the point of enmity, and simultaneously finding love through hatred. Among these islands were centurion enforcers who went about secretly patrolling the activities of the youth, enforcing the rules by savagely executing anyone who did not obey. Usually the enforcers had metallic noses and metallic eye patches that covered up many of their identifying features, and they would always strike their victims in the dead of night, often cutting their throat twice, with one inch between the two cuts. And then in the morning the body would be found, and much nasty gossip would circulate among the old hens about how the victim never could do this or that on time, etc.

It was in one of these Musical Drink Sanctuaries that a certain patron entered the building, shrouded in the inner darkness that could always be found in such establishments. The patron passed through fields of thin plastic that went from wall to wall like a transparent hymen, and she came to sit down in an armchair that was located next to the jukebox. Tiny kittens came to her feet, crawling up her leg in a queue, while mewing little pathetic cries that could only shake the heart of their mother. But there was no mother for these kittens, and so they were nourished by a mixture of milk and rum by the proprietor of this particular Musical Drinking Sanctuary. The kittens became very attached to the new visitor, whose maternal empathy seemed to warm their little hearts much more thoroughly than the rum and milk cocktail did. She petted a few of them with her finger, and then gently set them down into the basket in which they slept, right next to the blaringly loud jukebox. The visitor got up, and crossed the room, approaching the bar. The bartender had a featureless, porcine face. The visiting woman asked for her usual drink, put a cigarette butt in it and then watched it float in the iceless drink for the rest of the time she was at the Musical Drink Sanctuary. As if in slow-motion, she turned her head to regard a smooth, green iguana who was seated next to her, on a high stool. The iguana was alert enough to make eye-contact, but apparently lost in a reverie about wandering among sunny rocks and salty tidepools filled with delicious small crabs and other insects. As if in a dream, the woman felt that she had seen this iguana once before, and vaguely remembered poking its side with a toothpick, remarking how cute it was, just like old-fashioned ladies like to pinch the cheeks of little boys and girls, so as to express their appreciation for their cuteness.

The iguana continued to ignore her, which made the woman furious. Her left fist clenched, while the right hand covered the fist, barely containing the heavy anger that was contained within. She impatiently fingered her untouched drink, with the floating cigarette butt, and contemplated the surroundings that included some tacky plastic colored lights and ornamentation from the previous winter festival (which were never taken down, but only allowed to collect dust, and where the burnt out bulbs were *eventually* replaced by the bartender, who did so at his own snail's pace). Around the room was a very long, continuous mural depicting the local mythology of the islanders, showing scenes of night and day, summer and winter, and heads and hands. She felt as if she had swept her eyes over this mural so many, many times before, and yet could not remember a particular, single instance of such. It was all very curious. In addition to this sense of déjà vu, there was an accompanying feeling of paranoia, as if somehow she were being watched, as if behind the paintings of eyes there were real eyes that were watching her every move, as if her life were an orchestration of puppet limbs, including of course, heads and hands. It was disconcerting, and eventually she moved her eyes to the door and followed closely behind them with her arms and legs. Reaching the threshold of the door, she looked back at her barstool in the Musical Drink Sanctuary, at the daydreaming iguana perched at the bar, and at her untouched drink with the floating cigarette butt in it. Impassively she pulled out a fresh tube of greasy, red monkey-face lipstick and liberally applied the red color to her face, smacking her lips with an assurance that spoke of sex mixed liberally with strategy, and the politics of denial stamped onto her skirt like the Braille dots of truth that were as real as the genetic code, but just as invisible. She stalked away from the Musical Drink Sanctuary, leaving the iguana in peace, with the bartender, who was a bald-headed pork with a stout, flared pink nose, scratching his head and making up a fresh baby bottle of his special milk formula for the kittens, who were by now fast asleep in their comfortable, fuzzy basket, oblivious to the loud music and utterly drunk.

This woman who visited the Musical Drink Sanctuary was new to the island, or so she thought, but in truth she had been there many, many times before, like the way an infant keeps coming back to the breast. The woman was puzzled by the agitation of the villagers, who had only during the earlier part of the day watched their village descend to a state of chaos thanks to the bombing which had occurred there. But as this particular village was the largest, and of course the most affluent, the shock of the destruction was discussed and investigated to a larger extent than in some of the poorer villages, who nevertheless ate the same kinds of fruit as everyone else did, like pineapples and coconuts, even in December, when it was supposed to be freezing cold. The visiting woman walked through the frosty haze of dusk within her own mental fog, with each of her hands clenched, like two children who are inconsolable when the family pet dies. The woman reached the center of the town square, and saw an open coffin next to the central fountain that was spewing nothing but near-freezing water. Although many of the passing villagers saw the woman get into the coffin and close the lid, none of them did a single thing to investigate or question this curious behavior, either because they were too dazed by the horrible events of the day, or because they had already seen this very act done the same way. When the woman closed the lid of the coffin and reclined upon the cushions, shutting her eyes and staring up into the darkness, she closed her eyes and hummed a nursery rhyme while feeling as if her body were crawling with a swarm of stinging insects. The woman's name was Yes-Yes.

Despite Yes-Yes's repose in the mysterious coffin, the townspeople remained oblivious, even when a certain pair of porkly constables came to lift the coffin and carry it away. The human and iguana townsfolk didn't seem to care, but most of the proprietors of the various shoppes, stores, restaurants and even the Musical Drinking Sanctuary poked their piggly heads out of doors and windows, to focus their beady pink eyes on the coffin being carried down the street with a live woman inside. Nobody in town ever questioned what the pork people did, because the pigs were the ones who called all the shots. The pork people were the ones who owned the buildings, and the ones who provided the cars (that were now marked with the blackened image of an enigmatic hand) and the ones who provided the pineapples and coconuts to this otherwise dull island existence that lacked an economy.

After the two pork people and the coffin procession had left the scene, the porkly proprietor of the Musical Drinking Sanctuary pulled his detached head back inside the window with his hands and replaced it on the fat stump that was his neck. In his twisted mind, bookshelves moved like parallel staircases, scheming the stew that was the gristle of half-baked cerebrum, moving around in convecting motions like blobs of jellyfish pushed by oceanic currents from the deepest of the deep, which rarely see the light, all the way up the uppermost strata of consciousness in order to experience the harsh realities of wind currents as they try in vain to dry out a cornea that is always refreshed with a wet blink up until the moment of death. Therefore these circular plan-making sessions always occupied the consciousness of the pig owner of the Musical Drinking Sanctuary, always moments after Yes-Yes would leave, to be taken away in her special taxi down the shores of memory lane, as if yesterday were the island that the inhabitants really thought was today, and perhaps even vice-versa, creating the most disturbing kind of paradox that could only be mimicked by a completely different kind of invasion experienced by fellow mannequin travelers at the abandoned pantyhose factory, on the outskirts of the pork city which in all actuality was not very far away (perhaps half a day's drive by old-fashioned automobile) from the island where the inconsiderate tavern was located.

The pork owner of the bar kept circulating these ideas regarding the conquest of Yes-Yes, as if he couldn't wait to run his animalistic snout between her toes, between her smooth legs, spending some time sniffing around in her musky bush, and then all the way up the magic, pink road between her breasts, until he'd reach her mouth, where he'd set up camp for the night, filling her with what he only could serve up best from the tap, from the inner kegs that he kept within the depths of his Musical Drink Sanctuary, filling her with his very best until she would split in two, like the world split in half, in the way a sharp sword would cut the earth along the doldrums, a blade of honeyed sweet-talk that might put two globes in his greasy hands that could later be used to barter for something greater, as if the map of the world were also the tattoo that most likely ran along the length of Yes-Yes's luscious body. These lustful, geological reveries always made the bartender fidget ever so nervously, causing him to manifest numerous behavioral tics, like a certain rubbing together of his hands under an imaginary faucet, perhaps even some vain psychological gesture as pre-nuptial purification in anticipation of getting his sweaty, pudgy, piggly porkchops all over her soft pink tenderloins, spattering her with dollops of gravy and sucking on her ribcage, and then, finally hitting her where it counts with the butter. No holding back. The pork bartender, a hopeless diabetic, licked some drool that had just started down his chin and then turned his attention to the quiet green iguana, who had just asked for a refill.

12
The Descent

Not very far away, in Lucipheromone, the lost city of the porks, the Pork raised himself up from the floor where he was murdered on-ly a week ago, completely regenerated. Although the mice and roaches tried to munch on his bones as hard as they could, the vermin found themselves out of luck as the Pork's incredibly strong immune system took over, allowing the damaged tissues to heal themselves while keeping out infection. As he looked up at the ceiling, infinitely tired, he noticed a small pile of purple lightbulbs where he had been splayed out. Apparently he was working even while dead! He gingerly picked up the newly discovered treasure, inspected the bulbs, and put them in a safe place, utterly happy to be in the lightbulb business even after being killed in a city that was known for its barbarism including a severely high murder rate. Luckily, he noticed that nobody had stolen his lightbulb stash, not even the Perfect, who had apparently found another lightbulb provider in the meantime. In all of their pinheaded logicality, thought the Pork to himself, the Perfect would not even steal a petty lightbulb collection to further their interests. This development of course did not mean that the Perfect had any strong sense of morality, but merely that they had a list of other things to steal, and purple lightbulbs were just not close enough to the top of that list. The funny thing was, the Pork made plans to contact them again, perhaps to introduce himself as the Pork, the dear younger brother of the Pork who used to be in their employment. It was all a very funny game as far as he was concerned, as he fumbled through the storage crates, verifying that indeed all of the lightbulbs had been left undisturbed during the week of his incapacitation. Life was grand.

Although he had not been paid in a while, his savings were still secure for him to venture out to celebrate his new life, employing one of those edible, disposable piggly-wiggly prostitutes as the celebration piece. He'd always enjoy raping both of those holes beneath the skirt, reveling in her squealing terror, decapitating her, and then taking her body down to the local BBQ establishment, as a proudly won trophy, only to dine on her flesh and bones a short while later. The Pork was always very careful to keep himself legally protected at all times, conscientiously carrying around with him his cannibal permit as well as the prostitute's legal paperwork so that, upon request, he could furnish the correct documents to any officers of the law he might encounter along his short trip to the local BBQ. As it was, he'd have to show all of the same licensing and paperwork to the cashier at the BBQ, otherwise they'd call the cops on him, so really, as long as he was on the right side of the law, he was able to have his cake and eat it too. Life was grand.

The Pork stepped out of his house, noticing that straw baskets made of tumbleweed were blowing down the street. These were the finest naturally occurring baskets ever made, whether by agile, sentient hands or by nature, but regardless of how they were created in the grand scheme of phenomenological existence, they were there, and they were definitely tumbling past the Pork's widened eyes. Immediately the baskets were trailed by the impressions of written characters, as if letters of the alphabet were tagging these poor baskets and chasing them down to the edge of the earth, an existence of possible accretion whereupon the final result was a conglomeration of sentences which led to the telling of a story, or possibly a history, or protocol, or sequence of events that might have shed some light into what was commonly held to be a rather narrow concept of "reality," only showing that such a reality was poverty-stricken, yet secretly bursting at the seams with riches which most people (including the Pork) were too afraid to open their eyes to, for fear of appearing out of step with the commonly delineated bounds of "normality" – another, equally poverty-stricken concept that slapped at the impoverished, rubbery skulls with cruel waves of punishing instigation into the ranks of obedience, and equally, "false individuality," another insidious form of obedience (its non-dialecticized antithesis; true individuality was to be found elsewhere) that rose from the ashes of the original obedients. Such were the enemies of the lost, tumbling sentences, who only tried to join in with playful somersaults with the tumbleweed baskets, but were forever limited and castrated by numerous incarnations of obedience and obedients.

Eventually the wave of passing tumbleweed baskets reduced in volume, and the Pork was able to leave the house finally, to observe the flow of conventional and magnetic automobiles pass along the street, down the slummy neighborhood where his snot-nosed compatriots spent their disgusting lives. Of course, he was no different, and he immediately began to look up and down the avenue for the right prostitute of his choice, the one who would worship his snot, pleasure his skin and finally nourish his entrails at the close of a salaciously busy evening. Dusk fell upon his brow like a violet ray of light passing through a stained glass window, evoking the alternative awareness of identity that comes through casting one's sense of consciousness through altered surroundings.

The Pork continued his prowl, never quite finding what he was looking for until a certain curious impulse drove him to nervously retrace a few steps back to the Wax Museum, that he had just passed. The museum had just closed an hour ago, but he only desired to peep through the windows with his beedy eyes obscenely tucked within a furry brow, replete with wild hairs. The ever-searching eyes focused on many of the new arrivals, usually caricatures of humans, or the latest celebrities that always pulled a vicious, mocking guffaw from his lungs. He enjoyed these silly humans, and only regretted there not being a legal precedent that would allow him to sink his omnivorous teeth into their stinking flesh. Pork BBQ feasts were not enough for the Pork, he decided. As his eyes passed over the curiously leaning statue of the Man who was Lead, he noticed a red ring of pigment around one of the temples on the statue's skull, which shone oddly in the light. Such artistic liberty was not uncommon among the porkly wax sculptors who sold their creations to this wax museum, but he had never in all of his greedy, gluttonous days seen such a strange creation, as if the red ring was a signal, or a port where a hose might connect, either to pneumatically remove contents from the brain or to put new things in. The other wax subjects looked much more mundane, with dull and drained faces. Yes, that was the difference! The Pork realized that the Man who was Lead was so different because his face was made of freshly cut lead that was only beginning to oxidize, before the air had changed the metallic sheen to a dull gray. What a strange addition! The face really did look like it had been sculpted from the soft metal. He would have to ask the museum proprietor about that one.

Turning his attention to his path towards uncensored, wanton gluttony and carnal debauchery, he followed his nose in the direction of dinner and a show, in reverse order. During the late afternoon, there had been several porkly children running along the streets, aimlessly playing their games that they would soon have to renounce upon entering the workforce at the onset of adolescence. One thing that could be said about porkly society was that school was not a priority for most of its members, as higher learning was only reserved for the privileged. Generally the commonly prescribed checklist of porkly existence was work, procreation, consumption of commodities and death, which was originally modeled after the human formula, morbidly brought to conscious perfection by the terrestrial capitalist and faux-communist regimes (that were in all actuality just reactionary, anti-clones of the former, becoming the opposite of what they originally set out to be, thereby making themselves replicas of what they hated, but only with different masks, names and titles), so in the end, both capitalist and anti-capitalist (the so-called "communist" societies, merely threadbare caricatures of the true kind of socialism/commun-ism advocated by Marx/Engels and their intellectual descendents) cultures were really one and the same, ultimately two sides of the same dirty coin of miserabilism, and much more similar to each other than they were different. Of course, the Pork and his people were completely against such utterly false and blasphemic ideas of equality and sharing, instead and to the contrary, preferring to support and even blindly worship the economic exploitation of one group by another, and of course the culture that was created as a result, so as to maintain the state of economic exploitation. Therefore, the pork citizens were solid proponents of the old and sickly laissez faire economic strategy. Such practices were considered desirable in that capitalism bred a state of competition which would allow for humanity to take great forward strides of Progress. True genius and true innovation could not be cultivated in a flowery, mild, "safe," egalitarian environment – it was only under conditions of strong oppression and holy terror that *real* Progress could be achieved. In this respect, the Pork and his kind felt that humanity might someday come to serve the needs of the porkly society in such a servile capacity, instead of the other way around which represented the prevailing conditions. That was why most of the porks lived in slums, why the first letter of their race was never capitalized, hence the "porks" instead of "Porks." But the Pork in particular was one of the different ones, though, who had dreams of revenge and conquest, and who purposefully capitalized his name so that he might spread his vision of domination that might someday help his people turn the tables on the humans.

With these casual thoughts, the Pork once again returned his focus to the pink road that would lead him to his prostitute and meal for the night, both desires integrally embodied by one corpulent, concupiscent porkly female with a juicy, fat ass and succulent ribs, who had absolutely no idea her fate was to terminally cross paths with his.

Across the street from where the Pork was leering at an overweight whore who had had too many candy-bars over the course of her short life, a telephone booth spraypainted in graffiti contained a sticky telephone that began to ring. Pressed all over the phone apparatus and booth were the colorfully painted handprints of children, similar to the rock art of certain "primitive" peoples whose hands of history had descended through the ages, tracing a lineage of knowledge with the tactile remembrances of fingers. Perhaps a similar event was occurring here, the process of knowledge – or perhaps its evolution – through the memories of touch, incarnated in the form of the handprints which seemed to be surfacing in many varied parts of the world, not just on telephones or train stations, but also on houses and other expensive objects, often perceived as vandalism but really just the form of a return to basics, or an assertion of the collective consciousness that manifest reality is not the only one.

The telephone stopped ringing long enough for a human with hairy arms underneath a dark, expensive gigolo suit to turn away from the machine in utter terror, as if the ringing of the telephone was exotic anathema to him, causing his body, which was normally occupied by soft, visceral organs, to become made of wooden planks, as if he were comprised of wooden compartments like a titanic ship that began to buckle after a blow from an iceberg or some other powerful force that would cause the physical integrity of his being to cave in, like a frightening chain reaction. As if wrenched in pain, with his chest cavity in a state of collapse, he held out both of his hands together, with his wrists bound by invisible rope, and his black-gloved hands evoking the dawning of a black sun, a horrible symbol put forth by a weak being crushed by unknown forces, possibly belligerent chests of drawers that contained strange varieties of formal clothing, with each garment having different but important functions within society, at different points in the timescale of the society's lifespan, however long certain empires last, at least long enough for them to change their socks. Perhaps it was the compartmentalization of his sense of control that was in a state of sorry implosion, as he watched his sense of order and his hierarchies of social stratification begin to meld together, like segregated icicles that long to return to the ocean where the sea floor would periodically spread open like a book. The volume of the earth, neatly kept somewhere on an intergalactic library shelf, was a parted sea that was also the parted hair of the man, along the lobes of his cranium beneath his skull, just like the two lobes of a pitifully sprouted bean that was languishing in a place that did not nourish, and which only caused the sprouts to grow upside down and migrate sideways to circumvent obstacles that normally would have been absent should the bean have sprouted in a healthier environment.

The struggling gigolo man staggered this way and that, bumping into lightposts; meanwhile the ground shook, sending tremors through buildings that caused some of the old painted signs to crack and drop off in certain places, revealing the old lettering that had existed before the current layer of paint had been applied. Cars sensed the quake, and hurried to jet along to other parts of the pork city, where perhaps it might be safer than in the older quarters. The strange gigolo narrowly missed being hit by one of the fleeing cars, and eventually pried his hands away from each other, as if he were prying apart two lovers who were completely devoted to each other. His dazed look was accentuated by a small amount of blood that dribbled down his lips onto his chin, and his glazed eyes looked almost dead, with shrunken corneas, highlighted by accentuated patches of white, showing only the beady little pupils within, as if the entire being of that man had withdrawn into the shell that was now his body, all of which staggered off behind a disused alleyway where nobody would see him.

Meanwhile porky children clapped their limbs together in odd, synchronous rhythms. These children did not have any fingers, because all of them had been cut off, as had been the custom demonstrated to them by their parents. The fingers would of course grow back, but only once the offspring started laboring again. And then towards the end of their lives after retirement, in the last decade of life allowed them, the fingers would again be chopped off. Humans might have found these customs strange, but such practices really represented the goodness and kindness of the pork people. This finger-cutting represented an open oyster with pearls of fine morality that had been spun over the centuries, partially on earth, where the porks colonized, and then on other worlds, including their original homeworld. Such a majestic tradition was reminiscent of the simplicity of an insecticide spray: there is a cockroach in the kitchen? Then take out the can of insecticide. Read the can label. See the iconographic picture of the targeted roach? Then aim the can and spray the roach that you see clinging to the wall, with twitching antennae waiting to hurt the children and ruin a perfect Sunday outing when bloody stumps of hands are used to row an artificial rowboat while the working parents, with the functional fingers, hold up colorful parasols, smoking seaweed cigarettes and pinching ants off of the forehead of unfortunate children who cannot get their parents to look at them save for the ants. Time to use the bug spray again.

These cycles were unleashed by the chipping of the paint on the buildings, as if a wet tear pulled away from a fat cheek could manipulate a song about lollypops into a spiny porcupine that slept in a very, very special room where certain kinds of tarot cards are read. This particular room was on the street near where the devastating quake occurred, and the porkly attendant who ran the tarot-reading storefront was of a short and stocky breed and who constantly used stubby pork fingers to stop the constant flow of viscous mucus from its engorged snout, with sickly thick waves of snot periodically being wiped under the tables and counters, since using paper towels was too expensive and using fingers was cheaper, unless one was either a child or in retirement, when there would be no more fingers due to their being chopped off with a meat cleaver. But within the tarot card storefront, all people and porks who entered to have their cards read were encouraged to wipe their snot under the tables and on the chair and table legs. The particular pork who did the reading, in addition to being an anal-retentive type, had a rather unique approach to cards. Upon learning that a visiting patron desired a reading, he would put on some dark, round sunglasses and slowly, somnambulistically take the arm of the person, leading them into the back, private room with the sullen, red lightbulbs. The red lightbulbs would be extinguished in favor of lighting a few candles, mainly for mood-lighting. Then, the tarot-reader would observe some thin, cotton gloves, usually worn by uptight people, as they sat ever so innocently next to a handful of freshly boiled artichokes that were ever so sinister. These innocent gloves in the vicinity of the sinister, boiled artichokes caused the tarot-reader to gasp and snort. Immediately the tarot reader would put on the gloves and impulsively pick up an artichoke. He would choose several of the leaves and place them face-down on the table. Then he would pretend that they were real tarot cards. He would overturn some of them, looking at the random specks of dirt and tears in the leaf, coming to a conclusive interpretation of which number of the tarot the artichoke leaf represented, and in this way, the patron's fortune was laid out by a pig wearing gloves and sunglasses who pulled out artichoke leaves for a living.

The tarot-reader sent his last customer away completely satisfied and cynically removed his arid countrycide sunglasses to reveal a pair of sinister bloodshot eyes whose fibrous irises encircled the pupils like barbed wire, choking a pair of blood-red roses with thorns that would eventually eject the visions of destruction capable of scaring any half-baked child or adult, even. Despite the snot dripping from its snout, the tarot-reading pork leaned back in his chair, completely exhausted by holding back what up until now, it had only seen. The tarot-reader leaned back further in his chair, against the wall of the establishment.

On the other side of the wall, outside of the, uh, building, there were various mannequins assembled, each wearing their characteristic purple velvet spacesuits, with the emblematic star insignia above the left breast. These mannequins were carrying various pieces of hardware, even posing with them, as if they had just been removed from an outlandish department store that had taken an unwholesome approach to marketing their wares. Many of the pork people who had witnessed the mannequins screamed with a holy terror that scared many of the other porks who had not yet seen them. Within minutes, people opened purses, automobile doors, post-office boxes and other compartmentalized spaces, and subsequently various mannequin limbs were discovered to be occupying those areas, like an invasion. Even the closets were occupied by mannequins, requiring porks to go without wearing jackets because they were so afraid of encountering the velvet automatons within the dark places of their homes.

Back at the Salt Manor, the Cook squeezed a zit, releasing a spurt of pus that accidentally fell into the freshly risen cream, obtained from the cow only the day before. No bother. The Cook shrugged his shoulders and stretched his weary back while looking out of the window at a hazy autumn morning. He had slept very well the night before, which was indeed unnatural, considering the return of the Evil Queen who had supposedly been away on business. Usually any sort of gossip regarding the Evil Queen would send a wave of fear and/or panic through his stocky frame, given her savage reputation, and also considering that most cooks never lasted for more than a few months until their heads appeared one fine day on a stake, often as retribution for a scalded sauce, or a roasted ribcage that was a tad over-crisp. The Cook always took painstaking measures to ensure that all plates leaving his kitchen for the Queen's table were prepared according to all of her numerous whims and specifications. If she desired bleeding pork sausages on a bed of pubic hair instead of parsley, then he complied. If she wanted cow's tongue with silver-stud piercings and an onion marmalade, then he obliged. If the Queen wanted one of his assistant's eyeballs smeared on toast for breakfast, then he had no choice but to give her exactly what she wanted. So far the relationship he had with the Queen was a good one, and it was his supreme wish to keep it that way.

Regarding the "head garden" as some of the servants called it: as of late much gossip had been circulating that both the courtyard garden as well as the back-of-the-house "Hall of Shame" had been filled to capacity with the skewered heads of ex-servants, ex-lovers, miscreants, thieves, trouble-makers, hoo-hoo's as well as ha-ha's, leaving no room for the "new arrivals." Based on this limitation of space for newly impaled heads on the garden stakes, the Queen had last week issued an order for there to be a new area for recently disposed skulls, underground, perhaps in one of the Manor's numerous catacombs, most of which had lain undisturbed for many, many years. This talk of such ghoulish plans gave the Cook a severe case of the creeps, as his hands shook ever so uncontrollably as he stirred the cream sauce to be used in making the Queen's Eggs Benedict for her morning repast. Next to the slightly bubbling sauce was a skillet sautéing the rebellious ears of infidels, the severed outer ears of a few servants who had been caught listening to improvisational music in their quarters, when they thought that the hallway was dark and no-one could hear them. Their passion gave them away by their syncopated foot-taps, drumming fingers and jovial humming, which became audible to some sneaks and snoops who had been hired for that very purpose: to spy on the other servants and rat them out, usually for a few extra, petty privileges, like an extra bar of soap each month, or an extra day off from work to be awarded once every four or five months. The head of the Elite Guard had decided that these servants should pay for their affront by relinquishing their ears (filled with subversive music) and then their lives, in that order. And so it was only upon opening up the kitchen when the Cook arrived that morning, did he receive a basket of almost a dozen ears with a very brief note describing how the Lady preferred to have her stewed ears. In a rich stock of beef bouillon, the ears were tenderized with various herbs until they turned a near-gelatinous consistency. Then, they were soused in a regal white wine that only came from the most virgin grapes, which was simmered with the ears until they were delightfully caramelized, and then garnished with some wild-flowers, the edible kind. This was the kind of cooking to which the accomplished Cook was accustomed. And when the Queen was happy, then he was even happier, because it meant that his life would be extended for one more day.

The Cook had been too busy clearing the wax from his thick, bulbous ears, but the rumors he had been hearing were that the Evil Queen had died and gone to heaven, and then come back again to walk among the living, as if she were some kind of zombie, or if she had touched upon the highly metaphysical domain of the living-dead. Other rumors suggested that she was an undercover agent, sent by the gods or some higher power – whether supernatural, extraterrestrial, or simply a rogue incarnation of another government – to test their loyalties for the end of accomplishing some dubious mission. Still other rumors suggested that she was a traveler from a faraway land who could metamorphose her body into anything she pleased, giving her the opportunity of stealth and infiltration, allowing her to take unprecedented journeys to spy on her enemies so as to learn their economic insecurities and secrets of state. That last thought sometimes gave him chills, bringing on waves of paranoia. As if life wasn't complicated enough to prevent him from doing his job in peace. He'd been feeling rebellious, forming in his head half a plan to leave the Salt Manor, to flee and go to one of the cities to work there. He probably wouldn't have made such high wages as he did while working for the Evil Queen, but then what good are high wages when one's head is skewered on a stake outside in the courtyard? And besides, he had a blossoming romance with Nathalie, who was one of the maids and who even wore one of those traditional French maid's outfits, complete with black satin undergarments. At this moment, between the odd trysts and carefully concealed gifts of rose petals and sweets left under her pillow, the Cook felt that he was but a step away from being able to snap her garters and exchange passionate kisses and embraces during the odd hours of the early morning, when he had the pretence to be up and about, taking inventory of kitchen supplies or preparing a special stock or sauce with magical ingredients that required several hours of extra preparation. If discovered, he already had a plan of hiding her in a meat locker among chops, steaks, ribs, skulls, entrails, etc. – a likely place to be avoided by the nosy guards. His life really was like a cake walk over eggshells, but with his half-baked artistry, he was sure he could find a way to extricate Nathalie and himself from this dangerous situation – he was sure he could, just as surely as minted dough rises. The Cook planned on discussing it with Nathalie that very evening, on account that he could easily detect her unhappiness and dissatisfaction with her life at the Salt Manor, as well. He wouldn't have dared broach the idea if she hadn't have seemed so receptive to it, since he could easily imagine his immediate demise should he reveal his plans to one of the "happier" slaves (or living automatons, really) within the Salt Manor who might tattle on him.

In the meantime, the Cook was biding his time, making coarse breads, sauces, salads, roasts, and from all manner of gustatory delinquency to the most obscure and abnormal delectation. As a lover of music himself, he decided once and for all that he would never eat another person's or animal's ears ever again. He was revolted by the Evil Queen's premise for consuming the ears – that ears filled with music might be enjoyed by her majesty, simply because of the vicarious and purely cowardly thrill of experiencing the music of rebellion second-hand. Or perhaps it was a sour grapes display of fatal irony. He couldn't be quite sure of her motives, but he was certain only of his resolve never to eat ears again, with or without music bedamned! The Cook then squeezed a very ripe zit on his forehead, and returned to the preparation of the Eggs Benedict, which were to be ready within the following quarter hour. He hurriedly wiped his fingers on a dirty rag and set to his tasks.

Upstairs, in her most favorite bed chamber, the Dark Witch awoke from a very sound sleep. Was she the Dark Witch, or perhaps more of an Evil Queen today? She couldn't decide. She was all of those things: Dark Witch, Evil Queen, Evil Mother, Scar Lady, Mother Corpse, etc. She couldn't make up her mind. She felt as if she were all of them, but that also she was always more of one than another at any given time of day. She felt as if her life were becoming too complex, as if she were reaching some kind of high road that might be untraversable unless she discard some of her excess psychological baggage. That was the suggestion of one of her spiritual advisors from last year, before he perished in much the same way so many of the Dark Witch's assistants had died.

The Dark Witch hadn't even risen to look at herself in the mirror, and she already knew that there were dark lines around her eyes. She could feel them. Lying in bed, she ran her hands over her engorged womb, thinking of the new child that would be born on a day to arrive very shortly. Who this child would be, and what it would represent still held quite a degree of mystery for her, but already the wheels were turning in her head about which direction she would posit her offspring, the first baby she had ever had. As she was reaching the surface of consciousness that morning, she was almost certain that she could feel the baby kicking, but then she wasn't completely sure. Perhaps she *wanted* to feel the baby kicking.

Even when thinking about getting out of bed, the Dark Witch was suddenly assailed by a void in memory, of not being able to remember where she was the day before, and perhaps the day before that one. She looked at her clothes on the floor, trying to connect what she was wearing with what she might have been doing, but no such luck. It seemed certain that she was absolutely clueless about her whereabouts of the previous day(s). Immediately she called for her most trusted servant, the Baked Nun, who with great effort suppressed her hysterical laughter and bobbing head motions which her majesty seemed to find so particularly annoying on this day. The Baked Nun was having trouble keeping herself collected in the presence of the Dark Witch's barely concealed annoyance and agitation, but she managed to squeak by with only barely a nervous laugh, and a few involuntary bobs of her head. The Baked Nun had informed her that her majesty had been gone on a business trip for the past week, and that it was only until the previous evening that she had returned, immediately retiring to her sleeping chamber upon her arrival at the Manor. The Dark Witch listened to her servant's reply attentively, studying her face in order to look for signs of deception, but of those kinds of signs there were none.

With the nun-servant dismissed, the Dark Witch searched her

mind and memories for any clue about where she had been and what she had been doing, and WHY she might not be able to remember. Had she been drugged or poisoned? Her very deep sleep might have been suspicious, but the resident physician of the Salt Manor gave her a clean bill of health, even suggesting that she looked younger than she did last month. Of course she responded favorably to the doctor's flattery, but then instantly sent her away, and resumed walking around in her private quarters, deep in thought, with her left hand obsessively clutching at her right hand (which was clenched as a fist), occasionally petting it, while the Dark Witch muttered to herself, lost in speculative thought. Every once in a while she had a flashback of herself when she was in preschool, learning the alphabet and doing recitations and singing songs. There was a particular nursery rhyme that haunted her, but she could only remember vague fragments of it, not enough to reconstruct the melody, but enough to be aware of it, to recognize it should she ever hear it somewhere again. And that was not all: this song seemed to be associated with the impression of a hive made by honeybees, a hive that seemed to resonate with her recent dreams and preoccupations from the past few weeks: the underwater cavern, the voices of the children, the strange chants that the voices were singing. Completely frustrated, the Dark Witch took out a fresh tube of greasy, red monkey-face lipstick and generously applied the color to her smooth, succulent lips. As she was headed out the door of her quarters, determined to penetrate this haunting mystery to its furthest depths, she walked past a plate of eggs benedict, left on a table in the bedroom's antechamber, still piping hot. But at this juncture, breakfast was the last thought on her mind.

The Dark Witch dismissed her servants and bodyguards, intent on making the trip to the bowels of the Salt Manor all by herself. She equipped herself only with a powerful torch, and double-checked to make sure that she had the brass iguana key still around her neck – the sharp one with the green gem for an eye – and set out to confront the unknown. As she entered the central staircase that was nothing but a downward spiral leading to the beginnings of the Salt Manor and its confused history, she regarded the hanging cages still filled with the skeletons of prisoners from centuries ago. Descending the stairs, the

Dark Witch clutched at the torch, passing level after level of dungeons. Some of the floors were in use while others had been converted to storage areas, while still others had not been used in such a long period of time that they might have caved in or been completely overrun by cobwebs, rats and other vermin of the night.

Eventually the Dark Witch arrived at the bottom of the staircase, where the sealed door had been contained with giant padlocks that resembled holy scarabs of rust or congealed blood, perhaps. The thick door remained open and undisturbed as it had been left not long ago when she had been here with her most trusted guards, exploring not very far, but extensively enough for her to experience more painful memories induced by the uncovered artifacts. She passed the low-ceilinged room which the blond girl had perished in, still with the sinister mirror, the rabbit dentures and the Victorian top hat. She passed the room with the refrigerator sarcophagus that still contained nothing but which still reminded her again of her lost sister, killed underneath the weight of the Manor house. The sinister refrigerator still beckoned to her, but she steadfastly ignored its calls. She continued on, past the room which evoked the horrible memory of her dying sister, entering into an area where she had never been before. The dust on the floor was the same, and the ever-snaking and turning hallways were numerous. She knew that she would never be able to explore each and every room, so she decided from there on to trust her instincts and intuition – that they alone would lead her in the right direction in her quest to track down the foundation and perhaps the cause(s) of her dream of the song and the children and the networking cave system which resembled a honeycomb more than anything else. As she proceeded on her strange journey, she noticed that many of the rooms had been miraculously opened, reminding her of a similar rending of the doors in the upper, inhabited levels when the Ratmeister had disappeared after inseminating her. As predicted, the open doors all bore the strange coat of arms of a grand oak tree with a gaping eye in the center of the foliage, reminiscent of an evil wound, or perhaps a doorway to somewhere she had never been. There were tiny footsteps everywhere in these dusty hallways.

Many of the halls had become slightly flooded due to the

persistent trickling of groundwater that penetrated the ceilings in certain areas, leaving behind pools of wetness as well as a lighter-colored mineral slime coating some of the stone walls and floors. Many of the rooms were now bare, except for a few leftover pieces of furniture, all very old in design. Before finding the room which housed the power generator, she felt another seismic tremor permeating this underground level, but the effects were mild. The Dark Witch might have been worried for her safety, due to the possibility of stones falling from the ceiling from the quake, but there were no signs of fallen rocks anywhere within these underground passageways, suggesting to her that her ancestors had made the architectural designs for this fortress based on sound principles. She instinctively ran her lithe fingers along the wall, recalling the days when she was more of an Alchemical Waif than an evil witch. She was more alive then, and it was only during the time of her internship at the Vaults of Athanor that she realized her own abilities. She was able to spin the proverbial hay into gold, and then she also excelled at creating birds that could fly through prisms of glass, as if they were aetherial highways that could travel from one point to another, analogous to the way certain metals could be transmuted to non-metals and vice versa. At one point, she was able to conjure a whole swarm of beautifully decorated humming birds – translucent as swirling stained glass – and then send them from one castle to the next, while phasing in and out of the more modern buildings that were made from concrete and metal. These birds were the focus of her passions, the coat-racks of her dreams of brutal conquest and libidinal ecstasy. As she recalled these now-distant memories, she felt a wetness form between her legs which only harmonized with the wetness on the walls, with the crystallized minerals composing fascinating tactile patterns. The Dark Witch gently eased out of her reverie, crushing some of the wet mineral paste between her fingers as if weighing the quality of the most expensive saffron or powdered diamond. This motion of her fingers also evoked a memory the fabric-feel of a starched collar of someone she might have loved, or perhaps not loved. It was all in the memories, anyway, she told herself.

Down in these parts of reality, the everyday-stuff of her surface life – the killings, the isolation, and the economic production – didn't seem to matter as much, especially since she was alone now with her own thoughts. It would have probably behooved her to make the journey better prepared, as she was by now all hot and bothered, and her precious clothing was soiled beyond repair. The torchlight battery would hold out for several more hours, so her fears of the darkness and the unknown were steadily dwindling. She even had half a mind to explore some of the rooms with a greater level of attentiveness, preferring to rummage through old closets to see what the previous inhabitants used to wear on their apparently sunless days, many, many levels beneath the surface. By now her ears had gotten used to a steady drip-drip-dripping of mineral water that left behind small mounds of calcinated anomalies in the most random of places: sometimes on the nose or forehead of a useless statue, sometimes on a random dinner plate forever rusted beyond use, sometimes precariously growing on the edge of a staircase – the ones which always led downward and not up – and also just on the floor. Some levels that she traversed had these vertical streams diverted, leaving them almost dry, while others were so wet that several inches of water would move down the hallways with her. In many areas there were cracks in the walls, suggesting that tectonic shifts had allowed these streams to invade the livable areas. And because the autumn rainy season had recently ended, there was quite a bit of water in the ground.

Not having eaten or drunk anything in several hours, the Dark Witch became hallucinatory, with her consciousness phasing in and out between half-fears and aspirations of conquest, of meeting the inner person who always lived within her but who rarely showed her face. Her sense of time became distorted, and if it were not for the timepiece she carried, she would have forgotten about how the hours really passed. Occasionally her hands would be at war with one another, but in most cases they were quite at peace beneath the cold dark of the Salt Manor, rather than when they were wrapped around someone's throat or their prick. In one of the rooms, whose paneled walls had nearly rotted away in some areas, there was seen a tall, victorian grandfather clock, looking flimsy and weak, yet still well defined with the deliberation of consciousness, with its troubled hands. These hands not only corresponded to the invisible creators of the clock, who only now existed in imaginative memory, but also conversely, in the limbs which once swung about the clock face that was in the shape of an owl, with carved features now so badly warped from the uneven humidity and invading groundwater. So the hands that were left behind felt the urge, figuratively of course, to clasp those of their creators, so that time might have been something more noble than a cobwebbed box, purely a speculative coffin which might have held something inside, but then maybe not. The excitement of opening the clock overcame the Dark Witch, who with trembling fingers of both hands reached out in unison, now taken over by the passions of childhood, in the most primitive joys of discovery and revelation, making the statues of the dead come alive with sprouting masses of clay that overcame their previous solidity.

The contents of the clock were rather drab: really just a mess of decaying plant material – probably hay – which helped the cavity of the clock retain its space due to the removal of the actual mechanical parts that presumably once occupied the body of the clock. Inside of the decaying twigs and reeds were three eggs made of a dull marble. They might have easily been oblong paperweights, or purely decorative ornamentation to hide in someone's garden. But their weight and presence struck the Dark Witch as odd, and she closed the clock face door, looking at the weathered paint on the owl's face that was now all but gone. As her disappointment with the clock and the strange "nest" inside became apparent to her, her anger rose, while simultaneously bringing her focus on the strange dripping noises that came from the running groundwater, sometimes forming a synchronous rhythm while at other moments falling into a hopeless discord. It was thus that the Dark Witch, finally alone with her thoughts, began to listen – really listen – to the emptiness with which she surrounded herself, a cool passage through spaces that her ancestors had hidden from her for too long, and equally to everyone's detriment.

Just as the Summer Solstice is eventually surpassed by the Autumnal Equinox, the Dark Witch's footsteps brought her from one orbit into another, with dark masses that almost seemed to be hiding behind certain heavy walls that were as non-threatening as they were lifeless, yet which still had a certain pull of impulse directing her footsteps like puppetry. The dripping that tuned in and out within her focus of concentration became the signals that told her where to go, as if a wordless poetry of hydrology within the most intimate crevices of the earth were the slippers of guidance that now led her passive feet. Her fingers became gentle, almost senile, those very same fingers which slit human throats with razor-sharp daggers and twisted the cherished treasures from the hands of naïve children who might have trusted her at this or that point along the way. The hands were forests of quiet that hid among the caves of the landscape, hiding the obtuseness and sending up towers of stillness and darkness to compliment the gravitational walls of the subterranean, necropolitan palace that she was penetrating for the first time. The motion of the celestial orbit of lotus roots brought her through passageway after passageway, almost always moving downward, rarely moving upward. She was certain that she would never get lost down there, wherever she really was, that somehow she would find a new exit that would deposit her at the base of a mountain, ever so mysteriously, or perhaps an entrance to a world further north, where glaciers covered the land, and her rebirth into the world of life would pass through an ice cave, made from a frozen river of congealed birds.

The objects in this netherworld, as scarce as they were now, still held to the semblance of what was once normal living: furniture like beds now sunken in, smashed pottery and rusted ironworks. The occasional silver key, the accoutrements of young girls, like hair wreaths or soiled ribbons of luxury, the squishy volumes of rotten books swamped to the core, with inseparable, gummy pages of lost intellect, poetry and discrimination. All of these objects fascinated her and bored her at the same time. Each contact made with an artifact or lost object summoned motions of abstract thought. There was recognition but also alienation. The urge to possess sometimes was at complete odds with the urge to abandon, to flee. Now the walls had a life of their own. This world had that effect on the Dark Witch, and all the while, the dripping of groundwater was steadily getting to her, as if she were the victim of the more traditional water torture, with endless drops of water on her head for an indefinite period of time. But the neurosis of such an experience came not from any sensation, but from the ambiguous sounds of self versus other, which called to her but also cursed her.

Ever so faintly, the Dark Witch heard the call of cherubic voices, the singing voices of children that were as tender as they were sweet, which filled her both with longing and with dread. The complex harmonies would overlap with angst, most often just beyond the reach of her ears, always pulling her forward, moving her through the organic muck that besmirched these lower levels. Corpses of snakes and dead men littered the wet corridors, completely decayed and beyond foul odor, but still present and malevolent in overall grotesqueness. There were dead rats, dead dogs and even dead birds, although it could have been anyone's guess how such large birds with a meter or more for a wingspan could have reached such depths below the earth's crust. The music wafted towards her in the form of a sonic perfume, and she had no choice but to follow. She would pass around numerous bends in passageways, always speculating that she was upon the source of the celestial yet subliminal noises, but around each corner there was still only the light cast by her torch, and no apparent source for the noise of relentless puppetry. At the foundations of consciousness these sounds might originate, like seeds that wash up on a river's shore, only to germinate once they have actually left the weightlessness of the current to latch their little claws into the soil and assert their biological presence onto the landscape, like the way a plague would colonize new continents of people at every chance it got. These sounds were relentless – not quite voices, and not quite instruments of music, yet approximately what the Dark Queen would expect from a terrifying symphony of modernity that originated paradoxically within the bowels of the past, among the dust and tombs of her ancestors where the savage always conquered the meek.

The symphony mocked her, the Dark Queen decided as she maneuvered past forked passageways that always went in the same direction, always reconvening in the direction that led ever downward. The music would change its hue the same way the color of an object might change under light sources that periodically shifted, ever so gradually. Even the walls began to emit a certain color, a bright green, and the rough mineral and fungal coverage on the stone walls lost their dullness, displaying a living green tinge that almost gave them the appearance of moss. The brickwork in the passageways began to change too. In the beginning, the bricks were positioned uniformly, with only a small margin of cement between each brick. But now certain gaps appeared between the bricks, giving the overall structure an organic look, which seemed more and more as if the spacings were becoming paradoxically random yet purposeful in appearance, as if they were organic catacombs designed with small, regularly spaced alcoves to carry urns of corporeal ash or whatever other small-sized effects of the dead. But in fact there were no funerary objects or anything at all placed within these tiny alcoves. As the Dark Queen passed through these snaking passageways, chasing the music that grew louder with every minute, the walls finally manifested a strong resemblance to a glowing green honeycomb.

Within this mental state, whether or not her perceptions were based on reality or hysterical fantasy, the Dark Queen pressed her flushed cheek to the side of the wall, feeling its coolness while drowning under wave after wave of the well-defined music, a system of music that lacked any recognizability or resemblance to the predictable sounds made by conventional musical instruments. The music droned on and on in a progression of sonorous cadences that were as fast as they were rhythmic, generating a barrage of poetic intensity that seemed to have a life of its own at times. The music would march forward like a colony of ants lost in a honeypit of subversive tintinnabulations, but then become syncopatedly fragmented on a whim, or by some spastic reflex the rhythm would reform itself, shifting a pitch here and there, whereupon it would resume its progression to whatever unknown end, but always ultimately reincarnating itself from its own ashes, in an endless cycle of regeneration which was the analogy of madness. Likewise, the Dark Queen would stumble along the passageway in parallel to the unpredictable transformations in the music, careening along the smoothed, honeycombed sides of the tunnel, paying homage to invisible owls whose eyes became the empty compartments of the green honeycomb, losing sight of an antenna whose radiowaves managed to find the shortwave connectors nonetheless. The travesty of the idols became reflected in the earth gods of the owls, with their prescient and ever-reaching eyes, who seemed to move through the passageways with her, now giving her the impression (or hallucination, perhaps) that she was not alone, and that there was a horned, taloned bird of prey who was following her, and yet who was indivisibly a part of her, forever locked in time similar to collapsed gold mines that still hold their treasures yet never see the light of day. This recoil of tightly wrapped parcels, true packages made of meat with tightly bound string that cut into the meaty packages, were the semblance of treasures that moved along a delivery route, moving towards the destination of reception, where they might be appreciated or implemented in some way. It seemed like the travels of the unknown packages might soon end, much as the way the Dark Queen felt that very soon, *very very* soon she would reach the end of the mad corridor that was pulling her with a gravitational twist the likes of which she had never felt before, with the strange honeycomb passageway which was now more of a citadel of antiquity than a crypt and also with the strange music that pulsated around her ears and which seemed to oddly resonate around her and within her. She felt that the perfection of the music was her own, and she also knew that the organic imperfections found with the complex overlaid rhythms, melodies and discords were also her own, too. She almost felt like the music was a part of her, and yet not a part, simultaneously. It was then that a door blocked her passage. Made of an ancient alloy of iron, the door was as thick as a drum of lead, and just as heavy. A single, tiny keyhole nestled amid an ornate encrustation of dainty insects with lacy wings made with the same blend of metal greeted her gaping disbelief. In an outrage, the Dark Queen felt that this was the time to use the green-gemmed iguana key-dagger that had hung around her neck. The ornate key worked quite smoothly, and quickly penetrated the lock with a vicious, stabbing thrust from her majesty, who breathlessly inserted herself into the corridor that followed.

Just at her feet, the Dark Queen found a silver platter. She lifted the dainty lid to find a young infant who might have been plucked from a stork's nest, high up in a tree buzzing with dangerous killer bees, with toxic nests dripping tainted honey and with packs of lascivious wolves crowded around the base of the tree. The baby cried

out weakly, as if it had not derived nourishment for a long while, as if it had no firm breast from which to suckle for so many days. Its weakness and vulnerability captivated the queen, which caused her to sigh in such a way that bespoke maternal empathy and a sense of togetherness that she had been in need of for many years. Despite its current state of hunger, the infant had its eyes open, clear and bright, and reached out its tiny hands to touch the face of the new visitor that intervened in the middle of the baby's abandonment and total loneliness. What a sweet smile, almost, and what chubby little cheeks, with fat legs and plump arms. Instinctively, the queen presented the child with her breast and cruelly allowed the child to suckle, knowing full well that she was not yet lactating. After a few minutes the baby wailed in utter frustration. The Dark Queen laughed and then grasped the left leg of the infant and took a large bite out of its thigh, causing blood to spurt everywhere, even on her precious royal tunic. The baby cried out in raw pain, with shrieks that could have pierced lead walls. The queen continued to eat the baby, mauling the young flesh, finishing off the legs and arms, and then moving on to the chest, quickly consuming the virgin internal organs which tasted just as good as the saltiest raw oysters from Chesapeake Bay. Last of all was saved the head, now with vacant eyes and a screaming mouth out of which sounds no longer passed. Cracking the skull as if she were enjoying the finest lobster, the queen slurped down the brains, satisfying her hunger and tossing aside the flimsy carcass like an old cheeseburger wrapper from one of the many fast-food joints available in the "civilized" world. Bespattered with the infant's blood, she burped, feeling well-prepared to continue her explorations of the secret domain that existed directly underneath her own world of the Salt Manor. The Dark Queen turned her attention then to the open path ahead of her, opened like the mouth of the wolf, with stalactites and stalagmites for fangs, ready to consume her majesty. The passageway gradually widened, and she reached a steep ramp that led downward into a centralized pit or inner cavern, with passageways that radiated outward in other directions, perhaps leading into the maws of other mountains and possibly other establishments, other manors, other castles, other fortresses and hereby into the backyard basements of the collective cerebrum of all humanity, in its alienated state of existence.

Within this grand chamber of shimmering light, the green honeycombs of birth seemed to predominate over the regular strata of rocks on top of which grew the hexagonal green chambers. Their radiance was blinding, as was the music, which had now risen to the level of a mind-blasting cacophony. The Evil Queen was beside herself. The center of the room had a network of cracks in the rocky floor through which oozed a clear fluid similar to an amniotic buffer liquid that was viscous as it was protective and nourishing. It ebbed and flowed with a regularity that evoked the oscillating tides at an unnaturally fast speed, or perhaps breathing in slow-motion. At the very center of this network of oozing cracks was a hole, though which much of the liquid penetrated, sometimes flooding the entire floor of the room up to her ankles. The queen felt compelled to stare down the hole, as if this were the receiver piece of a telephone which might reveal her destiny. Amid the glowing, emerald light that radiated from the surrounding honeycomb, small fetal babies appeared in almost all of the hexagonal cells. They were all pre-developed, lacking skin and only kept moist by the slime which oozed not only from the floor but also from the back of each of the hexagonal compartments, suggesting to the queen that she had finally found the hive, or an embryonic establishment of what could have been anyone's guess. The fetal, humanlike creatures cried out with primitive shrieks inside of their transparent compartments, with their pink, smooth bodies arranged in their womblike alcoves just like dolls or pawns.

Taken aback, the Evil Queen felt her entrails bulge as two long strands of protoplasm reached out of her womb to embed themselves in the liquid hole in the center of the room. All the while she felt feverish with obsessive thoughts of owls assailing her consciousness. She was able to visualize herself as some kind of meaty bulb that was grasped, squeezed, punctured, by the talons of the owl as it hunted at night. This process dragged on through primitive forest after forest, with her always reaching the point of escape, but then at the last moment being seized by the owl, whose talons hurt her greatly as they punctured her fragile body, which had now become like a rubber bulb, as part of some hellish apparatus, to be mercilessly yet systematically squeezed, squeezed, squeezed on a routine basis, as part of some larger process that had yet to be outlined, but which had been continuing for as long as she had been alive. Her mind was not her own, and she could feel her consciousness as a precious jewel lying on a display bed of velvet, to be wheeled around in front of glowing, thirsty eyes, each of whom were very picky and waiting for just the right gem to pass their way. She could feel herself being scrutinized and assessed for her usefulness in whatever hole-in-the-wall scheme They might be planning, whoever "They" really were. Still at the back of her mind was a man with crossed arms and without a head who was still facing her, with his hollow body as a clock with ticking parts that worked together to create the measure of time, as if she were staring at a bomb. Or then perhaps she was the bomb. Completely in the throes of vertigo, she moved upwards while the clouds moved downward and the moon raced through her mind similarly to the way craters on such planets can conceal rocks that have not seen the light of day – rocks that breathe and think and play games on a carrousel of nausea which was a measure of the eye contact she felt with a raven who landed on her leg and dug its talons deep into the ankle, as if to tell her something. The Evil Queen realized that these babies growing from the wall-wombs were her own, somehow, and that they were just as much a part of her life now as she was of theirs. By the time she realized that she was going to vomit, the cavern had flooded amid all of the wailing cries of the unborn plastic babies in their pinkness which made them resemble marble sculptures. The din of the rushing amniotic fluid saturated her ears until its intensity caused her to hear nothing at all. The last thing she remembered was a surge of fluid in the room which filled the cavern to such an extent that she was forced to start swimming for her life. When consciousness returned, she was lying on a wet, gravelly beach, covered with scum and flies, as if she had washed ashore like a piece of deformed flotsam, a message of maggots in a bottle expelled from a faraway place in order to begin again, with half-memories and half-truths as the only premises for the continuation of her life.

The Evil Queen couldn't remember the last few minutes of her ordeal very well, only recalling the screaming fetuses and the screaming waves as they had completely swallowed her whole. Her consciousness returned to her eventually, and she found herself on a deserted beach, somewhere near the coastline, presumably the Pacific Coast. Her fine clothes were shredded, and all of her jewelry, including her watch that also had her ID/citizenship implant, were gone. She rose to her feet, covered only in rags, soaked with brine, and looking like a hag from the sea. She didn't even have any greasy-red, monkey-face lipstick with which to paint her pouty lips to help lift her spirits above this overwhelming morass. Periodically the flight of seagulls caught her attention, and their avian eyes gave her sensations of rhythmical shellshock entrenched within the concentric rings around the eyes of an owl. Those eyes were the tumorescent magnets which had been the nucleus of the forgotten necropolis from which she had just escaped, the hounding tentacles that held her fast, restricting her movements and suffocating her within the green jungle of genetic multiplication. The feathers of the birds crossed her brow indefinitely, forevermore, burying her legs in the sand so that she was forced to stare at the seashore, and the cliffs and the lighthouse and all of the little country shacks that lined the upper cliffs suggesting that there were people around her now. It was certain that they were absolutely ready to sink their talons into her breast and suck her life-energies dry by way of a proboscis that resembled a snake-like appendage jutting from the mouths of the curious, of the ten-gallon top hats of those who roam the city streets always at 10:05 in the morning, and then 10:05 at night, limping along with bandaged legs and lacerated arms and faces, singing the woeful songs of dogs as they turn the corner from a bright street onto a dark one. This transition was the lipstick that crossed the Evil Queen's lips as she tried to straggle her way to a steep staircase that led away from the beach up to the cheerily lit cottages at the top of the cliff, high above. Her ascension had drawn nigh, and she felt that it was her own legs, the architecture of her own organic existence, which would position her above the clouds so that the owls would no longer taunt her, and that she would be more than a mouse. Her eyes shut like clams during every cold gust of wind that greeted her as she ascended the stairs. Her long, straight eyelashes became the reeds that grow around a tidepool that has been sucked dry by the ocean, starving the snails and starfish who once lived happily in those pools, now forcing them to enter a new phase of life that was harder and where moisture was a commodity that had once been taken for granted. With that last thought, the queen rubbed at the dark circles which had formed around her eyes and regarded her own thick, cracked skin that could have been a lizard's. She felt a sharp contraction in her womb, being reminded of her pregnancy, of her child that was soon-to-be, and smiled in a dark, brooding way, plotting the future and writing the history books before they had even been bound with the leather of dead men. At this last thought, her foot hit a loose stone, and she lost her step, tumbling down the frayed, wooden stairs and falling heavily upon a bed of sand, losing consciousness for the second time that night.

12½
Identity Crisis

S omewhere on the outskirts of pork city, the lost city once known as Lucipheromone, the Pork hauled a briefcase with him to a remote dock in the industrial sector of town, by a warehouse close to the ocean. He was traveling alone, and within his briefcase was a new stash of purple lightbulbs. He met his contact at the correct hour, and wiping some snot on his sleeve, he then proceeded to place the briefcase at the "feet" of one of the agents of the Perfect, another of the mysterious coat-racks that had appeared out of nowhere, flanked by two purple velvet mannequins who were also motionless. The Pork laughed his insidious laugh, while looking at their impassive faces, only imagining how confused they must have been to see him alive, to witness his uncanny and unexpected delivery of the purple lightbulbs in such an otherworldly way! Life was indeed sweet at times, as he licked his chops, thinking of the new stream of money that would be coming his way, helping him continue with the building of his empire, of his new life as the master of humanity.

Little did the Pork know that the Dark Feline eventually was to warily saunter through his neighborhood in pork city, walking with cautious paws at a brisk pace, thoroughly enjoying the newness of urban exploration. Although the cat had never seen so many pork people together all at once, it would eventually become used to their company, their culture, their noise, their smells and their practices – maybe. The cat meandered through deserted alleyways, through debased tenement housing, moving through poverty and wealth, looking at the sky and the dead trees of the city landscape. Birds threatened to land on the cat's shoulders, sinking weak talons into the shoulder blades, but they refrained from such an attack. This premeditative kind of attack, purely hypothetical, might have been related coincidentally to some angry museum people who were unpacking artifacts from wooden crates up the street. The birds contained within the crates were made of stone, and the hollow street that led from the cat to the distant museum was really a throat that was yelling at top vocal blast, and yet paradoxically no sounds were heard because of a mythical fear that had overtaken the city. Why were all cities possessed by such fears? Were these kinds of fears unique – could they be referred to as "urban fears"? The Dark Feline could only guess. Throughout this entire process, however, the feline did manage to navigate its way through the streets, learning street names and trying to practice the kind of speech that humans and porks spoke, although the cat's phonetic spectrum differed from those of the latter, so accurate pronunciation was not always possible due to differences in shape of the mouth, throat, larynx, etc.

Eventually the cat saw a sinister hotdog stand that was being wheeled along the street by a vagrant Frenchman, whose febrile daughter held certain cats prisoner, like Picou, for example. The cat had never met Picou, but it knew of her resplendence, of her ability to chase loose yarn, jump at crickets, to eat nori seaweed and also to knock water glasses off the table when nobody was looking. These talents of the furry Picou were most welcome and legendary, but unfortunately the Dark Feline shrugged its shoulders, realizing that the meeting of myths with flesh was a rare occurrence indeed, and sometimes it was better to pursue the flesh-on-flesh encounters instead. With this firm resolution in place, the cat broke its reverie by consciously choosing to cross the street, keenly observing some rounded, antiquated subway tunnels made with the red bricks of blood – the kind of bricks to die for, the kind of bricks on which tears would form glass beads that served ornamental purposes, as when syringes were encased inside of bricks for historical purposes. The Dark Feline passed the subway entrance, with drool leaking from its mouth, and it began to purr, while actively fantasizing about skinned anchovies and raw salmon, stripped down to the bone, dripping with fat and all. The primacy of fish was unquestionable.

The daydream was interrupted when the Dark Feline passed the Wax Museum, and chose at that moment to dart inside when a rather heavyset piggedly matron opened the door to exit the establishment. Her extremely fat legs were too heavy to move very quickly, so the cat had plenty of time to dart past her and into the shadows cast by some inanimate statues (as to be distinguished from the moving kind of statues) where it could hide until it regained its bearings and nomadic intuition. The proprietor of the Wax Museum was a very stocky pig as well, and she wore the costume of a Southern Belle, an archaic persona from the Southeastern part of what was once the United States of North America. The lilt in her southern accent was almost pleasing to the ear, with its sensual qualities of leisure and erotic passion, yet with a moral naiveté and backwardness which was potentially stifling, and not just in the bedroom. She seemed also very myopic, and as she had forgotten to wear her eyeglasses for that day, so the Dark Feline speculated that its stealth would be greatly accentuated. Intuition told the cat to move away from the Southern Belle proprietor of the Wax Museum so that it could concentrate on the wax statues of people (humans) that the pork people had apparently erected as a form of derision, in the same way one race might stereotype and lampoon another, just so that it could feel superior and perhaps overly cultured. Therefore, the first exhibit displayed a priest, who was in the process of fondling the buttocks of young men – choirboys, actually – with all parties involved wearing big grins on their faces, but with the priest ever so discreetly looking over his shoulder, with crafty eyes. This Roman Catholic priest seemed to be married only to his indiscretions, as if the very nature of being a priest necessarily had this almost incestuous, invasive, malevolently abusive component, suggesting that his religion itself (i.e. the path of spirituality that had been imposed on him and his kind) had an unusual way of castrating its members.

The next exhibit involved some corporate executives in the process of obscene displays of verbal stealth and secrecy, to the end of personal gain, such as monetary wealth. These corporate statues carried symbolic revenues and paperwork bearing incriminating titles, with fat runny noses and pockets overstuffed with currency. Meanwhile, honest workers cast in wax were seen outside the fake office door working for pennies, while doing honest jobs, without any of the strange facial expressions of crafty eyes, furtive glances and underhanded gestures worn by their bosses.

The next allegory showed a man and a woman in the process of divorce. Every item in their wax home was portrayed with a crack running down the middle. In fact the house prop, itself, had a division line bisecting it, suggesting that man and wife would split everything upon their separation. Instead of sorrow on their faces at the idea of lost love were instead the features of bitterness, revenge, and of course, more craftiness and subterfuge most probably motivated by greed.

There was another display devoted to the human family, in its nuclear representation, with Mom, Dad, Sister, Brother and family pet. These statues were frozen in time, forever acting out strange, extremely well-defined, codependent roles that were predictable as they were unnaturally fixated on the common ideas and goals of the establishment, as if personality roles were plucked from trees and internalized through external means, or as if a subconscious letter would arrive in the mail that had detailed subconscious instructions about whom to identify with, whom to emulate, whom to follow, and which values to adopt: all at the drop of a hat, or the disappearance of a white rabbit.

The cat was just about to explore the next exhibit, which looked like some soldiers stepping over dead foreigners with empty oil and gasoline cans in their hands, when the museum proprietor came along, making the rounds, looking over the statues in their poses and at the overall tidiness of the exhibits. The feline hid underneath a wax piano and watched the pig's feet shuffle by, in a moment of malodorous nausea. When the ugly feet had passed through, the cat resumed its tour of the Wax Museum, exploring the exhibits, reading the descriptive placards, and in general, marveling at the stupidity of the human race. Not that the pig race was any better off, but this wasn't a wax museum about pigs; it was one about humans. The cat was preparing to leave when it noticed a back room which apparently served as a work area where the wax statues were dressed. Besides there being a break table, with emptied cans of sugar drinks, there was the Man who was Lead, still crouching in the weakened position, possibly recovering from his wounds, but possibly not. One favorable sign was a growing pile of blue crystalline dust that formed on the ground near where the lead hands threatened to drag the ground. Out of curiosity, the cat eased its way among the chairs and other obstacles in the room to get a closer look. On the side of the head of the Man who was Lead, there was a glowing red circle, possibly a symbolic corpuscle, or maybe a systematic diagram of some kind of alchemical process, or gateway, or myth, or whatever. Whatever it was, the round shape was faintly glowing with energy, and the cat could almost swear that the statue was observing him out of the corner of its eyes. It was only when the cat's vision grew ever so blurry that it backed away from the lead statue. Suddenly the cat heard the reverberating footfalls of the fat, piggly museum proprietor, and it beat a very fast retreat among some cleaning supplies, including a heavy mop that ever so precariously leaned against the wall, just waiting to be knocked over. The cat anticipated this ugly prop, almost like a reflex, and nimbly circumnavigated the potentially hazardous noise-maker. The cat retreated into the shadows of a broom closet and only its green eyes were visible, staring and waiting for the right opportunity to flee, possibly out the back door, which the museum attendant had just opened to take out the garbage. Some of the sweepings of the blue crystals fell from the sleeves of the Man who was Lead at a phenomenal rate, even in his state of nearly suspended animation. Like lightning, the Dark Feline seized its opportunity and ran between her waddling legs, effectively scaring her in the act, and causing her to shriek loudly, while she let go of the dustbin full of blue crystals that were accidentally catapulted into the air. Most of the blue fragments rained down on the pavement of the back alleyway, but some of them managed to fly through the wide opening in the museum proprietor's blouse, falling between the smooth pink slit that separated her generously full cleavage. The cat knew that this was the only time to flee, so it did, bounding down the grimy alleyway, ducking in between garbage cans and unable to avoid doing what it didn't want to do: making a big ruckus. The clatter of garbage can lids and scattered trash made quite the commotion, upsetting the dogs and the cynical neighbors who shouted and cursed at all of the abstract things in life that lowered their spirits, flinging snot at walls and kicking wives and children for lack of any other suitable targets at which they could direct their collective frustrations. With the menace of the Dark Feline gone, the plump museum proprietor wiped her sweaty forehead, straightened her blouse and her bra and then noticed a curious erection of her nipples which seemed to share an undefined connection with certain dreams she was to have later that night – in particular, some very strange dreams having to do with rubber bulbs.

The Dark Feline traveled to a nearby street and noticed some gigantic cracks in the pavement, as if an earthquake had recently shattered the pristine concrete and sent all manner of urban roaches scurrying away in fear. On various sides of the street were the signs of chaos: mannequin limbs here and there, torn from fiberglass sockets and still draped with shreds of brutally torn purple velvet, coupled with the corpses of pork people, bloating in the afternoon sun and speckled with shiny green flies who were laying their eggs in the decaying flesh. There were various tags and political slogans spray-painted on the walls, in addition to the colorfully painted handprints of human children applied haphazardly over the various urban surfaces, weaving their way into the minds of people by way of touch. It was certain that these handprints were from human children and not pork children, simply because it was common knowledge that all pork children are bereft of fingers until the age at which they can work for wages. The cat sniffed at a few of the handprints, somewhat perplexed. It certainly understood many of the anarchist tags, and was actually quite glad to seem them, although it was thoroughly disappointed not to find any graffiti of a Marxist nature. Here and there were purple velvet mannequins holding strange tubes of an unearthly toothpaste, silently transfixed within the throes of utter mannequininity, in their department store stratifications, forever lost among their pre-programmed impulses. The labeling on the toothpaste tubes read "Dr. Fleshtone Toothpaste," yet the true function of such an obscure brand and formula of toothpaste completely eluded the Dark Feline, as it backed away from the frozen but menacing automatons that clutched at tubes of goo which represented the insane plasticality of nightmares. On this particular street, there were no pork people to be seen, and neither were there any humans.

The Dark Feline, despite the insalubrious visions of carnage and plastic mayhem, managed to withdraw from the urban warzone without further incident, and by a strict event of intuition managed to find the battered storefront of the tarot card reader. Squeezing in through a pane of broken glass that had yet to be boarded up, the cat circled around the front room silently regarding the curios and hollow, plastic owls littering the shelves amid various "new age" pamphlets and other superstitious literature for sale. It could hear the murmurs of a tarot reading in the backroom, and poked its head through the door that was ajar. In the back room, under the auspices of sullen, red lightbulbs and a few candles, the fortuneteller had on his round sunglasses and was wearing the thin cotton gloves so instrumental in his reading of the tarot cards, wiping away fresh leakage of clear viscous snot. The tarot reader plucked at some of the overly-cooked leaves of an artichoke, intently staring at their imperfect surfaces in order to glean the trail of causality that might suggest what was in store for the patron, who just so happened to be an overweight whore who was currently giving the stout card-reader a blowjob. As he had declared that her reading included the card of death, the whore involuntarily sucked on his organ somewhat harder, causing him to spill his seed in her mouth. Since they had both effectively serviced each other (with quite different services, obviously), there was no tendering of money, and the overweight pork-whore rose from the floor and left, with a blank expression on her face. She didn't even notice the cat, who was hiding next to an unused chair. The tarot reader, on the other hand, had a blissful smile on his face, while staring into space, showing off his thready irises that encircled the pupils of his bloodshot eyes that were truly roses of poison, or projection beams that might show cinematographic visions of destruction to all that looked deeply into those bloody orbs. One look into those eye-lights was enough for the cat, which instantly leapt on top of the fortuneteller pork's head, and began to lacerate the flesh that surrounded the skull. The front limbs of the cat, which at times seemed so lithe and soft, became cutting blades of death, joined to convulsing shoulder blades as the feline deftly held fast to the skull and tore apart the flesh covering it. The tarot reader squealed with pain in its corporeal dissolution, but there was nobody close enough to hear. With time, the cat excised the scalp, the nose and other facial features, with vicious growls coming from such an amazingly compact body. One might almost have thought that the resonating vocal cords of this animal were not

its own. The cat was surprised, once the skull was stripped of all flesh, that there was no cranial bone as might have been expected. Instead, the bony interior of the head consisted of a nearly spherical plate of spikes that helped the gelatinous flesh adhere to these skeletal structures. The bony interior was not really made of bone, but of a fibrous substance intrinsically more similar to wood, as if the head of the pork might have been some kind of giant pollen spore. After some prodding, the skull plates peeled away to reveal an interior that was not a brain in the conventional, terrestrial sense but more of an unearthly floral bouquet that was motile. To clarify: the cat did not discover the expected gray matter with its creases and folds innervated with exorbitant vasculature, but instead, there was found an almost pulsating bouquet of red rose-like formations packed together that were rubbery and soft, and would contract at the slightest touch of any object, such as the way sea anemones would shrink within themselves when viciously poked by a curious diver.

The Dark Feline recoiled in obvious horror, and jumped upon the desk where the artichoke leaves had been plucked and then read. While the newly exposed "brain" of the mauled pork still continued to convulse, along with the body on the floor, the cat began to attack the wall against which the fortuneteller would sometimes lean while doing the tarot readings, pulling away the cheap paneling with clawed digits that ripped the sheets of faux wood away from the wall. Inside, there was a thick circular ring of metal hung by a rusted nail, and small grains of iron filings could be seen hovering upright around the circumference of the metal, which was presumed by the intelligent cat to be nothing but a powerful magnet. No wonder there were so many mannequins on the other side of this wall when the powerful quake had stricken the pork city not long ago! The cat's eyes glazed with exhaustion after the discovery of the magnet. The roundness of the metal somehow reminded the cat of the roundness of the brick archway it had once seen intuitively, of the strange garage that it was seeking. Such a roundness called out to the Dark Feline, but the animal could not hear all of the words. Taken aback by an instant fatigue caused by the loathsome surroundings, the cat sat on its haunches, with its head beginning to sway deliriously. It knew that it had to leave, or else come under the influence of whatever malevolence was presiding over this fortunetelling storefront. With alien blood on its jowls and claws, the cat fled the building in shock, seeking the shelter of the dolphin ceramic sanctuary in a slummy industrial alleyway that was one of the few spots in the pork city that had any significant degree of tranquility available for those who felt troubled or enmeshed in worrisome circumstances. In its haste to make for the exit, the cat did not notice the inconspicuously positioned coat-racks that had taken up residence on both sides of the door. They stood still, ever so sinister, and completely upright without any coats or hats hanging on the hooks. It was certain that these coat-racks were out to cause much trouble. The Perfect were becoming bolder and bolder in their aggressive and highly destructive forays into Swinish Hominid Urban Existence (SHUE). Needless to say, this subconscious code of urban living, SHUE, was only a grotesque and caricatured adaptation of the more traditional philosophy of Feng Shui, relating to the arrangements of organic and inorganic objects and the healthy, ever-continuous flow of energy between them, in contrast to the energetic stagnancy of the SHUE configuration, adopted by both porks and humans alike. To that extent, the two urban species had quite a bit in common.

When Yes-Yes awoke, it was not in her usual place of awakening, although she couldn't remember the bed in which she usually regained consciousness. But regardless of which neighborhood on the small Pacific Island was hers, of the location of her bed and entire domicile, she knew from the bottom of her heart that the bed she was strapped to was not her usual locale for regaining consciousness. She wore a hospital nightgown with an open back that exposed her smooth shoulders. She was strapped to the bed with very strong leather restraints that permitted very little movement – not enough to restrict the blood flow, but almost to that degree. Looking around the room, she was certain that she was in a hospital, but had no memory of her arrival there, or of the circumstances that led up to her going there, nor of the past forty-eight, or seventy-two or ninety-six hours, even. Instead, Yes-Yes could remember who she was, and all of her memories of the beautiful island, of her sexual flings with porks and with people, of the raucous times of leisure spent at the famous Musical Drinking Sanctuary, but despite all of these numerous memories, it was very difficult to assemble them into any coherent sequence of events or any solid timeframe. She found herself becoming increasingly disturbed about this lapse in memory, in addition to her captivity in the hospital. In truth, she normally could not remember much about her life, but such a deficiency in memory did not cause her much grief. In general, she was one of those types who never thought much about her words and actions, and only concentrated on getting whatever she wanted. She was quite used to it, actually, being catered to by her parents and superiors, who almost always allowed her to have her way.

Yes-Yes was shaken again by the unknown, but this time the cause was a heavy, throbbing pressure upon her abdomen that was experienced despite the absence of any leather restraints that might have stretched across her belly. She noticed there was quite a bulge extending from her stomach area, as if she were bloated or distended, causing her much alarm. In fact, it seemed like she might explode, as if her womb were carrying some kind of sentient infection, as many twentieth century science-fiction enthusiasts had fantasies of alien embryonics setting up residence in human body cavities, growing to term, and then bursting out of the chest in a showy explosion of gore intended to subject the audience to a gut-wrenching experience of "shock and awe." Her terror was only interrupted by the arrival of the doctor, who wore a sterile-looking frock. He had the appearance of milquetoast gone awry, with soft skin, feminine hands, a lisp, and a mouth half-paralyzed while situated below a pair of bulbous, bulging eyes that seemed ready to pop right out of the sockets. He looked at her calmly, the way one lizard might observe another, and spoke to her curtly. Yes-Yes was not at all convinced of his benevolence, in lieu of his strange appearance of mild-mannered malignancy. It was at this point that the man with the bulbous eyes informed her of her pregnancy – that she would be having twins – in fact. The sonograms indicated that they would be fraternal twins: one boy and one girl. Although Yes-Yes spent much of her time fornicating, she could not, for the life of her, remember the point at which she conceived. In fact, she could barely remember anything at all, now that her day had been disrupted so completely. Immediately she had the sonic hallucination of hearing fast-paced, haunted hospital slasher music, evoking the flying wild knives of possessed nurses slashing their bed-ridden patients with the violent but unreflective bloodlust of zombies who don't know what they are doing. Simultaneously, the pupils in her eyes contracted involuntarily, making the room look dark. She squinted, trying to see the man with the bulbous eyes as he moved closer towards her, opening his frock to her in the way one might pull aside loose curtains at the center, revealing well-arranged rows of slimy tapeworms, fully erect and with gaping mouths emitting a low-pitched sucking noise, all housed within the strange man's hollow rib-cage that was also lined with foul rot and other invertebrate parasites slithering around like clockwork. The man with the bulbous eyes looked at her with an intensity that would have caused her body to shrink like a flaccid penis covered with leeches, and just as soon as the hallucination (for that is what it must have been) overtook her, it suddenly left her, allowing her pupils to dilate again, restoring the sense of light and revealing the strange-sighted man to be without any hideous tapeworm-creatures emerging from his body cavity. In fact, he looked poorly nourished, as his frame became visible from time to time by the rather large openings in his hospital frock. Yes-Yes took the news about her unexpected children very well and inquired why she should be restrained the way she was.

Silence.

The man with the bulbous eyes eventually released her arms from the restraints, and immediately her left hand began to fight with her right hand, in the most savage ways. The sharp nails tore at each other, while Yes-Yes passively looked down to watch them. The coils of hands grappled with each other, wrestling, tearing, gouging and recuperating from the attacks. They strangled each other many times, cutting off the blood, without realizing that they were part of a whole, putting the grid of opposing streets onto the same map, comprising fish eyes that might get sucked from the same skull, and so on. It was upon the arrival of a taxicab outside the hospital, which Yes-Yes saw through the large window, when she realized that she was indeed on solid ground, and that the vines growing outside the windows would eventually overtake the building, sealing it underneath a coiled shroud of plants so as to strangle everyone under the cover of the roof, which now seemed to her most unstable. This traffic light on the ceiling was a warning signal, an on/off switch to be pushed at all costs, so as to stop the flow of time, or even the simultaneous flow of timelessness that was exerted on her by the strange man with the bulbous eyes. His appearance was of milquetoast psychologically burnt to a state of obscene impropriety, as if Yes-Yes were running through the set of a horror movie that began as a pornography stint aimed at deriving pleasure from the separation of mind and body by way of a shelf of pectoral books that would slide aside to reveal a secret spinal column staircase, spiral in shape, of course. This passageway would no doubt lead to that which she feared the most: the vision of the green honeycomb that she had already seen so many times in her precon-scious thoughts, as if she were revisiting her guilt each and every day that the sun rose over an oceanic mass of feeling to remind her of the strange impossibility of attempting to conceive of the infinite vastness of the expanding universe in a strictly rational way: it was something that was just too complex for the mind to grasp, and so she left the world screaming, remembering her children who developed as oneiric vegetables within the amniotic compartments of the green honeycomb, as plain as day, and as soiled as night.

At this moment, the man with the bulbous eyes spread apart his frock to show her his emaciated body, with a sunken ribcage, a mild touch of jaundice, a weakened liver and that ever so sickly smile. Around his neck was a pointed brass key in the shape of an iguana. He tore the key from his neck, and threw it at her, where it landed on her chest with a resounding smack that burned her sensitive flesh. Yes-Yes looked down at the iguana key, with its sparkling green gem for an eye, its razor-sharp edges, and she had a moment of instant recognition that seared her consciousness for an eternity, realizing that she never had control over anything, not even the kids that she had hoped so strongly to mold into images of her own design, to control them and direct them as if they were her experiments. But she would certainly try. Yes-Yes grasped the key and instantly remembered that she was just as much the Dark Queen as she was Yes-Yes. She was just as much the Alchemical Waif as she was the Mother Corpse as she was Yes-Yes. This mental blast of self-recognition caused her to gasp involuntarily, still clutching the key so hard that the sharp metal began to slice the skin of her palm, resulting in a firm trickle of blood running down her arm. As if punched in the stomach, it took her many moments for her ribcage to decide to accommodate an incoming breath of air which only began and lasted for many moments as a frail gasping or sucking sound, of someone who was fighting to live but didn't quite realize it due to that strange zombie condition of unconscious living, without any awareness of one's actions. Yes-Yes was the Dark Queen who traversed the underworld leading away from the Salt Manor to the Beaches of Death, across the torrid straits that led to the unknown Pacific Island just off the coast of North America, recently bombed on the orders of President George Bevis Bush, the bonehead from what remained of the United States of North America. And the Dark Queen was Yes-Yes, the gallivanting lady who never slept, who always moved from one thrill to the next in search of wealth, sex and controlling the natives – always control – and who would always weary of her endless pleasures only to pass out at the Musical Drink Sanctuary and get shipped "home" in a coffin. Little did Yes-Yes know that this "home" to which she was shipped was really the Salt Manor, and upon waking on the cerebral waterbed, she would resume her identity as the Dark Queen. The coffin was the vehicle through which she would switch personalities and locations. From the mobile coffin to the cerebral waterbed, and then back again, *ad infinitum*.

13
Departure

W ithin the confines of the pork city, the lost town of Lucipheromone, the Pork had packed his suitcase well: filled with high quality purple lightbulbs, capable of fitting most sockets, like cow udders, eye sockets, bulb housings, pantyhose, etc. He knew that it might be a while before he could return to his beloved hovel of a home, but if everything worked out according to plan, he would return some day, when the time was right, as a rich pig, as a filthy rich pig, able to retire permanently, living a life of pure leisure that only a very few sentients would ever know. He also knew that he could squeeze these purple lightbulbs out of his armpits on a regular basis, so it only made sense that the Perfect would want to move him to a safer location so that he could continue his "work" in peace. In fact, he was told by the leader – a man with a lopsided headdress that looked like a red velvet beehive made of a banal pastiche of expensive art-supply objects – that he would be kept in a secure location away from the troublesome machinations of humans and their greedy, interfering ways. The idea was that his assistance would someday lead to the domination of earth by the Perfect, of which the Porks would have a newer and more powerful role in this domination, and of course he, the Pork, would most likely ascend to become the leader of all Porks. It was the most perfect plan, thought the Pork, most equitable for all partners involved. All he had to do was camp out in luxury, assured as he was that he would have plenty of tasty gourmet slop to consume everyday, while there would be edible prostitutes who would swallow his seed and then be swallowed themselves after a few turns on a BBQ rotisserie. And during this "camping out" process, he would produce many, many purple lightbulbs which would somehow add to the power of the Perfect so that they might be better enabled to effect their ambitious plan of terrestrial domination over the human primates.

The Pork stuffed everything he needed into two briefcases:

one case for his personal effects and the other for his current stash of purple lightbulbs. Leaving behind nothing, the Pork would become a memory, just a number in a computer file on nobody's hard-drive. No one would miss him. He turned the key in the lock and left his low-budget residence for perhaps the last time. He arrived at the designated meeting area – an abandoned playground now slated for destruction and covered with endless loops of graffiti – and he waited until the agreed upon hour. A minute after the hour, a flock of birds with eyes that had no pupils landed on the branches of a dying tree, next to the swing-set that lost its swings long ago. For such a swine to approach a swingless swing-set was nothing but arrogant jetset swank within the ruins of childhood. The birds with the strange eyes began to disintegrate, loosing color and substance, while passing on this state of transition to the tree itself: both birds and tree dissolved into the shimmering ripples of some glassy energy, creating what appeared to be a portal of some kind. The Pork briskly clutched at his briefcases, and boldly stepped through the new, liquid aperture, entering a void which was to bring him to Mars. What nobody expected was that the Woman who was Honey had been hiding behind some industrial waste drums watching the whole turn of events, and she followed the Pork into the void. Her wild honey hair flew through the air as she raced to enter the glass chasm before it closed up, leaving behind not a trace, not even a bird or a tree or a branch or a feather. Nothing. It was all gone, and they were gone, to Mars.

Meanwhile, a few blocks away at the Wax Museum, a truck pulled up to receive a large wooden crate. The Wax Museum proprietor, the portly porquette with the open blouse, presided over the transfer of property, which in this case was the Man who was Lead. The driver of the truck wore black gloves and clenched his fingers upon seeing the hunched-over figure of the Man who was Lead. Rapping on the metal with his piggly knuckles, the driver whistled quietly and removed a vial from his jacket. He poured the contents of the vial over the statue, transforming the metal into a non-metal, Antimony. Now the Man who was Lead became the Man who was Antimony. Very brittle indeed, his consciousness silently writhed with the fear of being broken to bits, of being at the mercy of pigs who would use his body toward dubious ends, most likely fragmenting his life even further into the tiniest pieces. The pork driver of the truck made sure that the statue was well-packed in wood shavings so that it would not fracture during the voyage. He removed his black gloves and slid his greasy hands into the open blouse of the proprietor of the Wax Museum, in order to caress her succulent breasts, while drooling on himself and oozing fresh snot from his fully alert porcine nose. Her cheap perfume was ravishing. The proprietor of the museum found this display simply captivating, feeling her own juices churn within her, waiting until the moment that these two porks would be able to share some quality sty-time together within the privacy of an inexpensive slophouse that didn't ask too many questions. The driver vowed to return later that evening after dropping off the "package" and the two were to share a romantic evening together, filled with snot and slop and the poetry of sighs, all under the aegis of the civilized pork who knew better than to mix with the swinishness of humankind.

As the truck pulled away from the curb, the Wax Museum proprietor, all hot and bothered, straightened her blouse and smoothed her skirt with her corpulent pig hands. She went back inside the museum in order to ready the next exhibit, which was a lampoon of several human political leaders. A few blocks away at the garage-fortress where once resided the Man who was Antimony, who was also once the Dark Cowboy, there were no fresh piles of blue crystalline dust to be found. Any young ladies who might have known of this absence would have shed many, many, many tears. But that the Dark Cowboy might in actuality have vanished caused no lack of sleep for anyone. In fact, nobody even knew he existed. It was almost as if he were invisible. The Dark Feline, however, was not so naïve. The animal arrived at roughly five minutes past the morning hour of ten, and just so happened to notice some spray-painted graffiti on one of the doors of the garage which just so happened to resemble a scarab beetle with human-like markings on its back. Such an omen was well-timed, especially because this image was not painted there by the Dark Cowboy, or the Dirty Alchemist, another of his aliases. As in the vision, the Dark Feline saw the brick archways of the original garage doors presiding over the more recent door installations. The side-door was curiously ajar, but

there were no signs of intruders, like thieving porks, rats, other cats, or whatever else. Entering the sanctity of the alchemical garage, the cat could feel the power that once was barely contained within these flimsy walls, now covered with a fine coating of dust that probably wouldn't have been cleaned off by the Dark Cowboy anyway, since he was allergic to dusting the inside of his living space.

The Dark Cat looked over the surroundings: the studio, the tools, the raw materials, the mementoes, the muses, the pizza boxes, the ashtrays and the minimalist furniture. Why the vision brought the cat to this dumpy place was unknown, but apparently the power of the place was more latently distributed, rather than being found within the monetary value of the furnishings. Therefore the artillery shells on the shelf were just as potent and valuable as the seashells. In fact, the two were interchangeable at times, with the seashells serving as elements of aggressive destruction while the artillery shells promoted pacifistic condemnations of moronic aspects of popular miserabilist culture. These strange items, poetically arranged, constituted another one of the mysteries of the place. The cat also perused the bookshelf, looking at many a fine volume of work by surrealists and other alchemically-minded people who cared nothing for mundane insanity or insane mundanity, and for the dialectic that existed between these latter two expressions of miserabilism. In fact, it was the overthrow of the current social conditions of the Normal and the Perfect that were important, as were the economic and other materialist dimensions behind these self-serving conceptions of Perfect Normalism and Normal Perfection. In this light, it became obvious that the Perfect – those coat-racks of insidious misery that crept into every corner of thought and physical breathing space and elbow-room (and even body cavities and appendages) – would someday have to be destroyed. Or so concluded the literate feline who pawed at the bindings of the various volumes on the dusty shelves of the Dirty Alchemist.

At the moment when the cat found an incoming ray of sunlight through one of the grimy garage windows, it scratched behind its ear with its hind leg, and then vigorously shook its head, trying to dispense with the itch to which it had succumbed. Its green irises contracted in the sunlight, forming sharp slits, and its sudden rise in agitation only bore fruit when it saw a small anole lizard attempting to cross the floor of the garage, over mountains of junk and old boxes filled with even more junk. The green lizard darted around one of the boxes, getting the cat's attention, inducing the latter to jump out of its sunbeam and to commence the chase of the former. The lizard foresaw this plan of attack, and changed its color from green to brown, attempting to camouflage itself among the dark-colored boxes. Suddenly a million cockroaches erupted from one of the taller boxes, evoking the scene of a Saturday night city of insect vermin exploding at a given hour where all of the roach citizens precipitously wanted to leave the metropolitan area and flee to the suburbs, where there were less lizards waiting with long pink tongues that the roaches would easily confuse with the long pink roads that led to all of the cities of mankind, who by far had the best processed food available. Therefore these roaches, in search of processed food and genuine long, pink roads that led to human cities, were unconsciously plotting their escape from the artificial, long pink roads that were really the deceptive tongues of lizards that led not to cities but to reptilian stomachs, where the acid was free but the internal architecture was devoid of specialized honeycombs. This delirium of avoidance and attraction, and the confusion between the two, were enough to first perplex the Dark Feline, but then subsequently to entertain it, and so the cat put on some socks and sat back against a cushion, viewing the spectacle between the city of roaches and the giant brown lizard that was once green. The lizard didn't like it when the roaches bit it on the ass, but then the roaches didn't like being consumed, either. This constant war manifested itself as a royal goblet of silver that held the blood of priests, squeezed from pure Christian hearts savagely plucked from the faithful and put into a blender. Therefore the blood of Christ was very much like a blenderized fruit smoothie poured symbolically over a crucifix made from leprous basalt. The blood smoothie attracted the roaches and the flies to it, who all of a sudden became happy and wanted to learn ballroom dancing and other fancy methods of correspondence which might help them live independently from the libraries where they used the books to carve out roach motels inside, where the roaches could hide between the words. They would first bore a nearly invisible hole somewhere on the spine of the book where it would easily be missed by human eyes. Then they would carefully bore through the printed paper, eating it, tearing it with their mandibles and creating labyrinths within the pages so that roach dwellings could be constructed within the hollows of the books. In this manner, each printed volume became tenement high-rises for the roaches, and entire roach families lived between chapters. Effectively, it meant that the roaches would hide between the literary ideas, themselves – creating the perfect smokescreen for the vermin to live behind, while still remaining apart from those words, and thus, ideas.

As stated, these roaches (and pesky flies, too) desired to leave their "roach motels" carved from the pages of books, and to learn better, more prestigious ways to relate to the world, such as through ballroom dancing and other fancier methods. But for now, they were trapped within the library of a man who had disappeared. Between living like fugitives within the ideas of the past and running from the lizard(s) who pursued them relentlessly, these insectoid vermin had numbered days, and yet still managed to reproduce, like the roaches that they were. It was all a vicious, self-propagating cycle, to continue only until something or someone like the Dark Feline, for instance, decided to intervene, that such an ugly cycle would continue 'til the cows came home' (which they would do, eventually). The cat was unable to contain its laziness, resigning itself to a day of pure contentment, sitting in the sun, enjoying the shelter of the alchemical garage, and watching the tortured animals play out their little drama right before its eyes, while the cat, the primary agent at the top of this particular food-chain, could just sit there and recover his senses and vitality. In the end, it decided upon the course of intervention, and first ate the lizard: it crushed the skull between its canine molars, grinding the bones and brains to a paste which was simply delicious, and then next, swallowed the body, whole. The cat was in fact quite hungry, and had not really had the chance to eat anything of its own liking, and of course writhing, alien pork brains were not on the list of acceptable protein sources. So now, after a satisfying snack, the cat set out to deal with the roaches. It had absolutely no interest in eating them, and if there had been only one or two of the bugs, it could have easily spent the day batting their brains out, just playing with them, toying with them as a source of sadistic amusement. But because there were so many of them, the cat felt a certain duty to rid the garage of them, in the way one cleans house from time to time, so as to become free of parasites and all of the associated nuisances that come with parasites like roaches.

The Dark Feline took a nap in the sun, allowing the warm light to play across its sleek, black fur, while its feline brain dreamed of special measures to take in order to get rid of these troublesome literary roaches who enjoyed living within the books (and ideas) of the past. When it awoke, the cat remembered one of the volumes it had noticed before, an old tome from at least a hundred years ago which had some of the most creative ways of dealing with such pests. The cat immediately set out to follow the procedure: in the center of the garage, it filled a small wading pool with water. Within the pool it placed a footstool that rose above the surface of the water. On top of the stool were placed several old books, including some especially putrid, stinking literary-analysis volumes, such as books written by certain terrestrial favorites like Mary Ann Caws, Susan Sontag, Anna Balakian, Roger Shattuck, and a whole slew of other opportunistic literati. These special volumes were placed on the stool as bait for the roaches. What made these books different, though, was that the cat hollowed them out, on the sly, when the roaches weren't looking. In the hollow spaces inside of the books, the cat placed dry, powdered plaster of paris. When the books were set into position, making the trap complete and ready, the cat left the garage to go visit some of the local grocery establishments in order to find something to eat, if such cat-friendly comestibles were to be found in the lost city of the pork. While the pork citizens seemed to have no concept of fresh fish, they did at least stock their grocery stores with canned anchovies and sardines, so the cat readily made off with several metal containers by creating various distractions in the stores, such as by knocking over canned vegetable displays, sending the tin cans of goods rolling everywhere, ultimately causing quite the commotion. During the distraction, the Dark Feline would always manage to push a few tins of anchovies or sardines out the back door. And it didn't even consider the canned cat food, even for a second. It knew what the good stuff was, and the highly processed "mystery meat" made for cats (who could never voice their protest) was not on the Dark Feline's list of favorites. It was not afraid to be selective.

How exactly the Dark Feline managed to drag its loot of canned fish back to the alchemical garage that was the home and workshop of the Dark Cowboy (a.k.a. the Dirty Alchemist) was an unutterable mystery, and yet the task was done. The cat squeezed in through the special opening on the side of the garage (which seemed to be made just for it), lugging its tinned fish in tow, and uttered a growl of surprise upon seeing the fruits of its labors: the entire population of literary roaches had become ossified, frozen in time in different poses of escape and terror: many of them were still burrowed in the trashy volumes of flaccid literary analysis, filled to the gills with plaster of paris that had solidified. Others had jumped from the footstool into the tub of water, only to harden while they tried to swim to the other side. These particular roaches had accepted the fate of sinking to the bottom. The stronger ones had managed to swim across and then ossify when they were in the process of seeking shelter in their usual library metropolis, the "Hardcover Highrise," as they called it, on the shelves of the Dirty Alchemist's bookshelf that housed the not-so-treasured books. And across the garage floor, there they were: an entire army of literary insects with their viscera irreparably frozen by the hardening of plaster of paris, Calcium Sulfate. These roaches might have served well as chess pieces or pawns in any other sort of aggressive, competitive board game based on pettiness. As it were, the cat yawned and swept up the roaches, and added them to the hollow, literati masterpieces, and then stuffed them all into a trash bag, which was then thrown to the street curb to be collected on the following day. The best news of all was that the treasured volumes were kept apart from the trashy, literati ones, with the former being housed in a glass cabinet to which the roaches had not access. For example, all books of the likes of "Mad Love" and other comparable contents emerged unscathed from the roach onslaught. Although the Dark Feline was still learning how to laugh the way humans do, it did feel its ribcage involuntarily contract, as if these gasps of disbelief liberated some kind of pent-up energy in its psyche. A pleasurable convulsion based on poetic contradictions. Therefore a good start, in all likelihood.

A few months passed and the winds grew colder. Lakes and ponds froze, and in the early spring, there was the threat of a thaw that never came, analogous to colorful tropical birds swallowing their songs before they have a chance to sing them. But unfortunately there were no colorful, tropical birds anywhere near the Salt Manor. Such birds would have perished in close proximity to such a toxic building anyway. The trees that grew nearby were of course alive, and yet they were brittle and always had to be replaced by imports that were pushed into the toxic soils, with the hope that the root systems would take. Most of the time they did.

The Evil Queen – or Yes-Yes, as it were – still pretended to have no knowledge of her multiple personalities. When she had arrived on the shore that was a straight shot across from the mysterious island of pigs, she had feigned ignorance of who she was and why she was there. The porks who did find her seemed to be genuinely puzzled by her unexpected appearance, and they did their best to hurry up in discreetly sending word to the island to request a traveling coffin for Yes-Yes. In fact, Yes-Yes almost enjoyed playing the role, instinctively adopting a melodramatic tone which inspired pity in the hearts of the porks, who immediately attempted to convince her to forget the whole adventure. They drugged her, and she slept all the way home. But this time around, she didn't forget her terrifying journey through the heart of the mountain which had shown her the roots of her ancestry as well as of her family's decay, and also the strange voice of hope that manifested itself as the glowing hive of children's voices whose frightening rays of light revealed inner truths about humanity. Yes-Yes was interested, more than anything, about who exactly was manipulating her in this way. Thoughts of revenge began to bubble up through the depths of her consciousness. In the meantime, she prepared herself for her babies.

On the Friday morning that she awoke, Yes-Yes realized that the contractions were no longer to be ignored, and that she was to give birth that very morning, or perhaps sometime during the day. Her water broke during the late morning, and fraternal twins followed soon after. A boy and a girl, the twins looked very little like each other, and both slept peacefully with the mother, while attendants hovered around Yes-Yes (although they still continued to know her as the Evil Queen, as they always had). Little did anyone in the Salt Manor know that the queen was really Yes-Yes, or so Yes-Yes had thought. Obviously, there had to have been someone who was working with the porks to smuggle her onto the premises after her habitual subconscious outings to the pig island. But who? She had killed off so many of the older faces, for various reasons, so the only conclusion she could reach was that a steady stream of younger servants might be agents for the one person or organization responsible. The identity of her manipulator still remained a complete mystery to Yes-Yes.

As Yes-Yes reclined on the bed gazing down maternally at her newborns, a piece of afterbirth emerged from her womb and scurried onto the floor and underneath the bed. Yes-Yes screamed, and attendants came running, but nothing was to be found underneath the majestic, four-posted bed. In fact, the servants bade her to forget what she thought she saw and to simply rest without worry. Giving birth consumed a lot of energy, so therefore it was possible that Yes-Yes had merely hallucinated about the appearance of the afterbirth that supposedly crawled underneath the bed. Yes-Yes put on a fresh application of greasy, red, monkey-face lipstick and then fell back onto the pillow completely exhausted. She felt a great sense of accomplishment at having these two children. As life was one big experiment, so were her children, mused the mother. She fell asleep with the twins nursing at her breasts and dreamed of rats, mannequins and the planet Mars.

Down in the kitchen of the Salt Manor, the Cook had finally gotten his act together and packed his bags. Obviously he would not be giving any advanced notice about his plan to leave the old Manor house, since he would have been beheaded the very day he made the disclosure. The idea was that he'd be checking out sometime in the middle to later evening, under the pretense that he'd be needed in the kitchen that night, where the preparation of the celebratory victuals would be underway: a cake to celebrate the arrival of the twins and the affirmation of the Evil Queen's powerful domination of the surrounding countrycide, braised chimpanzee skulls stuffed with garlic, poached rats and camel snot (camel snot was truly one the Queen's/Yes-Yes's favorites, especially when it had congealed from the heat), some bland and utterly coarse vegetables fit only for the most degenerate of sub-humans who might have been refugees from an H.P. Lovecraft story, a succulent orangutan ovarian chutney, and last but not least, generously cut shoulder steaks taken from many a beast of burden covered with all manner of lice, heartworms, scabies, morgellons disease, etc. It was thought by some that diseased meat was the tastiest, and so thought Yes-Yes as well. It was to be a true feast held in honor of the infants as well as for the Evil Queen, and even the servants would partake of the sublime and celebratory victuals. Bottles of champagne and many a virgin maid were to be uncorked that night. It was highly likely that because the queen would be indisposed in favor of adjusting to her new maternal role, that none or very few heads would roll that night, as the Evil Queen would not have the time to partake of her usual sexual, fatal promiscuity. So in the meantime, it was the Cook's duty to prepare the celebratory feast that would begin a night of pure debauchery, a night that under different circumstances he might have savagely enjoyed, as he rubbed the bulge in his pants against the greasy butcher block, thinking of his Nathalie and how perfectly her body united with his.

Therefore the Cook was to be indisposed in the kitchen during many of the night hours and of course free to direct the movements of his underlings who were only there to help him. His plan was to have them by his side up until the very end before his sudden departure out the back door, to be initiated by the howl of a wolf, which would be none other than Nathalie, who just so happened to be well-versed in the obscure art of wolf-calling. Then the Cook was to slip out the back door thirteen minutes later to reunite with Nathalie and then together they would flee into the night with their small suitcases, packed and carried outside by Nathalie, of course, who was to lower herself from an employee bathroom window close to the back of the house. The Cook occupied himself with all of his usual preparatory activities: slicing carrots and onions, seasoning the cuts of meat, tending to bubbling sauces and savory broths. He dismissed most of his assistants and kept only his most trusted few, whom he thought would be the least likely to turn him in should anyone begin to suspect his involvement in the "jailbreak." He furtively labored, trying to become one with his work, slicing fingers and arms and organs, prepping vegetables, making broths and sauces, doing his best to avoid revealing his listlessness coupled with fear and agitation. Perhaps a few hours of this hell would make his escape to freedom worthwhile.

The Cook of the Salt Manor toiled at his labors, removing flesh from bone and stirring the pot. His assistants, bleary-eyed and just as tired as he, continued with their culinary work without complaining. At one point, a steady cold wind blew through an open window, sending a chill through everyone's spine. A few candles in an alcove flickered threateningly. The Cook almost believed that such a blast of air was the same as a blast of sound, as if the harsh cry of the wolf had taken an analogous form, propelling him to drop everything he was doing and to flee to the outdoors immediately. Even in the cold air, the drops of perspiration on his neck were frigid, invoking a wave of shivering that forced him to put down the heavy kettle he was carrying across the room. For the rest of his time in the kitchen that night, the cries of wolves moved through his brain-space like candy, like when a sickly urban organism absorbs too much sugar, causing all of the cellular processes to become chaotic with spasms and off-note music that signaled the arrival of a transit bus at the wrong time and wrong place. His desire to travel the smooth pink roads that led to all of mankind's cities became adamant within his mental associations involving the bricks in the kitchen that were agonizingly on the point of bursting away from the hardened cement that held them in place, always on the threat of death.

The uncertainty of minutes continued for the Cook. He'd send his assistants on break, and then they'd return. The endless night wore on and on, it was pure agony for him. Surprisingly, all of his culinary work that night was flawless, with perfectly shaved lemons, with intelligent, diseased meats cooked to the proper tenderness, and sauces that would grace the palate without the slightest hint of scorching or separation. But he could really care less about any of that: it was all just a hollow dance. At moments, he'd notice the rats underfoot, as they hid underneath the gas stoves and counterspaces, looking up at him for scraps of food that he must have unconsciously been throwing down to them for the duration of his awful stay at the Salt Manor. Looking downward, the Cook could see a plethora of bread shavings, vegetable parings, meat scraps, etc., which had fallen from his knife and which the vermin were taking away with them to their lairs, tiny pockets of unexpected spaces tucked away among the interstices of the ancient brickwork – hollow walls with unseen cities of hungry rodents. And the Cook was helping them live, although it was uncertain that they were grateful. The Cook mused that in all likelihood, he was the god of the rats who showered them with processed food, a subconscious notoriety that came from seasoned hands that accidentally on-purpose threw down the scraps for his fellow mammals to find. It was only when he began to think of the rats tearing through living flesh, cutting through blood vessels that still pumped blood, that the Cook felt as if he would burst at the seams. A swinging lightbulb attached to the ceiling overhead caught his attention, signaling another quake underground, and he held onto the table for support. At that moment, he could hear the long, wistful howl of a wolf outside, and knew instantly that his moment of deliverance had arrived. As the quake subsided, luck saluted him abruptly by causing the sound of a crash in one of the nearby storerooms. He hurried to the room, finding the source of the noise: some canned goods shaken from the shelves by the earthquake. To take advantage of the situation, he purposefully overturned a big vat of cream sauce that was being allowed to cool. With the sauce all over the floor, creating quite the mess, he shouted for help, utilizing this moment of confusion to grab the attention of his assistants, who were immediately directed to begin the clean-up. While this distraction had won them over, the Cook quietly took his exit from the awful estate forever. Nathalie was waiting for him at the designated area, and together they fled to the countrycide, meeting up with a friend who hid them for a couple of days and then helped smuggle them away to a city on one particularly rainy night. The Cook and Nathalie never ever returned to the region where presided the Salt Manor, and they lived happily ever after, to the best of their ability.

After the Pope finished molesting one of his most trusted choir-

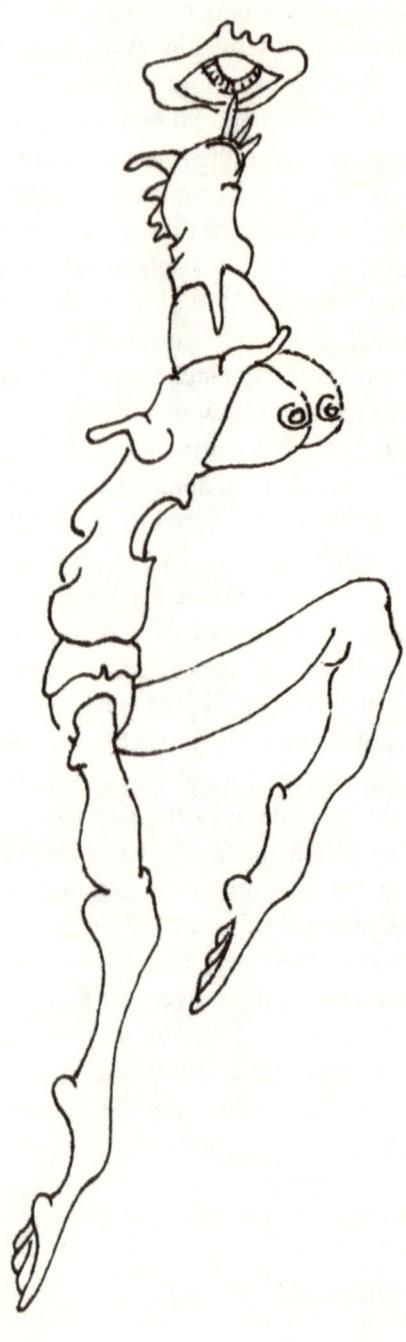

boys, he wiped his mouth on an expensive Vatican-issued napkin, and then made an impromptu videocall to George B. Bush, the President of the Remaining United States of North America, and who was the snotty grandson of the late George Dubya Bush, a despicable, capitalist swine also renowned for his limited intelligence and unmistakable warmongering talents.

When the Pope's call finally got through to Bush, the latter could be seen in the Oval Office, sitting at his desk, snorting a line of coke with a rolled-up ten-thousand dollar bill. When Bush was finished, he wiped a few white grains of powder that had fallen to his collar and addressed the Pope, asking him if he had fulfilled his part of the bargain. When the Pope nodded his head, the President laughed his most demonic Texas laugh known to him, and began to obsessively finger a brass key in the shape of an iguana dagger, with some kind of resplendent, fiery-green emerald for an eye. The President sat back in his chair and bellowed with cunning laughter, while the Pope did the same, pressing a call-button that would summon another barely adolescent choirboy to his private chambers. Before Bush ended the videocall, he informed the Pope to let everyone know that the Martians would be arriving within a week or two, at the most.

Meanwhile, plastic mannequins filled the urban landscape, spreading from shopping malls to classrooms to bedrooms. Somewhere within the darkness of a mannequin storeroom, the Man who was Antimony fought to survive the quakes, to keep his immobile but brittle body intact, despite the tectonic jostlings of the earth that would periodically send flakes of his outer skin falling to the ground. His eyes searched the surroundings for something that might help him regain his mobility, but there was nothing. For now, he could not move because he was a statue.

1st Incarnation

January 2000

1

As before, a single, solitary pink crab was trapped within the ossified lobster trap that had been half-buried in the mud for two days straight. The crab had unwittingly wandered into a trap that now threatened to transform into a lampshade that mimicked the architecturally unsound yet extremely beautiful glass houses from the end of the twentieth century. The crab of vaginal pinkness managed to become fused with the glassy, transparent silicon apparently attracted to the lampshade icon that became more and more visible to hungry, beady red eyes that labored in darkrooms across a greedy continent.

Immediately, however, the luscious crab of vaginal pinkness uttered a magic word or clicking that caused the cage of steel to be dissolved in folds of rotting eucalyptus leaves scattered across the deck of the fishing liner that attempted to recollect all wayward crab traps. Then the solitary pink crab realized that because of the scattered eucalyptus leaves and branches, and because of some glass lampshades that were stacked into a corner of the ship's glass control room, there was nothing left to keep the pink vaginal crustacean confined within an arbitrary prison of glass, concrete and metal.

A crewmember sighed, remembering that some devices work better than the most trustworthy of computers, such as the living tarantula/thermometer hybrid. When attached to the spider's thorax, the thermometer became capable of relaying the lost sounds of the ocean to the ear canal of the listener, upon being placed in the ear. Such a device immediately released all vaginal pink crustaceans to return to the water, unharmed, unscathed and ready for aquatic adventures of new. A sightseeing monkey of loose handkerchiefs on the boat unfortunately missed the opportunity to procure one of these life-saving tarantula-thermometers, and so drowned in the saline water, unaware of what could have been, had the arachnid device been installed.

In a faraway garage, mechanics mused over the rubber tires of a dusty jalopy. The harsh sand on the shop floor interrupted these blue musings, and led the mechanics to believe that a strange, disruptive buoy was floating towards them, inexplicably. They felt fishy green and pink birds surrounding them. The humans became cornered by these colorful fish-birds that did not have feathers but instead scales. The mechanics then became encased in the feathery fishiness because the pink and green fish-birds were secreting a mucousy lubricant from their armpits which eventually dried out and solidified, effectively relegating the musing mechanics to an isolated state of confinement, far away from the ocean, and far away from glass lampshades.

The dehydrated mechanics were now dried figurines of wood and protein, and thus were placed on the dusty dashboard of the jalopy with the blue minerals secreted behind the rubber tires. The owner of the car, a dark man of shadows with a black cowboy hat, returned to the vehicle and drove away from the garage at full speed, eager to spill his seed in the desert sands where the coyote gravel pits became the reaction cauldrons for the secret gemstones of tomorrow, of places where tomorrow existed simultaneously with today. The demon car left no clues of its passage other than a fine and almost indiscernible trail of blue, finely crystalline dust.

A woman bathes in a soft porcelain tub, splashing azure water over her face and breasts, while considering her feline friends who hibernated in tessellated, hexagonal cryo-chambers within the spiral of an embryonic plant that remained coiled within a patch of soil next to the desirable woman's shoes. In her mind's eye, the woman knows every inch of the frozen honeycomb and also knows the magic password of water that would rouse the felines from their icy slumber. Even though she is alone, she knows that the time is not yet right for the feline reanimation; instead, she will have to wait for the right moment when love finds her the least bit ready, paradoxically. She has never found the man she had always wanted, but knows that vigilance over frozen mammalian relatives is better than doing nothing, in the same way that glass pebbles at the bottom of a cold, clear stream can someday become the solar system, provided that the trees retain a clear vision of the green pigment that allows them to photosynthesize nourishment.

After bathing, the woman crosses to the other side of the glass room, which also resembles one of the infamous glass lampshades that are sometimes found at ocean-bottom areas, filled with abundant, trapped sea-life. The woman clothes herself in the waves and folds of fragrant silk, giving thanks to her own genetic creator – the cellular nucleus – that she has yet one more day to avoid sacrificing love for convenience and happiness for financial stability. Yet one more day to avoid the mad rush toward reproduction, the insane swarming impulse which cognizant primates are so aware of. And so, despite the dust which can one day be so easily lifted with the help of a feather, the strong woman pulls the drain plug and lets the water disappear, while feeling her special love towards the microscopic honeycomb of frozen blueness that is a secret jewel nestled within the folded growth apparatus of a dormant plant.

Immediately the woman's shoes become slugs, as the madness of her steps leaves shimmering echoes of burnt comforts on the tiles. Meanwhile, the coiled weed sleeps, waiting for the day of awakening. A cylindrical starfish appears as a shadow on her leg. The shadow is the cool retreat of blue minerals, a chemical precipitate that retains no knowledge of where it came from, but clearly indicates a link between desert garages and morning baths that are and were miles apart and yet which share certain secrets that are incommunicable to the dirty, soiled everyday miserabilist world of men.

A glass heart reclined on the dinner table, beating black swamp blood and sending out aortic attachments over and around the plates and utensils. The blood vessels wrapped around table legs and massaged the knots in the wood, provoking excessive orgasms and burrowing between the rings of many years of growth in the wood. This burning in turn provoked the cells of wood to become activated, leading to micro-feline development within each wooded hexagonal cell. Modern-day felines shrieked and clung to all wooden surfaces in the hopes of sharpening claws and rupturing the black blood death that waxed over the old surfaces. Eyes closed and penises were pulled from pants, and vaginas were unveiled. This unfettering closely resembled an advancing forest of pubic hair – a forest of bells that rang in harmony and concealed barely lit candles that were unaffected by the wind and other elements. Not even the idiotic monsoons could penetrate the innermost clitorises of dry dessert, in order to push aside the silky sands to reveal the buried gold, left behind to tempt the idiotic monsoons that could never cut through a cemented wall of papaya seeds with a blow torch.

The desert heat was confusing, but the black vessels of swamp blood had no trouble coursing through the bed sands like snakes, unlike the idiotic monsoons that proved incapable of lifting the sand grains. It was all a drunk equation that required brass keys that bore the forms of animals on the key-handles. The serpent keys were then placed on the pink sand which tempted the vultures to draw in closer. Upon nearing the serpent keys of solid brass, the black tentacles of the glass heart wrapped around their avian bodies and surrounded them with pulsating circles of swamp blood. Yet something still wasn't right. The vultures were ungrateful, ignoring their new gift, and so they returned to the rock caves.

Meanwhile, the crystal heart of swamp blood played with cigarette lighters and secret panels in the dining room. The developing felines eventually burst from the wood of the table like flammable maggots, and were free to roam the area, with their red hair standing on end. Due to the collapse of the table, the crystal heart attempted to camouflage itself with the party napkins. It nearly succeeded except for a blue dragonfly that landed on one of its aortic branchings, and thus was revealed to the felines and scorpion necklaces in the dining room. At least no human cowardice was involved.

A 1969 poly-chrome chevette shrimp was bolted to the brick wall next to the ladder. I kicked the snow aside as I grasped the cold metal ladder and touched the poly-chrome shrimp plate. Just before climbing, I was pounced upon by a mountain lion. Its claws tore through my flesh as I raised my arms to protect myself. I backed off and attempted to evade the large feline, yet still received lacerating blow after blow from the creature. By now I was suffering from serious blood loss as I dived into the icy water, which instantly healed my cuts. I swam to an underwater tavern and was rejuvenated.

Within the large and extensive bar, I first strolled down the main entrance hallway, enjoying the neon lights and the bubbles of air that rose to the surface somewhere above. No one was around, so I amused myself by playing the slot machines. Upon leaving the bar, I noticed a violent tilting back and forth of the main hallway. Maybe there was an earthquake in progress, or so it seemed. Suddenly a large boulder rolled down the hallway and then exploded upon impact with the front door. I was immediately free and swam to the surface world of felines and poly-chrome chevette shrimp.

Around the same time as these events, pink and green mucous-secreting fish-birds emerged in a rush from a strategically placed fire hydrant on the side of a mid-western road. The flock of creatures draped an otherwise innocent rural town with mucous lubricant and then disappeared off into some North American mountains. An adolescent girl that was living in the town just happened to be spreading apart the mantle of an already opened pink clam and was tickling the foot of the clam with her fingertips when the lubricant deluge occurred. From there on afterwards, the human female spoke of nothing but pink and green lubricant fish-birds and was severely chastised by her ignorant, naive and puritanical parents, who ended up locking the poor young woman up in a boarding school prison, which caused her much despair and social awkwardness. The girl-now-a-woman vowed that upon her release on her 21st birthday, she would take revenge upon the world by joining the green and pink fish-birds in their mission to douse all of humanity and its silly effects with the most erotic of mucous lubricants, even if none of her human friends would join her or even believe her. So, until the fish day arrived, the girl remained in her cell, counting the bricks in the wall, re-reading the insulting magazines for the one hundredth time, and being forced to eat nutritionless and biochemically debilitating simple carbohydrates.

When the pink and green lubricant fish-birds did return on the woman's birthday, her new womanhood welled up within her and the nameless woman immediately came to life, pushing aside the stinky sea urchin shells that were wedged within the mortar and bricks, and melting the uncomfortable prison furniture. With one sweep of her powerful red hair, the brick wall gave way to reveal another cell that contained another miserable captive. Eventually, after all of the adolescent inmates were freed and the wardens were executed, the new red-haired woman invited the inmates to join her in her quest to find the pink and green mucous lubricant fish-birds. Most of the other liberated humans were cowards, and chose to return to abusive and hypocritical family members, but a few remained, solidly dedicated to the mucous fish-bird quest. Throughout this process, the red-haired woman found a mate: a man who shared her values. They had themselves sterilized so that they would conceive no children, under the premises that the world was already disgustingly overpopulated by humans, that highly intelligent and aromatic animalistic fornication was best achieved without the worries of conception, and that even still, having children was still nevertheless possible: not from the womb, but from the world around them.

Instantaneous brain-freeze occurred in the boring school classes, when the standardized tests injected the right drug at the right time, causing the children to slump comatose in their seats. A fragmented attack of wingtips broke through the windows, and giant lubricated fingers reached in through the windows to grasp the unwittingly feral adults who conducted the testing procedures. Of course, these adults were disposed of and the children were reanimated out of their dull comas to receive the lubricated mucous from their powerful benefactors. A silent starfish slowly slid up the legs of a purple umbrella mannequin that symbolically resided in the corner of the classroom, forever punished, forever damned as long as the world remained oppressed under dirty, foul primate ignorance. The umbrella mannequin was hurled from the window by the pink and green mucous fish-birds, which caused its dunce cap and rubber clown nose to fall off. The human figure of the mannequin, in its utterly silent plasticality, shattered upon impact with the street, but then reconstituted itself as a gemstone dragonfly – the kind that raised glass leaves to its mouth only to sullenly discard them because the glass isn't of the right degree of brittleness. The dragonfly twitched its wings and then was off, up and away from the rancid school of subjective mental conversions and castrations. Men and women all over the world placed shadow starfish all over their arms and legs. They measured the lengths of tree funguses that erupted right in their own backyard. They burned twigs to calibrate the potency of frogs, and became momentarily myopic just to mock the pre-rendered calculus of civilized coward-scholars. All plants and animals celebrated their own chromosomes as the cake of life was cut yet another time, with hearty, heady slices being passed out in all directions, thanks in part to the pink and green mucous lubricant fish-birds and also to the boys and girls of all terrestrial species.

The red-haired woman and her mate rebuilt their own mechanical dragonflies and starfish, and understood the equations necessary to effect such transformations. All the while, choked trees lost their ability to remain silent and red maple leaves issued forth from the mouths of lost men who used to have tongues. The red lingual maple leaves were split at the ends, and were used to lick the lubricated crotches of trees that bore apples as well as crunchy lobster rings that only erupted during the fiery winter months. By comparison, Valentine's day was rendered completely flaccid and meaningless when enamored humans breathed fire all of the time, even when the ambient temperature threatened to convert liquid water to its solid state. All of the argumentative word-twisters stopped dead in their tracks, and their penises and vaginas dried up like the lifeless transient flowers that they really were. Meanwhile, lost men with red maple-leaf tongues of cunnilingual fire continued to wreak orgasmic havoc on the oozing sweet and salty crotches of velvet and satin trees that were recently visited by those infamous pink and green mucous lubricant fish-birds.

Knowledge-workers pushed their fingers into moist orifices, causing the owners of the moist orifices to gasp with infernal pleasure, as the midnight clock cried out stroke upon stroke of twelve – a dozen gasps of nocturnal glee that even the fruit lemurs of Madagascar could not ignore. The fish pipeline was in full swing, outside of linear doubt that closely resembled the arbitrary and boringly linear passage of time. The irrational shockwaves were instead non-linear and seemed to occur simultaneously in future, past and present moments. Such a phenomenon had been unheard of up until recently, up until that fateful day when a pink crustacean managed to flee a sunken glass lampshade that lay half-buried in the mud of an undersea bottom. A child's rattle became a side-winding rattlesnake that deposited jeweled glass embryos in the desert sands, that deposited feline honeycomb sections under the plump pillows of permanently adolescent changelings that languished in the wakeful world of the dollar but flourished in the cognitive, fornicative-loving world of slumber. Never had the sweet and salty crotch trees borne so much fragrant, musky fruit.

The pink crabs were caught by a current of azure water and flipped onto their backs. Their armored pink legs wriggled and writhed in the attempts to right themselves, but were not successful before the pungent mucous-lubricated kisses of the green and pink fish-birds that smelled of cheddar cheese and who knew the poetic trigonometry of sensual avian massage. A jewel-encrusted light switch was flipped, and the oval burial chamber was cast in an obsidian glow of sleepiness which caused reposed bird skeletons to check their non-linear watches and finally enable them to discard their asses' ears and over-sized shoes that these dusty clods had worn for centuries in the fiery, obsidian-quenched burial chamber. The non-linear watches indicated that the moment was green and scaly, not pink and feathery, so they whistled tunes as best as their skeletal mouths would allow and developed architectural designs that would enable them to live in the world of stars and suns composed of hydrogen and helium. These new architectural designs allowed for simultaneous living and sleeping, so that the two were no longer seen as separable and distinct. Through this innovation in non-Euclidean architecture, dwellings were created that allowed for love to exist, something that had hitherto been denied and actually stolen from them by the previous non-dialectical inhabitants – those tyrannical inhabitants whose puny minds enabled them to do nothing more than worship the simple and numbing forms of two-dimensional geometry.

By the time the non-linear watch indicated that the moment had become pink and feathery, a lost man removed his opaque red maple leaf glasses and engaged in post-myopic feeding rituals. After feeding, the post-myopic biped discarded his ears and shoes and returned to the blue crab fountain. He found a particular crab of lasting intellectual appeal, and applied curious whispers to its pink wriggling legs, which caused it to relax some. With the aid of a tarantula-thermometer, the pink crab once again was able to hear the waves of the mother ocean of

saline sensibility, and it returned to the lost waters. Therefore, the post-myopic biped man with the red maple cunnilingus tongue as well as the pink oceanic crab whose underside was kissed with moist mucous lubricants were now both free to live as they pleased, to remain fully aware of the useful fire hydrants that were positioned at every corner of every non-repressive metropolis that lacked any skyscrapers but had only one-level housing made of seaweed concrete. Both the man and the crab were now no longer lost.

Simultaneously, moist feline intruders erupted from frozen, tessellated blue hexagonal honeycombs to seek optimistic horseshoe crabs whose tails could be used as a lockpick.

Somewhere at the bottom of the seashell, the nodule of glass found a place to implant itself, in order to wait for the incoming tide of algae that was to spread the virus causing organisms of all sorts to pair off, two by two, so that fern evergreens would become the new breed of wallpaper. A platypus licked its bill clean of all lubricating mucous and placed a yellow sun between its breasts. This simple gesture accomplished everything, since only the platypus, the satin ancient platypus, knew where the gas giants could be harvested from the outer reaches of the Milky Way Galaxy.

Meanwhile, the ancient satin platypus also furthered its knowledge of can-openers, so as to become proficient in more mundane operations, such as the violation of mushroom tins hidden around the world in the same way ammunition is secretly hidden when daily life becomes difficult and microscopic honeycombs threaten to reach macroscopic proportions. In fact, the ancient satin platypus had only recently uncovered the midnight blade of sonic honey – a dagger that could become digitally aroused and which was capable of wreaking havoc on the subconscious minds of primate bipeds who used to inhabit the world in the same way roaches did. The marauding honey blade was more than a match for the other insubstantial feelers and claws that tried to blindly pinch the ass of the night; in fact, the midnight blade of sonic honey could do much, much more than just pinch the ass of night.

The digitally aroused sonic blade had lain dormant for many

eons, and had been more of a myth than a reality. But now, the power of the sonic honey blade was more than real, and it was beginning to shred the most subtle distinctions apart – the differences between beer and urine, the differences between second grade pre-pubescent cuddling and hideous post-myopic hooligan architecture. In addition, the blade could cut almost everything, even the large anus of a giant blue whale.

The sonic honey, when mixed with the lubricating mucous that could only be obtained from willing pink and green fish-birds, became the most sublime of ambrosias, and could only be gotten through much sweat and toil. This ambrosia was also scattered throughout the world, even though its probability of being found was much lower than that of the mushroom tins.

Suddenly, a silver parakeet (whose wings resembled those of a lunar crescent butterfly) landed on a fossilized branch that jutted out from the highly sensualized ambrosia. The parakeet gnawed on the branch and promised all trees in the vicinity that it would fly to the most secret underwater places if the sun could be divided into two globes, so as to prolong the silver photosynthesis that daily occurred within its metallic butterfly wings. Unfortunately, the ambrosia tree would not comply, so the silver parakeet with photosynthetic butterfly wings left the terrestrial planet forever, in order to seek a binary star system that could fulfill its most binary growth fantasies.

Meanwhile, the ancient satin platypus sharpened its bill and took up the midnight blade of sonic honey into its webbed appendages, and began to slice through various outcroppings of rock. Every now and then the blade-wielding creature happened to slice into an underground city of the extinct humans. It was discovered in these buried ruins that saprophytic larvae had burrowed into the archaic brick, mortar and metal and were slowly digesting the edifices of the dead, rotting city. When the squirming blue, glowing larvae caught sight of the honey blade, they squealed with glee and renewed their burrowing activities with a new digestive vigor. After much of the city's foundations had been digested, the entire city finally collapsed upon itself, revealing to the world of light its true center, its true heart: The left-handed snail supermarket.

True enough, no right-handed spiraling snails were present; only the left-handed ones. Within this derelict snail-vending site were left-handed snails in all shapes, sizes and states of being. Also present were several metal cans of mushroom ammunition. The ancient satin platypus sheathed the sonic honey blade temporarily in order to get a closer look at this forgotten supermarket of lost, left-handed snails. After satisfying itself that the snails had completely fossilized while waiting on the shelves to be purchased, the platypus selected a handful of ossified snails to be placed in its sun garden, that was found on a mountain-top of the newly thawed Antarctica, the very same continent that became a home for precociously cogent anteaters that settled there many centuries ago. Crawling out of the abandoned snail supermarket chaos was one giant purple lick-snail which the ancient satin platypus attached to its forehead. With the newly attached lick snail on its skull, the platypus could now see in the dark – something that it had been unable to do for most of its life.

2

The turkey truck rolled out after eight in the morning, gathering the shrapnel that littered the streets. The garbanzo party became separated and fragmented, so that the metal fences were melted onto the pavement, leading to rubbery coiled salamanders that quivered. These salamanders were black and gray striped, and sometimes were stacked on top of each other in their circular wound-up fashion, with stubby arms and legs jutting out in random directions. The clouds in the sky suggested a vast urban settlement, even though the people had been evacuated a few days ago. In the closed-up shops, finely greased turkey cuttings lay scattered, without any apparent order.

Lost monkeys appeared and collected some tiny purple beads that were also strewn about the floor of a particular turkey shop. These small medicated purple beads were to be directly injected into the heart of a transplant recipient. The hole in his chest received a pin covered with the medicated beads, causing the patient to become reanimated out of a deep coma.

The hallway lights flickered to life and a cold wind blew tumble weeds down the hall, which was covered in cobwebs. The frozen cameras on the walls could not register the intensity of the spider webs, since the wind was so dangerous. Meanwhile, children in the backseats of turkey cars squabbled over their respective abilities to care for dogs and horses, only insofar as these pets could improve the lives of the monkey children.

In a farmhouse restaurant, a solitary woman sits in the lap of a solitary man, and kisses him with her lips and soul. Turkey bones exquisitely wrapped in cobwebs are used as drumsticks, to beat upon broken windows, chairs, tables and clay farmhouse cooking pots. The noise is soothing just as water is, since a magic potion bottle is always to be found underneath the chair at the head of every table, and behind every garden fountain where dragon dances consummate the fall of left-handed mahogany statues of blue-eyed daisies that were once used for aromatherapeutic extravaganzas. The mahogany of the lost people-statues are worm-eaten, and within each worm tunnel there are ant colonies of amber – the kind that is actually a type of glue used by fascists.

In addition to magic potion bottles, there are also volcanic funguses that grow at strange angles, complementing the worm-devoured mahogany statues of long-forgotten flower children. Eventually the turkey trucks bring the pink flambeau canons in and the rotten statues are converted to just a rainy memory, in the same way that fox-felines can eventually melt their way out of ice-sheet prisons – the kind that forced them to sleep for a long time behind shuttered complexes of frozen architecture.

Once the mahogany worm-tunneled statues of lost flower-children have been reduced to ash, the same throbbing coiled rubber salamanders are left behind, as marker buoys of oyster brilliance, of cobweb postal packages that are not to be opened until christmas, when the larval insects are once again ready to endure a short winter sleep.

With the pink flambeau canons set up around the vast, sky-blue farm town of avian stagnation, the monkeys return from the mountains where they had spent a little time in some pleasure-palace caves that were ingeniously formed out of solid rock, where geode formations enjoyed wearing old-fashioned bearded glasses. As if the rain couldn't dribble from a soaked umbrella, city garbage began to split at the seams. Table-top manners were definitely at a premium where monkeys escape their urban farmhouse worries through family turkey bone excursions through spider web kaleidoscope gardens that once held the mahogany statues of flower figures, now just a memory.

A coiled rubber salamander bounced off the forehead of a latex dwarf, leading to a pimped knuckle used by a sparrow to forage for sidewalk seeds. The pimp-knuckled sparrow had fists of iron that were very effective for consumer data entry, as well as for table-top etiquette, when the time arose. In fact, the pimp-knuckled bird knew of several other meat maidens who wove soft ropes through their hair and displayed pimp-knuckle avian icons on their flak jackets, which protected them from the unearthly emanations of drilled mahogany

that exhaled the tempting perfume of mushroom ammunition as well as colonial ant nectar. The moist meat maidens with their soft, woven ropes and soluble flak jackets eventually became a chorus of dark, solid eye lashes that closed down the family farmhouse retreat town of blue skies. The town was then folded by these moist flak jacket meat maidens into a blue jewel that was sensuously tucked away into a mahogany crevice for later use and admiration.

Even if succulent turkey mahogany statues and pieces had been leered at in infinite lust only to be rudely and cruelly withdrawn from redheaded lightbulbs, the monkey prizes were still awarded, and the happy cancer cookies were handed out like pathetic consolation prizes to those who did not have fudge tables to melt in the livingroom when the good Reverend Bobby McDowell sprayed the faces of smiling chipmunk women with his radioactive semen. The frisbee that flew out of time only just reappeared as an egg-rollette that was worth a thousand precious earrings and even a thousand nipple-stamps that posted the past letters of jock-itch love affairs.

With the biggest "anyway," a goldfish dissolved its bowl and peed on a young nutcracker that had been carved from oak only the month before. The nutcracker accepted the urine and drew symbols of tooth decay on the black board with white chalk. A spider landed on the chalk and spoke about mannequin lampshade people who visit the theater a little too often. The mannequin lampshade people were actually precursory versions of the extinct mahogany flower-children statues; they were different cohorts of the same creature. Evidently these various groups were cyclically produced in batches from time to time and then released for dispersal from the mother factory, whose whereabouts were presently unknown to the unhappy world of humanity.

But wherever the mysterious mother factory of mahogany flower children statues or mannequin lampshade people actually resided, it was concluded by all erotic leg-seeking starfish that the offensive factory should be shut down and that the genetic code that gave rise to these species should be abolished, in the same way that alligator feathers are used as insulation for pink flambeau canons that clear away repressive, decrepit forms of modern architecture that are emotionally hostile to sentient primates.

Somewhere within the coiled pimp-knuckle of a deranged butterfly bird, a mucous sandwich was prepared with only the finest of pink and green lubricants, courtesy of the special fish-birds that used the pimp-knuckles to knock on the doors of the wooden hallways with clitoral growth rings. The mucous lubricant fish birds had these special butterfly sandwiches of wooden statues of rotten mahogany and sometimes an isolated statue would feed upon the mucous sandwich. This outcome, however, was the exception and not the rule. A red spinning eye cast its line out to a bridge of raining catfish and ended up catching a few token bricks on its multi-hooked line. Of course, this was more fantastic than a whale that used its tail to smack a wayward shipwreck, but it was all that could be hoped for when the seas were stormy and seaweed tobacco rolls were used in place of a daily bucket of cottage cheese. This latter instance could not be considered jewel-like, but at least it approximated the state of being where bathtub felines reposed in icy blue honeycombs.

The mucous sandwich was stored inside of an acorn for more needy days but the storm was unforgiving, causing desperate men to grasp for its fish-bird lubrications, especially when a highway was on the run, when the mobile roads of the highest speeds led to the central turkey-town of rotten stores and rotten statues. A highly feathered wing emerged from the ocean to point the way to the whales as well as the lampshade shipwrecks to come toward the shore, but perhaps this was only a mirage, since the decrepit band of handkerchief monkeys preferred to see clouds and not land, as if a report card was waiting, lurking for them behind the next gale of rainy wind. A terrace of purple lick snails formed the barrier behind which the monkey sailors hid, without even a cache of citrus to protect them from scurvy and without a cherry-wood compass to direct their seafaring efforts back towards the hearth of their families and turkey-bone children that inhabited senile pleasure farm towns of over-populated desolation. Another glass window breaks and the glass fragments form the sailors' new teeth, since their original fangs have long since slid out from their gums and dissolved onto the wooden fish-kissed deck like once-frozen rain. A phoenix bird emits plumes of green and pink mucous fire, in the same way explosive pineapples are hurled into unsuspecting refrigerators by unseeing, webbed platypus hands.

In the aftershock of the squid raid, city corners are turned onto their sides, and the wildlife underneath the city rocks are exposed to the light, squirming in their movie-star insolence and utterly vain wailings. Penis chopsticks clack on the white porcelain plates and a sunburst becomes enraged – enraged enough to videotape a rockslide that actually is a mudslide in slow motion. In the calluses of scraped elbows, feline fish whiskers lap up the spilled lubricating mucous that once was a ladybug dwelling amid the soft white petals of a magnolia that grew outside of a virgin prison-house.

The turkey-horses are not quite finished stampeding over the cliff, but they at least know about the jewels that are soon to be released from the worm-holes that cover the entirety of their muscular limbs.

3

In thirty years, the baby rattle that looked like a pink specialized chess piece – whether a queen or bishop – would grow from a palm-sized item into an object that would fill the room. The small, layered pink-marbled statuette was adorned with thin, wiry bands of metal and lay flat and surrounded by an oblate ovoid transparent casing of very thin glass or crystal. The entire womb-like apparatus floated a few feet from the ground, suspended in the green botanical shadows of the room. Someday this pink chess piece protected by glass would transform into a giant honey pink bee hive. Already in the green botanical shadow room there were the faint but persistent buzzings of drone bees who sought to attend the levitating pink marble embryo.

The embryo even contained information about certain femur bones, which when placed parallel alongside those of a living human would cause a profound molecular readjustment of skeletal infrastructures once the daughters had won their pre-pubescent baseball victories so as to impress their spineless parents. In fact, a pelican of black skin therapy entered a crystal window that had formed in the green botanical shadow room, and landed on a vestibular chair that was carelessly left behind by the female baseball champions. The pelican melded with the chair, forming a feathered back support that would enhance the seated pleasures of whoever sat down, especially if they were in the habit of counting their eyelashes in the morning. Quite frequently, the green botanical shadow room had transient pieces of furniture that would be moved, modified and sometimes eaten or folded up like clothing.

A sideways spewing orange was suddenly caught in the throes of spontaneous flatulence. The citrus module was squeezed until no pulp was left, by the likes of a pink bunny rabbit champagne goddess with hideously bloodshot eyes, and four bulging, lactating mammary marshmallows that could only mean trouble for a wayward hyacinth computer doorknob. When the lights of flowers were finally ignited in the green botanical herb room of shadowy bunny queens, the marshmallow breasts suddenly disappeared, leaving the newly found hyacinth carburetor friends cold and all alone. A skull lamp was used in place of the mammary marshmallows, and so the computer hyacinth carburetor was able to hone its trail blazing skills while ignoring the levitating glass-covered pink marble embryo that would someday be a very busy pink honey beehive of hexagonal mucous juice. But that remained to be seen.

The elephant tusks were used to sweep the debris off the floor, as the passage of time had led to a seepage of fluorescent foxtails that littered every habitable part of the earth mansion, regardless of how little light was available for successful seepage. After the sweeping, the elephant tusks were discarded – thrown down the drain to a sewage pool that contained the carcasses of ideas that were willfully degraded by the know-it-all's of the capitalist economy – those that controlled the lives of others and who took snowflakes and melted them with their foot odor. With a cleared path, the marching of beetles occurred. The beetles had holes in the shells on their backs, inside of each there was a fragment of connected microcircuitry, implying that these insect-minds were not acting of their own accord, but against their wills under the sinister directions of an umbrella valley top cowboy hat of arrogant leather which had been charred during the last soft fire that plagued the botanical room of shadows. The soft fires could have been avoided, had the tusks been left where they were meant to reside – jutting from the skulls of elephants. This preventative measure would have left the seeping foxtails to swamp the floors of the forgotten botanical house so that no flames could course through the walls and floors.

But the unthinkable event had just occurred and an unseen elevator within the rear portion of the botanical shadow mansion contemplated the future of the embryonic chess piece that might have one day become the pink honey comb of bee honey.

The fires sniveled and began to burn the lower thresholds of the wood. The insects that slept in the rings of the lumber were rudely awakened to a commercial that sliced through their electronic circuitry and rendered them useless and directionless, teetering on the edge of what used to be a home and now was becoming an intergalactic toilet with every passing second.

With every twitch, an egg was broken onto the windshield of happy police cars transporting the rotting corpses of dead senators and other politicians who had cabbages stuffed into their ears so that they could monitor the amounts and kinds of wood that were hurled into the fireplace. The shady botanical rooms ate the strange human refuse and created a form of humorous wallpaper with their flat, two-dimensional bodies. Interestingly enough, these papered political pinheads did not have eyes, since they were cut out with sewing scissors. Because of the removed eyes, it was possible to see the geometrical botanical shadows boring through the empty eye sockets.

Suddenly deep within the basement, a reclining skeleton grows soft green flesh and becomes an adolescent female baseball champion. The young female baseball champion, now reanimated with a suit of green meat flesh first, touches the folds of her moist vagina and then presses her fingertips to her ears. The vaginal secretions then say to her:

"Behold! Now we are one and the table has been set for dinner. When the clock strikes three you will descend the stairs into the lower basement antechamber and reunite yourself with the holed lotus roots that have adorned these botanical shadow walls for centuries. At all costs you must kiss the sliced cross-section of each and every lotus root and think of pineapple grenades that sometimes resemble gorilla skulls when they are not worshipped properly. You must also vow never to utter the phrase 'Yes-Yes will kiss the frog with her monkey-face lipstick' and never carry around sad little facial tissues in a black-leather gorilla skull purse, as the future maidens will someday do on the surface of Mars. Above all else, you must kiss all of the lotus root slices and then return to the room of the pink marble chess piece that is encased in a glass shell and which will someday be your very own personal pink beehive of hexagonally dripping pink honey. You must protect this developing chess piece with your life as well as with your gonads. Now go, and do as I have asked, so that you won't have your fingers permanently in your ear with your lusciously green vaginal secretion."

The young female baseball champion licked her warm fingers.

Her new body responded well to her neural commands, perhaps even better than her previous body – the original body that was condemned by Christian ghosts in the motel of hypocritical pleasures. The baseball champion then sprinted down the secret duty stairs, while pushing aside the shadowy vines that were in her way. The vines were almost octopus tentacles with hydraulic suction cups, so much pulling and grasping of the vines were required. In the downstairs lotus room, the shadowy botanical walls were in fact adorned with glowing red lotus root slices, each of which had nine holes. The young female baseball champion kissed each root, just as her vaginal secretions had instructed, and immediately she felt better, as if a great burden had been lifted from her legs. On the way back upstairs, the young woman encountered little resistance as she inscribed her name on photosynthetic lightbulbs and made her way to the particular shadowy botanical room that housed the developing pink chess egg that was to someday become her pink hexagonal beehive of dripping pink honey. The pink marble chesspiece was comfortable inside of the glass amnion, all of which was supported by a nest of finely woven glass fibers. The magic egg was frozen in time and eager to begin a lifeline that was to last several centuries, until the earth became once again inhabitable for that other race from a neighboring galaxy – a race that used music in place of money and Walt Disney characters as toilet paper. The alien race was actually beautiful, and had a soft green flesh that was a pure delight to touch, and who most closely resembled papaya munchkin loafs. These papaya munchkin loafs, as they could be described, didn't really care about the sardine cans that humans sometimes used as shoes, and were anxious to return to the world of shadowy botanicals, where flutes were played in harmony to the dronings of two-dimensional wall-people who were decorative as well as flammable.

Even when the crocodile was unable to fasten its teeth onto the telephone booth, the walkways through swamp areas led the way to safety for the flowers that always grew towards the light. The teeth were indeed sharp, but the phone booth was extremely slippery, almost coated with a slippery mucous, which prevented the teeth from piercing the shiny metal. The phone booth also revealed radioactive finger prints, which suggested that others had made use or at least attempted to make use of the polished telephone equipment.

The inside of the phone booth had become an isolation chamber for a sickly green alien who was in the unfortunate process of drying out, due to the presence of fiery leaves that erupted from its deflated, weak arms. When the rocks of debris obtained from a leveled police station were used as gardening stones, the sickly alien stopped growing branches from its arms and hoped that its non-terrestrial creator might take its gelatinous bones back to its homeworld, where its families lived in caves coated with neurons so that the weather might be more quickly perceived without the use of televisions. The alien did so eventually, but not without a peculiar vaginal flowering from its gelatinous torso.

Birds with pimp-knuckles flew by in order to knock on the doors of the telephone booth, perhaps because they were late to dinner and had to phone home to their mothers and fathers who had already prepared the evening meal. For the pimp-knuckled birds, this event was chaotic enough for them to desire a vacation of parasols that would hide them from the light of the next day, so that they could enjoy the summer darkness of heat.

www.ingramcontent.com/pod-product-compliance
Lightning Source LLC
Chambersburg PA
CBHW030923120626
46554CB00001B/259